THE HOUSE UNDER THE STARS
(A WHITBY STORY)

by
Jenny Hesketh

Grosvenor House
Publishing Limited

All rights reserved
Copyright © Jenny Hesketh, 2021

The right of Jenny Hesketh to be identified as the author of this
work has been asserted in accordance with Section 78
of the Copyright, Designs and Patents Act 1988

The book cover is copyright to Jenny Hesketh

This book is published by
Grosvenor House Publishing Ltd
Link House
140 The Broadway, Tolworth, Surrey, KT6 7HT.
www.grosvenorhousepublishing.co.uk

This book is sold subject to the conditions that it shall not, by way of
trade or otherwise, be lent, resold, hired out or otherwise circulated
without the author's or publisher's prior consent in any form of binding or
cover other than that in which it is published and
without a similar condition including this condition being imposed
on the subsequent purchaser.

This book is a work of fiction. Any resemblance to
people or events, past or present, is purely coincidental.

A CIP record for this book
is available from the British Library

ISBN 978-1-83975-846-1

Dedicated to all those kind readers who enjoyed my first two books and encouraged me to carry on writing.

Need to know who's who?

For a list of characters see the last pages of this book.

Some of the characters in this story were real people who lived in Whitby, others only lived in the imagination.

CHAPTER 1

1808.
In which Eliza goes on a journey.

It was a few weeks before the Christmas, I'd the breakfast nearly cleared and my young master and mistress were still at the table, when there was the sound of a horse coming to the front of the house and a sharp knock at the door. At once I went to answer it, dragging back the night bolt and opening the heavy farmhouse door. There stood the messenger boy from the post, with two small letters held out to me.

"For Master Curzon," he said. I gave him the customary coin from a saucer on the hall table, there at the ready for this very purpose.

At once, I took them to my Master and then started to pile up the last of the breakfast dishes.

He glanced at the first envelope and threw it onto the table without opening it.

"I know what that is, it's the bill from that bloody robbing horse doctor," and he took up the second letter and slit it open carefully.

"Well," he said thoughtfully reading it, "that's an odd to do and no mistake, though good news as well."

"What is Ben? Who is it from Dear?" asked his wife.

"Read it yourself, meself I've never heard of such a thing."

He passed the letter to her, turning to me he said, "well Eliza, it's from Jack."

At once I was all ears, Jack was not only the Master's cousin but also my own flesh and blood, my cousin's son (on my mother's side).

"That does sound strange indeed," frowned the Mistress handing the letter back.

"What Sir, please tell me," I was suddenly anxious for I knew there was a baby expected any time now.

"Here read it for yourself Eliza."

At once I pushed the letter away. "Sir, tha knows A cannot read."

"Sorry Eliza, I forgot. So, me sister Belle has had a fine son, Jack says he's healthy and strong..."

Overcome with relief I clapped my hands in delight, "thank the Lord."

"But, and here's what's an odd do, it seems that, though she is not laid up, Belle cannot care for the babe, Jack says she has a kind of fear of the child and will not have him near her". I did not know what to say as he went on, "so they've asked that you might go and stay a while at the vicarage and help out and that."

My heart sank, for I had not left the farm for more than thirty years and before then I had only been the four miles into Whitby a few times and never anywhere else. I knew nothing of travel and did not wish to know of it.

"But Sir, how could A get there?"

"Why it's only two stops on the stagecoach, I shall take you to the diligence myself and I'll write to Jack to meet you at the other end. You'll be fine Eliza, a bit of adventure for you, what think you wife?"

"I hope you'll not be away long Eliza, for I cannot manage without you," she answered, a touch petulantly.

"Come wife, me cousin must be in need of help, or he would not have written so, you know how proud he is, and Eliza is his relative, when all's said and done…"

"Ben Dear, could not your mother have helped out, and Eliza stay here?"

"I think her still with Cousin Penelope and her youngsters."

Now I was in two minds, for I did so want to see our Jack and Belle and of course the new baby, but in truth I was quite scared of the outside world, knowing very little of it. Thus, it was something of a heavy heart that I carried into the kitchen with me, as well as that pile of plates.

Naught remained a secret for long at this farm, and pretty soon Betty and Janet were fussing and telling me what I needed to take and how well they could manage without me. Of course, that was not what I wanted to hear, but the truth was, they were still young and strong, whereas I was an old woman of sixty-one, and not near as able as I once was.

"Come now Eliza, tha's trained us that well, we'll be managing as if tha were still here," said Betty.

"Tha'll be able ter see all t' town and shops and that, and a new bairn ter spoil, why tha'll want fer nowt," said Janet.

Later that day, I went up to my own bedroom and drew my wooden box from under my bed, to sort out what I was to take with me. That same box I'd brought when I first came to work at the farm, fifty years before. Newly orphaned and scared as a kitten, the old mistress had welcomed me, and she must have seen the fear in my face, for she took my hand and said that whilst so ever I lived at the farm, I would never want for anything and would never have anything to be afraid of. And this was the truth, for though the work was always hard and the hours long, I had only ever known kindness and respect from all of my three Masters and Mistresses, who had followed on one after another.

I was in possession of some quality clothes, better than you might expect in a servant such as myself, for when the old mistress had died, she bequeathed to me all her good clothes, though I had taken only the plainer dresses, leaving her silks for her granddaughters to cut up and remake, having no use for silk gowns myself. Thus I had a lifetime's supply of fine linens, several dresses which had required little altering, two India paisley shawls, a pile of good gloves, and an expensive beaver bonnet, which she had never worn, it being a present from her nephew and his wife and her not liking the new fashion for bonnets, preferring the large hats of the last century.

I folded everything as neat and small as I could, leaving my light summer clothes in the big chest at the foot of my bed, thinking I would be back home in a few weeks' time and not need them. But on my last night, when I would say I barely slept, I rose early, and through some kind of instinct, I took everything I had left in that chest and tied it up in a check shawl. I descended the back stairs from my little bedroom for the very last time, wearing a good dark dress, my fine beaver bonnet and both my India shawls, my box and my bundle in my arms.

"Eh, tha looks that smart Eliza, they'll not know thee, they'll think it's gentry 'as come ter stay," said Betty.

Janet hugged me, "tek all our good wishes wi' thee and come back soon."

My mistress wished me a safe journey and gave me a parcel of baby clothes she had worked herself, for she was the neatest of stitchers.

My master handed me into the gig and as we departed, I turned back to look at the farm for what I now believed to be the last time.

We raced along at great speed, for my master thought there to be no point to a horse, unless it was a fast one. The journey to the stagecoach passed all too quickly and next thing I was being pushed into that very coach and my luggage was tied to the roof with all the other boxes and trunks. Most of the journey I feared for my little box and bundle tumbling down and being lost forever, but at least I had my money on me, carefully wrapped in a handkerchief and pinned inside my stays.

"God speed Eliza," my master called after me, "I'll be along myself in a week or two's time to see what's what with Sister Belle."

I was seated between two portly gentlemen who rocked against me in a most unseemly way at every lurch and bump of that horrid vehicle. One of them broke wind more than once and I had to put my lavendered handkerchief to my lips to stop me from retching, so bad was the smell. At last, with a great rumbling and rocking, we pulled into an inn yard, but to my disappointment it was not Cookby and there was still another stop to go.

My legs were shaking like jelly as I descended the wobbly folding steps, and I had no idea where to go for the break whilst the horses were being changed. But as luck would have it, a kindly lady who had been sitting opposite me, showed me where I might relieve myself, and when I came back into the inn, her husband had ordered me a dish of chops and a large glass of port wine. I felt much better after this, for of course I had been too nervous to breakfast before my journey. So now I had friends to talk to for the last part of my travels and they took me to be a comfortable maiden aunt going to help out with a new baby and not a poor farm servant who could not read and knew nothing of the wide world. I confess I did not disillusion them, for I rather liked this invention of myself.

But oh, how pleased I was to arrive in Cookby, I almost fell into our Jack's arms as he helped me from the coach.

"Dearest Aunt Eliza, how good it is to see you. I do thank you for coming so promptly to help…er with our trouble…" and before I could ask him more of this, he went on, "I hope the journey was not too tiresome for you, for I know how wretched those stagecoaches can be."

"Not at all," I lied, "t' other passengers looked after me well, and arranged a dinner for me."

On that I turned and waved goodbye to my new friends as Jack picked up my box and bundle. He put them under one arm as if they were as light as feathers and offered me his other arm, he had always been a strong lad, though he looked thin as a rail now.

Together we walked the short distance from the coaching inn to the Vicarage. At every turn, hats were touched, and greetings called out and I was introduced more than a time or two as, "our Aunt Eliza, who is coming to keep house for us for a little while and keep us all in order."

A couple of people asked after the vicar's wife and baby, but Jack was dismissive and said she just needed rest and quiet and that the baby was as grand as could be, thanking them for their concern.

Although we met naught but civility and kind wishes, I was shocked by what I saw around me; poor tumbledown cottages, muddy streets with God knows what, running in gullies down the middle of them. At one point I had to put my handkerchief over my nose, so foul was the stench.

"Don't worry Aunt Eliza, you'll get used to the smell, it is in part from their lack of sanitation and part from the dye works where all these people have their work, including the children, I'm afraid."

But it was the sight of these people that shocked me most of all. Ill clad against the winter weather, thin and many of them sickly looking, with children standing barefoot in the slurry of the street. I own I had never seen poverty of the like and I was thus silenced for the whole of the walk and much relieved to reach the vicarage.

The vicarage itself was a neat four-square house of perhaps one hundred years old; a drawing room and our Jack's study to either side of the wide hall, behind them a dining room and a decent kitchen, this being the only warmed room in the house. Above were four sparse bedrooms. A servant girl, Elizabeth Jane, who could not have been more than fourteen, showed me around, our Jack having to go out on his calls to the sick and needy. I asked where her mistress was and she said she was sleeping, so I did not go in that room just for the moment. My own bedroom to be, contained a bed, a chair and a row of hooks on the wall. Jug, basin and towels rested on the hearth, there being no washstand; upon the windowsill stood a little jug of white flowers and winter berries.

"Are t' flowers thy doing?"

She nodded shyly.

"Well I thank thee; they give a nice bit of cheerfulness."

Which, God knows, was much needed in that gloomy, chilly room. I put my box neatly under the bed and laid my bundle upon the chair.

"Should tha like a cup of tea, Mistress?"

"Indeed, A should Elizabeth Jane and while it brews tha can show me t' pantry and outsides."

The pantry was hardly more than a cupboard with a stone shelf and a flour bin under it. But outside, I was quite surprised to find a run with a low water pan in it for two ducks and some chickens running about in it too. A shed contained a cross looking nanny goat and next to it an empty pig sty. Beyond was a decent sized vegetable garden, with a good show of cabbages, winter carrots and such.

"Who sees ter all this?" I asked.

"Master gets up at five each day, ter see ter t' animals and does a bit of gardening too, even though tis still dark. He's ter do it then because all t' morning he's out on calls and after t' dinner it's services, funerals and that and in t' evening he's in his study wi' his books and his writing."

Dear God, I thought, no wonder he looks so tired and thin, but I said, "it all seems in good order. Now is that t' bairn A'm hearing?"

For a loud wailing came from the kitchen. At once she picked up the baby from his basket and with one hand struggled to warm up his pap of milk, water and flour.

"Here let me take him," I said.

And certainly, he was a fine, big babe. Elizabeth Jane knelt in front of me and tried to feed him. I showed her how to tilt the feeder less so that he could suck and not choke on the liquid, he was fortunately blessed with a hearty appetite.

But a papboat was hardly a satisfactory way of feeding a baby and Elizabeth Jane must have thought so too, for she then said, "Mistress, may A ask thee summat? It is delicate and A cannot find right words ter speak of it wit' Master."

"Of course, Elizabeth Jane, what is it?"

"A dunt know a deal of bairns, but A know they need proper milk. Well it's me sister, she's needing work and she's ter stop feeding her bairn for he's nine month and he's started biting now..." I shuddered inwardly, and she went on, "she's plenty of milk, our mother'll look after her bairn if she came here as wet nurse..." She hesitated and looked at me wide-eyed.

"And where is her husband? For A could not tolerate no immorality in this house."

"He's passed Mistress; she's been widowed twelve month now."

"And is she a clean girl and decent too?"

"Aye Mistress she is, and we was brought up ter attend church regular. That's how A got me place here, for A used to come for lessons, t' Mistress used ter run a little school here, then when she became so poorly, t' Master took me on as maid. A've tried me best ter care for her, honest A have," she looked at me so anxiously, "but now t' Mistress is so sad A dunt know how ter speak wi' her...A could fetch me sister this afternoon if tha wants for we only live half an hour off."

I nodded, "then she may come over and I shall speak to her and see if she might suit, and if she does, then she may share thy bedroom wi' thee."

While Margaret Ann went off to fetch her sister and the dear baby was settled again, I decided I must at last seek out poor Belle. I made a pot of tea and set it with cups upon a tray. There was a plate of greyish scones in the pantry, so I buttered two of them and made a mental note that if nothing else was achieved in my visit, I would at least teach Elizabeth Jane to bake a decent scone.

Upstairs, I knocked at the bedroom door and went straight in. Belle lay upon the bed in a tangled heap of sheets, her hair was matted, her eyes red with weeping and her shift looked non too clean.

"Oh Eliza, you are come at last. Jack told me you were coming."

I put the tray down and sat beside her on the bed, whereupon she flung herself into my arms and sobbed out loud for a good few minutes, just as if she had been a little girl again.

At last I said, "come along now Dear, sit up properly and get tha tea, it'll make thee feel that much better."

She drank two cups of tea but declined the greyish scone and I resolved to sort out some tempting delicacies for her, for I had never seen her so thin. She must have lost about twenty pounds since I had last seen her.

"I have had a baby."

"I know Dear, I have seen him, a grand little lad."

She looked at me anxiously, "I cannot have it near me, I am afraid of it, while it grew in me, I felt it was sucking the life out of me. And now when I hear it cry, I want to run away but I have not the strength. Jack is so angry with me too."

"A'm sure he's not Dear, it is maybe hard for him to understand that's all."

"He spoke so sharp to me, and he never has before."

"Tell me what he said."

I think it always best to get the troubled mind talking, even though you can often find out more from what is not said than from what is spoken out loud.

"When it was born, I would not hold it, so Jack held it and kissed it, he was so happy until I asked him if he could ever love the baby. Then he spoke sharply and said of course he loved him, for he was our little son."

"And what happened then?"

"Everyone started whispering and they took it away, but I could hear it crying all night long."

I felt we had talked enough, for what new mother calls her little one 'it'?

"Now let's get thee washed and dressed, for A know tha'll feel a lot better when tha's up and about."

I knew she had not had the full two weeks of 'lying in' but I still felt it the right thing to be doing. This room was better furnished than the others, with a chest of drawers, a linen box, chairs and a bedside table. I made up a bit of a fire in the little bedroom grate and sat Belle beside it, in an elbow chair with two pillows on it for her comfort.

I could hear sounds from downstairs, so I said, "now stay here and rest quiet, while I go and see to arranging for a wet-nurse for little Jack, if that is all right with thee?"

"I cannot feed it; I could not do that." She shrugged her shoulders and looked away from me.

Elizabeth Jane and her sister were still in their shawls and bonnets. Margaret Ann was certainly a plump healthy-looking girl, of about twenty. She had brought her clothes bundle with her; I was undecided whether that showed her over presumptive or simply well prepared. But her interview was short lived, curtailed by loud cries from the baby.

"Shall I mek a start now Mistress?"

I nodded, for beggars cannot be choosers.

Her bonnet and shawl laid on a chair, she picked up the baby and cradled him as if he were her own. She hushed him on her shoulder, while she loosened her dress and then a wonderful peace surrounded us as he suckled.

Our new wet-nurse looked up at me and smiled and I had to smile back, with a simple relief for there is naught more agitating than a crying baby.

CHAPTER 2

The following days.
In which Eliza tackles her difficult task.

So, I set myself quite a strict routine to tackle my task each day. It would have been easy to shy away from Belle and her troubled mind, for I could have spent the whole of every day training up Elizabeth Jane and supervising the running of the household. She was a willing enough girl, and her mistakes stemmed only from her ignorance and lack of experience, but I just had to turn a blind eye to most things and let her get on as best she could, for my duties lay elsewhere.

Every day, our Jack rose well before six and without a bite to eat, went into the outsides to care for the various animals and milk the goat, in the dark and generally in a bitter cold. Myself, I was washed and dressed by seven and made sure whatever his protests, that he took something hot for his breakfast, before he was off out on his calls. It was a widespread parish and he often had quite a few miles to walk to reach the sick and dying. Then I'd give Elizabeth Jane instructions for the laying of fires, cleaning, laundry and preparations for the dinner. With a tray of tea and hot rolls, I would go up to sit by Belle as she slowly awakened, sipped a little tea and broke a few bits off the bread to nibble. I would let her eat what she could first and then try to get her talking, while I brushed out her hair and helped her with her ablutions. I think feeling cold can lead anyone to a depressive mind, so I always waited till the fire was really warm and bright before I wrapped her in shawls and a lap quilt, and we would sit to either side of the hearth to take up our knitting.

On the first day I had said, "our Jack'll need some new stockings A'll be bound, can tha remember t' pattern Dear?"

She had always been the neatest of knitters and I was much encouraged to see her pick out the five needles and dark wool from my bag.

"Eighty stitches?"

"Exactly, and twelve rows of the rib."

She worked steadily and industriously, without further comment and my heart ached to see her much withdrawn. I could not help but remember her first learning to knit when she was a little girl of perhaps five or so. Beside the great stone fireplace in the kitchen at the farm, she sat on a little low stool, working with some nice red wool when my cousin Jacob had come into the room.

He put his arm around her and said, "why if that int t' finest piece o' knitting A've ivver seen in all me life."

And she had smiled her sweetest smile with such pride, even though she had dropped two or three of the stitches.

Our only hitch was when a little later on, she heard the baby's distant cries, she twitched and pulled her shawl about her, rubbing her face in an agitated way.

"Is it still here? I thought it gone."

"Yes Dear, little Jack is downstairs," I replied firmly, fearing for her reason now.

But we carried on with our knitting quietly and no more was spoken between us about him.

****

Every day, that week and the next, we would work upon our knitting, mostly in silence, up till when I had to go down to see to the dinner. Sometimes she would carry on knitting on her own, but more often than not her work would fall to her lap, and she would stare into space, as if in a trance, until I returned with the dinner tray. Then, in the afternoons we would talk of times past, trying to keep things as cheerful as possible, sometimes Belle would rest in bed, she seemed able to sleep for a very great deal of the time. After several days of steady work on stockings, I began to knit a few bits of things for the baby without saying anything of it, but once or twice she seemed to glance across at them.

Since the presence of Margaret Ann, who I have to admit was an excellent nurse, hardly a peep was heard from the baby and a few days later, Belle said, "has it gone away now?"

"What Dear?"

"The baby, has it gone away?"

I had to answer carefully, "why little Jack is downstairs with his nurse, such a good little lad he is."

She nodded but said nothing.

"Should tha like me ter bring him up, and tha could see how well he's doing?"

At once she became upset, dropped one of the knitting needles, shook her head and tears welled in her eyes.

Taking her hand, I said, "don't worry Dear, Margaret Ann is looking after him very well."

Our difficult moment passed quickly for next thing, Jack burst into the room, two letters in hand.

"Your brother Ben will be with us tomorrow for a few days and the other letter invites us all to a Christmas party at your Olivia's, next week." He put his arm around her shoulders, "shall you feel well enough to visit? They are to send their own carriage to take us there and back…What think you Aunt Eliza?"

"A think it'd do thee a power of good ter see thy sister, tha'll be a month from t' childbed by then, and if we wrap thee up warm, A can see no harm in it?"

It was on the tip of my tongue to say it would be a chance to see Olivia's two little lasses as well, but I thought the better of that.

Of course, I knew that once Ben Curzon arrived, all our household routines would be turned quite upside down.

He arrived the next day, on his fine black mare. There was a great hugging and back slapping between him and our Jack, as I took a tray of drinks into the study. Ben threw his outer garments to the floor and rubbed his hands in front of the small fire.

"Bye, it's cold out. Now then, where's me sister?"

"Resting Sir, she'll be waking up soon though and knows tha's ter visit."

"And how about me new nephew, let's be having a look at him then."

I called to Margaret Ann to bring him in. Ben was always easy with a baby, as the second of nine children and with two little one's of his own, I suppose he had had plenty of practice.

"What a grand lad he is eh?" He stepped forward to take the baby's hand as Margaret Ann drew back his shawl to show him off. "Image of you Jack," he grinned, "no mistaking that."

Jack laughed; I had not seen him so relaxed since my arrival.

I saw Ben glance at Margaret Ann and smile at her. "He's just grand, isn't he?"

"Aye Sir, tis a pleasure ter care for him."

"Well Jack, if I don't have a son of me own, I shall name him as me heir, yes I shall."

"Nay, tis early days yet, plenty of time to have a son of your own, I think," replied Jack.

"Mmm well not so far, just two girls… not that I'd send them back for anything."

"Thank you, Margaret Ann," I said, indicating the door.

She bobbed politely and retreated.

"Well," said Ben a friendly arm around Jack, "it's not all bad for the little lad then."

"How do you mean?"

"Can't be all bad, spending the first year of his little life, nestling up with those two great big bubbies."

Jack could not help himself from smirking a little, he shook his head. "You've not changed Cousin."

"Nor why should I, nor why should I?"

Myself, I thought I would have to keep a careful eye on him and Margaret Ann.

"Now Sir, A'm teking a tray of tea up to thy sister, shall tha care ter join us?"

Suddenly serious, he said, "now truthfully Eliza, how is me Sister?"

I glanced at Jack, "in truth I would say she is a little better this last week; what say you, our Jack?"

He nodded, "yes, she has spoken more, and with reason too, but…" He raised his eyes to me, "but she cannot bear our babe near her still."

"No but A'm thinking it'll come with time," I said firmly.

Ben added, "well so it is with our animals sometimes, especially with a firstborn lamb, tis just a case of finding the trick to help them over it…"

Jack did not speak sharply, but I would say he spoke coldly.

"Cousin, I would remind you, we are not beasts of the field, we have our reason and our free will."

"Sorry Jack, forgive me I spoke out of turn, you know me, always weak on religion, much better with the sheep and cows."

Jack nodded and spoke again in his usual warm tone, "talking of animals, I have a few in our yard; come and take a quick look at them, while Aunt Eliza sets the tray."

From the kitchen, I could hear them talking as I put the kettle to boil.

"So, Cousin, who looks after this lot, while you're doing your vicaring and what not?"

Jack laughed, "why I see to them myself, I find with early rising it can be done before my morning duties."

"Well not while I'm staying, that is one thing I can do to help, every day I'm here, I'll get up and see to everything and you can have a bit of a lie in."

"That is kind, but there is no need…"

"There bloody is, no wonder you look so tired."

"I shall accept your kindness then, for a lie in or two would be a more than welcome treat. I'll show you where everything is…"

"No, you'll not, I'll find me own way about." He put an arm around Jack and steered him back into the kitchen. "I've been looking after animals since I could first stand up, and I know you, you'll have everything in the neatest of order. Yes?"

"I should like to think so."

I poured hot water into the teapot, I had made my master's favourite, a treacle tart, made with eggs and dark treacle, so some of that was on the tray too.

"Please, excuse me Cousin, I must return to my duties, for I have a funeral in half an hour."

After he had left, Ben said, "bloody saint, how come he's so good and me such a bad lad eh? What say you, Eliza?"

"Sir, his mother were very pious and A suppose he were brought up ter it."

"Mmm," he said thoughtfully, "she was lovely was Aunty Susannah. Made me and Robert stand on chairs at opposite sides of the room once, for fighting." He laughed, "usually she just told us kindly that God would not like to see us squabbling, God knows I loved her, we all did."

He took the tray from me and followed me upstairs into Belle's room.

"Now then Sister, how do I find you? A bit better I'm hoping..."

"Oh Ben, oh Ben..."

She could speak no more, and he sat upon the bed and took her in his arms as she wept. I think my master had never held a weeping woman before. He was a one for making everyone laugh before the tears came, his mother, his sisters, his children and even his wife, who was quite a petulant one by nature; he could always coax a smile at the very least.

When she had recovered herself somewhat, I left them sitting by the warm fire, they sat close, and Ben took her hands in his. They talked together intently and quietly for a good long time. When I brought up fresh tea, over an hour later they were still deep in conversation.

Over the next few days there were more tears, as they talked of their times as children and Ben told her of all his present doings on the farm. I knew she desperately missed her childhood home, never mentioning this to Jack, in case he felt inadequate in his provision for her. But I felt somehow that they were good tears that were shed, helping her rid herself of the pain inside her that she could hardly speak of to anyone.

****

Next day, I went into the kitchen, and to my shock there was my master, an arm about Margaret Ann's waist, whispering in her ear, telling her she was lovely and all that. To be fair, she had turned her head away and looked very uncomfortable.

"Margaret Ann, please attend to thy duties upstairs." As soon as she had left the room, I turned to him. "Sir, A'm surprised at thee, a happily married man, tha shouldn't behave so with a servant, nor anyone else come ter think."

He was meek and contrite, "I'm just a dirty dog Eliza, you want to give me a slapped leg, like you used to when I was a little lad."

"No Sir, A could not, for when tha were a little lad, tha dint know reet from wrong, and a slap were ter help thee to know, but now tha's got thy conscience and tha dunt need me ter tell thee what's reet."

I hoped I had not been too outspoken, I think I had not for he seemed to hang his head in shame, with only the smallest of twitches upon his lips, for I think he was laughing at me a little.

As Jack had so rightly said, my master had not changed one jot.

CHAPTER 3

1808. A week before Christmas.
In which a fine party is held.

A few days later, we were all to go to the fine party to be held by Olivia Fairfax, (sister to Belle and my master Ben Curzon). Her husband, a Mr Hartley Fairfax, was a rich man and quite the gentleman; with their own carriage to be sent to fetch us at six o-clock. The baby was to be left at home with the two servant girls and I was all day giving them instructions to keep the fire guarded, the doors locked, and windows shuttered, to cover the food, keep the baby well wrapped and remember to put hot stones in all the beds before our return. For I would swear before God, that house was colder inside than out.

"Tha can trust us honest Mistress", said Elizabeth Jane, "we'll do all t' things what tha said."

"We'll be sensible girls," promised Margaret Ann.

"Well yer best 'ad be," I said as firmly as I could, "else yer'll know about it."

Mid-afternoon, I put on my best dark dress and neat lawn neckerchief, for of course I had no party dress, not that it would be expected of the likes of me.

I raked through Belle's clothes and found a decent muslin gown; in her drawer was a most expensive silken scarf with gold stripes woven into it and a pretty fringe of tiny golden beads at either end. I showed them to her and asked her if she would like to wear them, she stared at the garments as if she had never seen the things before but did allow herself to be dressed. I spent a good deal of time brushing her dark hair, I was not much of a hairdresser, but she had such lovely long hair it looked well enough just twisted up and pinned.

Jack came into the bedroom at the last minute to change, he hesitated, clearly enamoured of her appearance. Putting his hand gently on her shoulder, he said, "shall you wear those little stars in your hair Dearest?"

She glanced at him blankly, as he opened a small green velvet box on top of the drawers and took out three paste hairpins shaped as stars.

I took them from him and said, "why they'd look bonny eh?" and pushed them into her hair at the back.

Then Jack spoke, "when we first lived here, Aunt Eliza, we called this our house under the stars, for all around us was such ugliness and foul smells from the dyeing factory, but when we looked up, we could always see beautiful stars above us."

"Well now, isn't that a nice thought?"

"Do you remember that Dearest?" he asked.

She did not reply, and he sighed turning away. I think it was only I who saw the tears on her eyelashes as she touched one of the starry clips with her fingertips.

"Does tha have long gloves Belle dear?"

Jack indicated the second drawer down. Quickly changing his linens, he put on a good coat, though I could see the cuffs had started to wear. He took Belle's arm, and we all went downstairs to await the carriage, for it was nearly six already.

We wrapped up in heavy shawls and winter bonnets. Jack and Ben, such handsome young men both of them, in tall hats and greatcoats, for it was a cold crisp night, on the edge of snow I'd have said. Just as the big old clock was striking, the carriage pulled up, drawn by two good sized bays. The coachman, a good-looking man, a year or two younger than myself, asked me if I wanted to sit up front with him as he had heavy rugs against the cold, and it was a pleasant clear night. Of course, I said no, and climbed into the carriage with the others to sit next to Belle to make sure she was comfortable, whereupon the coachman tucked a fur rug around us both. The inside of the carriage was most beautiful, lined with the softest cherry coloured leather, the upper part with a matching quilted silk and the fur rug, why I had never seen the like. It was a heavy whitish fur, sewn together in long strips on one side and the softest peach coloured velvet on the other. The velvet was cut away in flower patterns and there was a great tassel at each corner.

My master sat opposite me, he had already had a fair bit to drink and was speaking much too loud. He turned to Jack and said, "can't abide a bloody carriage, all this rolling about, give me a good horse any day, how about you Coz?"

"You'll not believe me Cousin, but this is the first time I've ever travelled in such a carriage and I'm finding it more comfortable than I would have thought. Of course, I've been times many in the stagecoaches to and from Cambridge, but a stagecoach is like a journey into Hell, eh Aunt Eliza?"

"There A've ter agree with thee our Jack, for A were terrified for me very life coming here," I said.

Here, Ben roared with laughter and took another swig from his brandy flask. It was offered around but

I took none, for the only time I ever had brandy was when I had the toothache and thus the taste always reminded me of such.

After a bit more drinking, Ben sang a couple of Christmas songs, and to be fair he did have a reasonable singing voice, though he was quite raucous by the time we arrived at Lockwood Beck House.

Olivia and Mr Fairfax had the most beautiful, new built house, I think I have ever seen. The outside was white with tall, pointed windows and everything inside was coloured white or the palest grey. The furniture was as dainty as could be, some of it painted with wreaths of flowers, some of it trimmed with gold. The downstairs rooms opened one into another and all was a sparkle, with what must have been a hundred candles, catching the gilt of the picture frames and the sconces in their light.

Olivia herself, quite resplendent in a silk dress, with tiny silver heart shapes embroidered over it, greeted us most warmly. Her husband, Mr Hartley Fairfax, who I had never much liked, called me 'dear Eliza', and taking my arm, led me to a comfortable chair by the fireside. Next to it, on a spindly little table, was set a decanter of port wine, a delicate crystal glass, and a pierced silver dish of nuts and candied fruits, some of the sweets in it were actually coloured gold and silver.

"Dear Eliza," he said, "Olivia has set this out for you. Of course, there will be a big supper in a couple of hours, but in the meantime please say if there is anything else we can get you."

I thanked him kindly, assuring him that I would be well pleased sitting there watching everything.

<u>Then</u>, as he turned to go, he said, "I shall show you our Mops as soon as all the guests have arrived."

Well, now I was aghast, whatever could he mean? Surely, when he had been so kind and thoughtful, he was not expecting me to mop floors. I poured myself a glass of port, decided to ignore his remark and enjoy myself as much as I could watching all those fine young people in their fashionable clothes. I will say that myself apart, there was no one there a day over thirty.

After some little while, when the dancing was just beginning, I saw Mr Fairfax offer his hand to Belle to partner him in the Cotillion, but she shook her head and looked away. An uneasy look passed over our Jack's face, for years before, Mr Fairfax had tried to steal Belle from our Jack, but in the end, he had settled to marry Olivia and it did seem they were quite as happy as could be now. She being so amiable, she would please any man, I would think.

Meanwhile Ben was handing his sister Olivia onto the dancefloor, and I had to smile for, as I have said, he had taken a fair bit of drink and he danced so vigorously he lost his footing and slithered to the floor. No one seemed a bit bothered and there was laughter all round as he was helped to his feet.

Next thing Mr Fairfax is at my side, pulling me up and taking my arm.

"Time to see our Mops Eliza," and we were off up the stairs and along a corridor carpeted in a pale blue; how they kept that clean I know not with little ones in the house, and dogs too. He thrust open a panelled door and there the sweetest sight met my eyes; two little girls sitting up in a white four posted bed. I saw at once, even before he said it, that they were the Mops, for each had a mass of tight golden curls sticking up all over their heads.

"Papa," they said with one voice, jumping out of bed and running to him. He laughed with pride, picking them both up together.

"Our Mops," he said simply, turning to me and they both reached out their little hands without any shyness at all.

Then, a voice was heard calling from the passageway.

"Quick," he said, putting down the children. "Quick hide, for it is Mama and she will surely beat you if she finds you out of bed."

Whereupon he lifted up his coat tails and the girls ran behind him and pretended to hide under them.

Olivia swept into the room, "Dearest, we have guests…"

"I was just introducing our Mops to Eliza."

"Whatever must you think of us Eliza?" she asked, laughing at the droll scene of her daughters clutching their father's legs and hiding their heads under his coat. "We cannot even get our children into bed."

"A think yer've prettiest little lasses, Mistress."

"And the naughtiest," she said tolerantly, "for they should be fast asleep by now."

Then they ran to her and begged and begged to be allowed to watch the dancing.

So I stepped up and said, "perhaps they could sit wi' me and watch some at' dancing and now A know where they sleep, A could put them ter bed for yer, for yer've both much ter do as hosts."

"Settled then Wife," said Mr Fairfax, taking her arm.

The little girls skipped along beside me as if they'd known me all their lives, back to my fireside chair; the youngest sat upon my knee and the other one leaned against me with my arm about her. The three of us took much pleasure watching the dancing, though quite soon the little one was warm and heavy in my arms, and I knew she was tired, so I said, "now each of yer choose a sweetie from my dish and if yer can get up them stairs quick, A'll tell yer me special story of Cinderella."

We were not far into that story when their slow rhythmic breathing told me they were fast asleep. I waited a few minutes more, just to be sure, blew out the candle and crept away, getting downstairs just in time for the supper.

I took an excellent repast which was served in the most elegant way imaginable, (though little of it seemed to tempt poor Belle). Afterwards, Olivia took me to one side, and I saw that there were tears in her eyes.

"Eliza, Ben tells me that Belle is ill and cannot care for her baby and will not have him near her. I had no idea of it till now, she will not speak to me of it, only shakes her head and looks at the floor and Jack told me to leave her be, quite sharply." She dabbed her eyes with a tiny lace handkerchief. "I cannot bear to think of that poor baby with none to love him…"

"Nay, nay, dun't fear for t' bairn, for he's loved by all t' servants and our Jack holds him upon his lap every day, even though he's so busy. And we have a good wet nurse." Trying to make light of it, for I see no point in making folks anxious when they can do naught to change things, I said, "even A think wet-nurse is good and tha knows how particular A am."

She smiled through her tears, and I patted her hand.

"So dun't fret over t' bairn, he's a fine strong healthy lad."

"Oh, is he? Bless him."

I took her hand now. "But as to thy sister, ter be honest, 'tis a worry. She's that quiet and thin and finds it hard ter tell of what she's thinking. She'd stay in bed all day if she could but A'm trying ter get her ter occupy herself a bit and hoping in time she'll be able ter pull herself round. Thy brother 'as sat talking with her a good while and says A've ter stay with her, so A won't be going back ter t' farm for some time yet. Put thy mind at peace Mrs Fairfax, while there's breath in me body, no harm'll come to thy sister."

"Thank you, Eliza." She blew her nose delicately on the tiny handkerchief. "I cannot understand it, a baby is such a very dear thing and such a gift, but I know no ill shall come to him if you are there."

I had not really thought of this, but of course, I knew it was not unheard of for mothers in their madness to harm their babes. I shuddered to think of it, and I could only pray God I would find a way to bring Belle back to herself.

As we were saying our goodbyes and wishing all a merry Christmas to come, Mr Fairfax took my hand and said, "Dear Eliza, I wish we could keep you, for our Mops have taken to you so. What say you wife?"

"Eliza is just pure gold," she said a little sadly, thrusting a large silver cardboard box into my hands, tied with silk ribbon. "A few sweetmeats for Christmas."

Whereupon, to my great astonishment, they both kissed me.

Out of the corner of my eye I could see our coachman listening in to all this, as he stood waiting for us by the front door.

When, at long last we were back at the vicarage, Ben, who could hardly stand for all the drink he had had, offered our coachman a warming brandy, which was politely refused as he said he had to get back to Whitby. For it turned out he was not coachman to the Fairfaxes but had only been hired for the evening to take us to and from the party.

As he turned to go, he gave me a most saucy wink and said in a low whisper, "well now A know where tha lives."

I was most surprised, but I could not resist a little secret smile to myself. Then he wished us all a very merry Christmas and was on his way.

Ben and Jack ensconced themselves by the fire in the study, Jack stirring the ashes into life and Ben pouring yet more drinks. Myself, I helped Belle straight up to bed; those girls had remembered the hot stones, so that the bed was warm and inviting for her. Indeed, everything seemed in order and the girls had been as good as their word, of which I was glad, for I had planned to give them my silver box of sweets as a treat on Christmas day.

Although I crept downstairs very quietly, in order to check the kitchen, my master must have heard me and called out from the study.

"Eliza."

"Yes Sir."

I went in and he grasped my wrist in a most inappropriate manner, but as I have already said, he was full of the drink, and I well knew what he would be wanting next for they always wanted toasted cheese at the end of a night of drinking.

"Dear Eliza…" he slurred his words a bit, but I knew what was coming next. "Dear Eliza…no drinking party is complete without…"

"No Sir, for Am tired beyond and my bed is calling me."

He was my master, and as his servant, I could never have refused him before, but here in my own cousin's house and away from the farm, I felt a whole new confidence to speak out.

"Nay Eliza, I beg of you, just one slice each. For are you not longing for it, Cousin Jack? Eliza's cheese on toast."

Jack laughed and nodded, "aye, there's naught to touch Aunt Eliza's cheese on toast."

My master put his hands together in a praying position.

"Please Eliza, this is my last night here and your cheese on toast is …is… sup…" He tried three times to say the word 'superlative', but could not, so instead he said, "have mercy on a desperate man."

"Very well Sir, but just one round each, and then Am ter me bed and yer both can shout all yer likes, A shall not hear yer for A'll be fast away."

And so, I sliced up bread and made cheese on toast, (and of course, I was rather flattered).

But there was something else, I was flattered about when I came to think about it, which I did as I was falling asleep that night. It was this: when I was at the party, all the servants had quite ignored me as a fellow servant to be invited into the kitchen but instead, they had seen me as a maiden aunt visiting her young nephew at the vicarage. And somehow this pleased me, I felt I had made myself anew and I rather liked this new person.

As to that saucy coachman, well I put him right from my mind as I closed my eyes that night, of course I did.

CHAPTER 4

The next day.
In which Ben Curzon shows he has a good heart.

Despite all the late merrymaking of the previous night, I heard my master rise at six o-clock to see to the animals, which he had done every day of his visit, as promised, so that our Jack could have his last lie-in. I turned over in my bed, which was still warm and comfortable, knowing I had another hour before I need get up and face the icy day. I lay there thinking what a sound man my master was, for all his fooling about, he had the goodest heart. Taking over the farm when he was but fifteen years old and his father had suddenly died, he had had to step up and be a man. For all he played the gentleman farmer, he never shirked from the work that was needed and made it clear to his outdoor servants that he asked nothing of them that he would not do himself.

When, at last I had got up, faced the cold of dressing, gone downstairs, stirred the embers of the kitchen fire into life and boiled a bit of water, he came in from the yard, rubbing his raw hands.

"Bloody hell, Eliza, me head's banging like a barn door."

He held his reddened hands out to the fire.

"Well Sir, if tha will drink so much, tha must pay t' price. A few good cups of tea and a raw egg will soon bring thee round."

With that I broke two eggs into a glass of milk and port wine and stirred them up.

"Bloody hell, I can hardly swallow, me mouth's so dry."

He gagged a bit on the egg mixture, but it seemed to work, for he was soon laughing at himself and tucking into bacon and bread fried in lard as he sat at the fireside.

"Now, while we're alone Eliza, I have to be off home today as you know, so what needs to be sent over? I know if I ask Jack, he'll say they need nothing. I'm thinking a cartload of wood and a barrel of apples. Belle was always fond of green apples, they'll not put flesh on her, but they might just tempt, eh? What else?"

I was touched that he had remembered Belle's fondness for apples. For when she was growing up on the farm, she almost always reached for one after her dinner.

"Maybe some cheese and some butter? For there's plenty at t' farm and ter be honest Sir, tis not a full pantry here."

"Aye, I see that, but Jack's a proud man."

"Also Sir, if tha might mention it to thy good wife, warm clothes will be needed for t' bairn, he's growing fast, and he'll be out of these little things in no time, and she might have some to spare."

"Good thinking Eliza."

He took a little ivory pad out of his waistcoat pocket and wrote a list with a stub of pencil.

Looking up at me with his bloodshot eyes, he said, "I want you to know how grateful I am to you, for taking on looking after me sister. I could not bear the thought of her being…being with strangers when she's… when she's lost some of her reason. I can leave confident that she'll be cared for properly but if you ever think there is aught I should know, then write to me and I'll come over at once."

"Tha knows A cannot write Sir."

"I've thought of that." He tapped the side of his nose and drew a sealed up letter from his pocket, "this is all addressed, just take it to the post lad at the inn if you need me to come and soon as I get it, I'll know to come straight off."

I slipped it into my apron pocket and then I was much surprised, for he felt inside his jacket and took out five gold guinea coins.

"For your Christmas box Eliza, with my deepest thanks."

"Nay Sir, A cannot tek these, tis way too much." And I put my hands behind my back.

"You can indeed," and he dropped the coins into my pocket, "There's no thanks enough, for my sister's most precious to me, I could not bear to lose her."

My master was rarely so serious, and I felt the weight of my burden, but I prayed God would help me to choose the right path for poor Belle.

I suddenly felt overcome and said, "Master, A knew thy father most of his life and one thing A do know is that he'd be that proud of thee… if he could but be with us now."

"I thank you; it means much that you should say that," he sighed. "God bless you, Eliza."

Later that morning, Belle wept copiously at his departure; yet his visit had done her a power of good, for when I went in to see to her, she had managed to dress herself for the first time, and with Elizabeth Jane's help, had got a decent fire going and had picked up her knitting.

When he left, my master had asked of our Jack, if ever Belle needed time away, she would be most welcome to come and stay at the farm and he would fetch her over himself. 'Get some roses in her cheeks,' he had said.

Jack had shaken his head and said, 'I know that is meant from kindness, but I have loved your sister all my life and we will be together until death, for good or ill.'

With that they had embraced, then my master gave two half-crowns to Elizabeth Jane, for her and her sister, mounted his horse and was gone.

True to his word, a couple of days later, a farm servant arrived with a great cartload of wood, baskets of dairy produce, linens, a barrel of apples and a piglet squealing its head off in a covered basket.

Thus, we found ourselves well stocked up for Winter.

CHAPTER 5

Two days before Christmas.
In which some Christmas baking is done.

Two days before Christmas, Jack came into the kitchen and sank into a chair at the fireside. He looked tired and pale, and I asked him if he would take some food, but he said he had no time, as he had not yet finished his visits for the day and had a funeral that afternoon. Of course, in this bitter weather many were sick and more than a few were finding their way to their graves.

"Just a bit of tea and bread, our Jack."

Without waiting for an answer, I filled a cup and as he warmed his frozen hands upon it, I cut some bread and folded it around a slice of beef.

He smiled up at me.

"Thank you, Aunt Eliza…I do have something to ask of you, and I hope it will not be too much of a trouble."

"Go on then."

"Well, it came to me that after the Christmas Morn service, would it be possible to give each of our parishioners a hot mince pie, for there will be many who do not go home to the good dinner we would expect on Our Lord's special day."

How could I refuse such a thing? "Of course, our Jack, how many will be needed?"

"I fear about a hundred, they need not be large, only so that each has something warm and cheering as they go to their homes."

"If we start on t' mincemeat today, it can be easy done in time, and then on t' day Elizabeth Jane can slip out at service and fetch them ovver in a basket. A'll line it with plenty of straw and laid on a cloth, that'll keep them good and hot."

"Thank you, dear Aunt Eliza," he said, but I could see he was thinking of something else now, as he pulled on his heavy coat and gloves.

So that very afternoon, I took Elizabeth Jane to the shop with me, early on before it started to get dark, for I did not like to be out too late in that village. We bought two pounds of beef and the same of mutton, a good lump of suet, plenty of raisins, currants and prunes too.

"The mince pies is it Mistress?" asked the shopkeeper in a friendly way, as he put cloves, mace and pepper into twists of paper.

"Sir it is, one hundred A'm meking."

He spoke pleasantly and said that nothing spelt Christmas to him better than a well-baked mince pie.

I took out my purse, for I had decided to pay for this from my own money. I did not need to buy for the pastry as there was already plenty of lard and flour in the pantry at home.

As soon as we got back, I had both girls chopping the meat very fine, grating the suet and grinding the spices. Of course, back in my days at the farm, I would always have added some saffron to give that special flavour, but the vicarage larder could not run to such luxury and nor could I. Here, we just mixed everything we had together, including some candied orange peel, I found in a canister on a high up shelf and hoped for the best.

Next day, Christmas Eve, I showed them how to boil lard and water without letting it spatter, then pour it into the centre of a large quantity of salted flour and I have to say, between them they made a very fair pastry. The little pies were filled, the tops pinched together and then glazed with melted butter and sugar to give a nice crispness. Altogether, we baked one hundred and eight pies, so that left a few over for us to eat ourselves, hot from the oven.

What with the baking, I had not had time to sit with Belle for the day's knitting, so I put two cups of tea and a couple of mince pies on a little tray and carried them upstairs to her room. There, I was much gratified to see her sitting up in a fireside chair, already at her work.

"See Eliza, I've remembered how to turn the heel myself on this one, so I've nearly finished the pair."

"Why Belle, A'm thinking tha'll have them done in time for termorrow ter give ter our Jack. For 'tis Christmas day termorrow."

"Is it?" she said, with little interest.

"Yes, and A know he'll welcome a good pair of warm stockings as a gift."

There was no answer to this, so I said, "shall tha tek a mince pie, while it's still warm?"

She crumbled up the pie and ate some of it. With tearful eyes she looked up at me and said the taste reminded her of being a child at home.

"I was so happy then, though I did not really know it till now; when we were all together and Papa was alive…We had all the horses and dogs too."

She wiped away a tear and reached out for her cup of tea. I drank mine too for there was nothing to say. Her childhood full of happiness and with little to worry of, replaced by a lonely life in a grim vicarage with a baby she could not care for and a husband she believed did not love her. Well, what could I have said to comfort that, for naught will turn back time?

Christmas day dawned a bitter grey day. Though I wore four petticoats (two of them flannel) and both my woollen shawls on together, I still felt chilled to the bone as we walked across to the church. I had given Margaret Ann strict instructions to keep the pies warm but not burnt, and at the last minute, to lay them out on linen cloths in the straw lined basket.

Our Jack gave the most beautiful and moving sermons, I have ever heard. The theme was how special each and every one of us is to God, and how He is always with us, even in our darkest hour of need. Lovely as it was, I thought that most of that congregation, ill fed and poor clothed, needed more than God's love to bring them comfort and health; though I knew it was probably wicked of me to think it so.

Just as our Jack was coming up to the final blessing, I nudged Elizabeth Jane and she slipped out quietly. Myself, I struggled to my feet, stiff with the dreadful cold of the church, indeed it seemed a touch warmer as we went outside. Just in time, Elizabeth Jane and I were holding onto either side of the big, flat basket as everyone came out. Jack stood in the porch with a kindly word for each and then with a touching gratitude, they all took one of our mince pies, excepting for a plump boy in a velveteen jacket who grabbed three, stuffed them all in his mouth at once and ran off laughing.

"Squire's son," whispered Elizabeth Jane.

It seemed that we had baked enough as the final stragglers came out and I was just shaking out the linen cloths, when I looked back and saw Jack talking to two children. There was a girl and a lad a bit younger; a lump rose in my throat when I saw that the boy held a stick with a rag tied around it and the way he looked about him, I realised that he was blind.

Next thing, they're all outside and us with an empty basket, so I said straight off, "now don't yo two think there's nowt left for yer, A've put by summat special for yer both."

And I instructed a puzzled Elizabeth Jane to run up to my bedroom as fast as she could and to bring back the silver box of sweets on the mantle shelf there.

"Now yo two tell me a bit about yerselves, whilst we wait."

The girl spoke up, "please Mistress, A'm Annie and this is our Billy, we live at Black Bull and A work there."

"And where are thy parents Dear?"

"They are both with God, Mistress, our mother died two years since and our father last year in an accident at dye works." Her voice faltered a little and I caught out Jack's eye.

"So where is it yer live now?"

"At Black Bull, we sleep in a cupboard there and A work in t' day for our bread, our Billy cannot work so much, for he's blinded after having the measles." She must have caught the pity in my expression, for she added reassuringly, "tis safe in our cupboard and we have two blankets and t' landlady were good ter tek us on, for otherwise it would've been t' poorhouse for me and Billy and we wunt have been kept together."

"Their father was a good man," sighed Jack, "tried his best to bring them up in Godly ways, but sometimes we cannot see God's purpose easily."

Fortunately, just then, Elizabeth Jane came running towards us, puffing and out of breath, carrying the splendid box of sweets.

"Oh, Mistress is this really for us?" gasped Annie as I put it into her cold little hands. "Our Billy 'tis t' most beautiful box tied with real silver ribbons."

When I helped her open the lid, she gasped with delight.

"Billy, 'tis filled with sweets...and nuts and fruits too. Some of them are gold and silver...like something in one of our father's stories."

Gently she touched them with her fingertips, then chose a candied fruit and put it into Billy's mouth. She curtsied low and thanked me profusely and on being nudged hard, Billy gave a little bow and thanked me too.

Elizabeth Jane looked at me and felt for her handkerchief.

Jack laid his hands upon their heads and said, "may God always watch over you," then more cheerily he shook their hands and wished them both a very merry Christmas.

I took Jack's arm as we walked back to the house.

"Aunt Eliza, sometimes 'tis so hard to do God's work here, to see such want and to be able to do so little to alleviate it. Their father died aged only thirty in an accident at the factory, but he should not have been working at all, for he had a sickness of the lungs and needed good food and rest; but with two youngsters to provide for, he had no choice," he shrugged. "The landlady who took them in is good hearted enough, but a rough inn is no place for children to grow up in, though I suppose it preferable to the workhouse?"

I agreed and tried my best to put it all from my mind and make sure everyone had a good dinner at home. There was a roasted chicken and a duck too with potatoes crisped up in the fat; I did two kinds of stuffing and a plum pudding flamed in brandy to follow. All served on the most beautiful of china and crystal set out on finest linen, which had once belonged to Belle's Grandmother Franklin, who had been what you would call 'well to do'.

Of course, I could not give the two girls the box of sweets now, but I gave them some fine linen handkerchiefs I had never used, and they seemed pleased enough. Myself, I was touched to receive a pair of well knitted gloves from Margaret Ann and a matching muffler from Elizabeth Jane in a very becoming shade of light blue.

After the dinner, they were to walk to their own home to spend the afternoon with their family. I knew Margaret Ann much missed her little boy. I had made him some warm socks and a little striped cap, and I gave them the remains of the meats and pudding to take with them too, for I knew their father was ailing and I guessed a bit of extra food would be welcome.

After they had left, I sat beside the kitchen fire with the baby. He looked at me most seriously and I said, "well, little Jack it seems there are to be no festive games and fun for us today, eh?"

As if he agreed, he closed his eyes and slept soundly for the rest of the afternoon.

CHAPTER 6

Two weeks later.
In which Eliza has a gentleman caller.

It was a Sunday, a couple of weeks after the Christmas. We had got the dinner out of the way and cleared up, the two girls were at the kitchen table chatting and doing a bit of sewing; myself, I was sitting by the fireside with my knitting. Thus, we were all cosy and settled, when, unexpectedly, there was a bold knock at the outer door. It quite jolted me, for I confess, I had almost nodded off. I jumped up, thinking it must be some kind of delivery but on opening the door, I was most astonished to see that saucy coachman who had winked at me when he had driven us back from the Fairfax's Christmas party.

He bowed low and said, "Miss Lawson, forgive me for coming unannounced like."

Then he looked at me very directly and I hoped my blush did not show, as I invited him into the kitchen. I took his coat for him, which I noted was of rather good quality and hung it on the back of the door, he laid his hat and gloves upon a chair. It was on the tip of my tongue to ask if he had brought a message or a letter for our Jack, but something held me back from saying it out loud and instead I offered him a cup of tea.

The two girls stared at him, open-mouthed, but when I glared at them, they said they had to go upstairs to sort out the linens.

He stood by me awkwardly while I filled the teapot and set out the cups. Then he thrust a cloth wrapped parcel into my hands.

"A brought this for thee, 'tis a cake what A've bekked me self."

In truth, I was astonished, but I unwrapped it and saw a most presentable fruit cake there.

"Why A thank thee Mr Thornton, that is most kind of thee."

"Does tha think it odd a man bekking a cake?" He asked, taking a seat in one of the fireside chairs.

"Well, A own A've nivver known of it afore, but it looks a fine cake ter me."

I cut two slices and indeed it cut nice, and the fruit was well spread through it, for it easy for the fruit to sink if one does not soak it thoroughly afore mixing.

"So," he said with his head on one side and grinning at me, "when me wife passed, three year since, A were missing a bit o' cake, so A thought A'd teach me self ter bake. A telled me self it couldn't be difficult if a woman could do it."

Of course, I tutted at that, but I could not help smiling too. Then, he had me laughing out loud as he told of his learning to bake; one cake was hard as a brick, another burst into flames in the oven and one was so soft, even the dog would not touch it. Truth be told, I cannot remember when I had last laughed so much. He told me he lived in Whitby, where he had his own cottage, and also had four more let out, divided in to eight tenements. I will say I was more than a little impressed.

After he had drunk two cups of tea, he said he had best go and pulled on his greatcoat. Then he took my hand in both of his, (he had strong, warm hands) and asked if he might call again. I said I could see no harm in it, so long as he was passing anyway. He said he thought he would be passing a fair bit, raised my hand to his lips to kiss my fingers, picked up his hat and gloves and was gone. For a moment I stared at my fingers like a fool, as if I had never seen them afore, but not for long, for his horse was hardly out of earshot, when those two girls came clattering down the stairs, full of giggles and questions.

"Now yo two," I said raising my finger, "A want none of yer nonsense. Yer can ask me one question each, which A shall answer as truthful as A can, then yer can each have a piece of cake and A want ter hear no more about it. Well?" I looked towards Elizabeth Jane.

"Please Mistress, what is that man's name?"

"Mr Thornton," I replied, "Mr Thomas Thornton."

I turned to Margaret Ann and raised a questioning eyebrow.

"Please Mistress," she said, a bit too bold, "as he come ter court thee?"

Here I did surprise myself, for I answered, calm as anything, "Aye, A believe he has."

So, I cut them each a slice of the cake and wrapped the rest of it up again to keep it fresh.

****

To cut a long story short, Mr Thornton and I came to something of an understanding by March, and I agreed to marry him; the wedding to be three months hence in the June. I thought this would give Belle plenty of time to get a bit better in herself. Indeed, after a such a difficult start, she was suddenly making good progress. In fact, only that very week, she had held the sleeping baby in her arms for the first time and had kissed his forehead as she laid him in his cradle.

So, on a bright Spring day at the end of March, Mr Thornton hired a gig and arranged to take me in to Whitby to see his row of cottages. I felt quite a rush of excitement when we got there and pulled up at the end of the busy yard. He helped me down from the high seat, with a secret little squeeze of my waist and I felt such pride as I took his arm and we walked up to his very own cottage.

Inside, I was pleasantly surprised, for I had thought that a man on his own for a few years would have let things go, but not so, everything was as neat and clean as a pin.

There was a big brick fireplace with polished irons and fender, with two wooden settles to either side of it. Four chairs surrounded a good-sized table, well-scrubbed and already set with the tea things. There was a great dark dresser, laden with blue and white cups and plates; shiny pans and ladles hung from the low beams. Below the sliding window stood a seaman's type chest with cushions on top, so it could be used as a window-seat and on the sill, pots of geraniums just coming into flower, giving such a cheerful touch of oranges, pinks and reds.

"Well?" He said grinning at me.

"Tha's a truly pleasing home Mr Thornton, A like it very much indeed."

For it was as nice and as comfortable as ever I could have wished for.

"Best not show thee t' other room yet awhile, Darling."

"But why?" I asked, puzzled.

"Well 'tis bedroom int it and A might not be able ter hold meself back wi' me passions and that."

"Oh, what nonsense," I laughed, slapped his arm lightly and boldly climbed up the narrow winding stairs.

There, I saw a four-poster bed filling most of the room, covered by such a pretty patchwork quilt and a chest of drawers with wash things atop. It somehow touched my heart to see his jackets and hats hanging neat from a row of hooks on the wall. All as clean and tidy as ever I could have wished it.

Upstairs again, in a light and airy garret with open beams sloping to the floor, were two narrow beds. They were both unmade but with piles of neatly folded blankets and ticking pillows upon them.

"Course when A were first wed, we thought our bairns'd be sleeping up here, but it weren't ter be."

"Did tha have no bairns then?"

He shook his head, "me wife were heartbroken ovver it, but as A said, it were not ter be. A nivver thought it would be difficult, A thought yer wed and young uns'd come along straight off." He sighed, "after a while A nivver mentioned it, for she got upset wi' herself ovver it and A dint want her ter think A blamed her for it, for she were a good wife ter me."

A little idea sprang into my head; it was an idea that stayed with me, though I did not speak of it for many months more.

"But tha wanted bairns?" I asked.

"Course A did, A wanted nowt more."

For a moment I felt shut out by his past, but not for long, for he turned me to him and kissed me in such a way that I knew now, that old as we were, ours was not to be a marriage of companionship but a true marriage in all ways.

As we sat to our tea downstairs, he looked at me very directly and said, "does tha think A'll do for thee then, Darling?"

"A think tha well might, Mr Thornton."

"And's me house to thy liking, for things can be changed if tha wants."

"No, A like it just as it is, 'tis a very comfortable home Mr Thornton."

Indeed, it was all exactly as I would have it. Somehow God had provided me with the house I always wanted and the kind of husband, I had only ever dreamed of.

After we had eaten, we drove along the quayside, I was hoping to catch sight of our Hugo (Jack's younger brother). I knew he would be sailing soon for the Greenland fisheries upon his cousin's ship the "Olivia Belle". But we were to be disappointed, for after driving down both ways, Mr Thornton pulled up the gig and asked a passing sailor, who told us the "Olivia Belle" had already sailed two days earlier, on account of the fine weather.

And so that night as I lay in my own bed, my head was full of girlish dreams of my wedding three months hence, my new home and my fine husband to be.

I was not a young woman, and you might say better late than never for all this. I knew I had wasted most of my life in a foolish yearning after my cousin, Jacob Curzon. In truth, though I believed him fond enough of me, he had never looked at me in that way. As our young years passed it became obvious, he would rather bed any woman, so long as it was not me; even bringing one of his bastards home for his then wife to care for. I shall not speak ill of this, for we all loved that young Hugo with all our hearts, but it was not a righteous thing to do. After his poor wife died upon the childbed, I thought perhaps I would have a chance, but that was not to be either, for she was hardly cold in her grave when Cousin Jacob started sniffing around Lydia Curzon. Not six months later, he married her, as she was well set up with a house and some money and him with naught, being the Curzon son born out of wedlock himself.

Now, at long last, Jacob was out of my head, and I had found an honourable and decent man to be my husband and for it all, I much thanked God.

CHAPTER 7

Two days before.
In which brothers are found.

Hugo Curzon went to sign up for his third voyage on the "Olivia Belle", bound for Greenland to catch whales, seals and maybe a polar bear or two. He was happy and confident as he stood in the muster line, chatting with others he knew who were to make up the crew of some forty men: some sombre at leaving wives and children, others like Hugo full of excitement with the prospect of a hunting trip. A couple of young lads were signed up too, one crying who could not have been more than eight years old.

Now he stood at the muster table to give his details to the First Mate.

"Name?"

"Hugo Curzon."

The First Mate looked up, he seemed to gasp and swallow hard as he stared at him.

Not understanding, Hugo repeated his name, and with shaking hand, the man recorded all his details. As he walked away, something made him turn around and he saw the Mate looking at him. Thinking little of it, he boarded ship soon after and of course there was much to do in preparations to make sail. High on the mast, he had the most magnificent of views as the boat rushed and bumped out of the harbour and suddenly rocked into proper waves as she left its safety. The "Olivia Belle" had set sail in the finest of weather. Captain Robert Curzon, cousin to Hugo and part owner, with a quarter share of the ship, had high expectations for the trip, hoping that by leaving early, he would reach the whaling waters before any of the others and thereby get the pick of those so profitable whales.

Climbing down the ratlines from the rigging, Hugo's next task was set by the Speksioneer, to coil and check the whaling ropes to be at the ready, even though it would be quite some days before a whale was sighted.

Absorbed in his task, he did not hear the approach of the First Mate, till he crouched down beside him. Hugo looked up in surprise.

"A think tha's me brother, in fact A'm sure of it."

"What?" Hugo reeled back slightly, thinking the man must be completely mad.

"Twenty year ago, me mother had a bairn, and it wasn't me father's so she took it away after just a few week ter live with t' natural father and we nivver saw t' bairn again."

"But that's not me, why should it be?"

"Bairn were called Hugo, he'd be twenty now and it's thy eyes, there t' same as mine, a yallery grey there's not many with eyes that colour, but me and me mother… and thee. A'd say we're of a height too."

"Well, there's many, same height as me, that means nowt, it definitely dunt mean we're brothers. Any road A've a sister Penelope and A've a brother Jack and it's not thee."

"Aye, they'll be thy half brother and sister, as A'm thy half-brother, and my sister Sarah is thy half-sister too."

Hugo felt angry and defensive now.

Ged went on, "A see A've shocked thee, A'll let thee think on't and tek it all in. We'll maybe talk more of it termorrow, eh?"

He stood up and walked away.

Hugo did not understand why this had disturbed him so, when this man, this Ged, was clearly deranged. But it had and Ged's words kept repeating themselves in his head.

Later, as he was sitting to his dinner at the end of his watch, a sudden thought came to him. It was as if someone had punched him hard in the stomach, for quite out of the blue, he remembered something from long, long ago, one of his very first memories. He had been sitting on his mother's lap and his Aunt Lydie had arrived; he must have been ill for she had bent down and asked, 'how is our dear little cuckoo baby today?'

His sister Penelope had asked why she always called him the cuckoo baby, everyone had smiled and Aunt Lydie, said it was because he had such a soft brown head like a baby cuckoo, and he remembered the feel of her hand as she had stroked his hair.

Now, this seemed to hold so much more meaning, for was not a cuckoo, a stranger in the nest? He tipped his meat stew into his neighbour's bowl and pushed his bread across to the man opposite him and leapt up. Without explanation he ran from the cabin to cries of,

"What ails man?"

"Bloody Hell what's wi' him?"

"Is he sickening?"

He ran along the passage, knocked at the captain's door and without waiting burst in.

Robert looked up from the chart he was working on and was about to reprimand his cousin, but on seeing the dark flush of extreme agitation in his face, he bade him sit down instead.

But Hugo did not sit, he gripped the back of the chair and said, "Cousin Robert, I must speak with thee, and ask thee summat most urgently."

"Very well," he said, carefully wiping his pen and laying it down neatly in its tray. "But please do be seated and try to calm yourself first, for you seem much disquieted Cousin."

He reached across to a galleried tray and poured two brandies from the wide bottomed decanter. "Here drink this first, and then speak of what is troubling you so."

Hugo gulped at the drink and Robert said, "what is it that you wish to ask me?"

"Can tha remember me as a bairn?"

The captain was astonished, of all the questions in the world, this one was one that could hardly have been anticipated.

"What? Yes," he said puzzled, "of course I can."

"Tell me, tell me what tha remembers."

"I remember when we were little, often going up to 'Hill Cottage', me and sisters Belle and Olivia, and sometimes brother Ben came too. Aunty Susannah used to read us stories and we always had little cakes. And Penelope and Jack were there as well, and Aunty Susannah had you in her arms... is that what you want me to say?"

Hugo shook his head, "no, can tha remember me being born?"

Robert thought for a moment; he had five siblings younger than him, who he could remember being proudly shown off as new-borns in his mother's arms as she sat up in her bed.

"To be honest Hugo, I don't remember you being born, only my own brothers and sisters, but what is this, why has this upset you so?"

"First Mate, that Ged Stone, says he's me half-brother, me natural brother and A've a half-sister too, and A were took away from them at a few week old to live with me real father…"

"Oh." Robert hardly knew what to say to keep his composure and hide his absolute amazement. "So er, what do you think yourself? Are you thinking this might be possible?"

"A dint, a thought he were bloody mad, anyone would. But then A remembered summat."

Here he told Robert of his memory of being called 'the cuckoo baby'.

"Ah," sighed the captain, he did not say it out loud, but he well knew his mama often spoke without thinking and if there was a tactless thing to be said, then she would be the one to say it.

"Does tha remember any of t' family saying owt about me being me father's natural child?"

"In truth, Hugo, I do not, but our parents were not angels, such things do happen and often I think, these things are not spoken of within a family. I swear before God, I have never heard aught of this before. But others must know of it, if it be true." Here Robert flinched a little, for despite his own deep Christian faith, he had recently fathered a child out of wedlock himself, though none of his family knew of it.

"But that? How could my mother, how could Susannah, bring me up and…and love me, when I was not hers?"

Robert shrugged, "I remember my Mama once saying that Aunty Susannah had lost several much-wanted babies, perhaps you filled that gap for her? For I do know she loved you, that I do remember."

"A thought she did, but now A'm questioning everything."

"And Grandmama loved you best, we all used to think you her favourite," added Robert encouragingly. Hugo nodded as Robert went on, "and another thing, I've sailed times many with Ged Stone, he is my good friend and there's no man more sound; if he says he's your brother, then he'll have a good reason for saying it, right or wrong." Hugo drained his drink and stood up slowly. "Cousin Hugo, naught can be settled for the next five months while we're at sea, then you can question Jack or Uncle Jacob or Mama, so I would ask that you put this from your mind as much as you can and put all your efforts into your labours. All must be working at their best to make this voyage a success for every one of us. There can be no shirkers. While you are in this cabin you are my dear cousin and we are bound by blood, beyond that door you are subject to the same disciplines as any other seaman."

"A know that; A would not want it otherwise. So tha thinks this could be true then?"

Robert shrugged again, "how can I know one way or the other? Ask Ged Stone more of it, and perhaps get a clearer picture. One more thing Hugo, tomorrow is Mothering Sunday, after the ship's prayers, all will be casting a flower or such into the sea and giving thanks for their mothers, whether in this world or the next. Please remember, that whatever the facts of the matter, Aunty Susannah was the one that cared for you and was a true mother to you, so think of her."

Hugo nodded. "A thank thee for thy time Captain," he said as formally as any other seaman.

He left the cabin and walked slowly down the passageway until the lump in his throat had gone.

He spoke no more of this to anyone and avoided Ged Stone where he could.

There was a great feeling of euphoria for the crew days later when it became clear that they had reached whaling waters before any other ships; in fact, they had to wait two days for the ice to break up and give their boat passage. Hugo worked hard throughout the voyage, he tried his best to put troubling thoughts from his mind, but he had begun to see, at least it was a possibility that he had been a cuckoo in his nest and part of a shameful family secret.

CHAPTER 8

June 1809.
In which Lydia and Jacob attend a wedding.

Jacob and I sat side by side on the edge of the bed after a simply dreadful, uncomfortable and sleepless night in the vicarage guest room. He rubbed my shoulders gently.

"Jacob, do you think her still a virgin?"

"A dunt bloody know." He laughed and turned away embarrassed.

"But Dearest, you must know, you and Eliza have lived near each other for most of your lives, as well as being first cousins… when you were young, were there no swains to court her? For she must have been good looking, still is in a way, for her age."

He thought a moment, "very many years ago when me Cousin Ben were at Cambridge, he brought back one of his fancy friends ter stay at t' farm for a week or two…"

"And so was there something between them?"

"Aye, A think so, A saw them disappearing in ter t' dairy a time or two. But of course, it came ter nowt, for she were only a servant, and he were an educated, young gentleman like."

"Was she heart-broken then?"

"No, A think not, for it were only a bit of a fancy like."

"So there was no beau that broke Eliza's heart then?"

He hesitated and looked at me very directly but did not answer.

"What, my Love?"

He shook his head and still said nothing.

Greatly intrigued, I asked again.

"Actually, A think that were me as broke her heart; A think that were why she nivver married afore."

Well now I was astonished, having had no notion of this before. "So she had eyes for you then?"

He nodded and sighed, "A feel bad about it even now… but tha can't help tha feelings can tha? It all came ter a head one Christmas, when A were twenty-two and she were a year older. Well she were allus gazing at me, or standing too close. So this Christmas, we'd all had more than a few drinks, and she puts her arms around me and pulls me close. Next off she's kissing me and saying as she loves me." He looked at me anxiously. "A dint want ter be cruel, but A think A were, for A pulled away and told her A thought of her as a sister and were glad ter have her as such. Then A turned from her and moved off."

"You have never spoken of this before Dearest."

He shrugged, "there were nowt ter tell, A were young and liked a bit of a chase, what man wants it handed ter him on a plate? She'd 'ave smothered me with love and A dint want ter be tied down. Liked ter play t' field, leastways till A met Susannah." I waited for him to carry on. "When A met Susannah, A thought of her every minute at' time, working out how ter get her, for she played hard ter get. And t' more she refused me, t' more A chased her. And when she finally agreed ter wed me, why A thought meself luckiest man alive and it seemed ter me she were t' greatest prize in Whitby."

I took his hand pensively, for Susannah, his first wife, had been my dear and true friend, God's own angel on this earth, who had been called to Him far too soon.

Jacob had spoken sadly, but as always, he quickly made light of it. Cupping my face in his hands, he kissed me and said, "what a fortunate old donkey A am, both me wives, finest lasses in Whitby. Me born a bastard, wi' nowt and wed ter likes o' thee, lucky old sod that A am."

He laughed and kissed me again.

And then, our little Martha Jane awoke, she had slept between us all night and had made that night so wakeful and uncomfortable for us both. Sleeping arrangements were not the best; we had to share with our youngest, and Octavia was doubling up with Eliza, which she was not too pleased about. But as I said to them both, it was only for the one night, so that we could all be there in good time for Eliza's wedding at nine in the morning.

Next thing, that fat girl, whose name I'd forgotten, but who seemed to be the wet-nurse, brought in a can of hot water. She placed it on the hearth, next to the jug and basin, there being no washstand.

"Thank you Dear," I said.

"Mistress," she bobbed politely.

Martha Jane stretched and rubbed her eyes. "What a very nice long sleep I've had Papa."

"Lucky for some," he said under his breath.

She climbed over him and pulled him to his feet.

"Dance with me Papa, for I'm going to be a BRIDESMAID today." She started to whirl him into a dance, singing, "I'm to be a bridesmaid, a bridesmaid, a…".

Jacob was none too steady with his bad leg and backed into the hot water can spilling all of our precious supply onto the floor.

As quickly as I could, I tried to mop it up with the meagre supply of towels.

"Surely there must be a spare washstand or two over at the farm, that they could have here?"

"Oh, sorry Papa, I'm just sooo excited."

She hugged and kissed him so vigorously that he had to sit down on the bed again.

"Bloody monkey's tea-party this," he laughed, trying to wash his face on a sodden towel.

And cross as I was, I had to smile at this, for he was referring to our trip to Bath, a few years since. Jacob had not much enjoyed the visit, but one thing which had amused him endlessly was a monkey's tea-party which had taken place on the green, opposite our rooms. Each day, an Italian man would arrive with a troop of half a dozen monkeys, little chairs and a table. Sometimes the monkeys would pour carefully from the tea-pot into the tiny cups and eat their cakes daintily, but more often than not, they chattered and shouted, spilt tea everywhere and threw the food at each other, playing I think, to the delighted audience.

Luckily, I had brought a hand mirror, for of course there was no dressing mirror provided.

"Now hold this steady Martha Jane, so that I can do my hair." I thought it best not to even attempt powder and rouge.

Then my Octavia, looking a picture of neatness, burst in and the generally sorry scene met her eyes.

"Why none of you are nearly ready and Aunt Eliza is serving breakfast in the kitchen for us all, right now."

She slapped Martha Jane's arm quite hard. "Get your bridesmaid dress on NOW, and don't forget your gloves and bonnet. Mama, sit down and I will do your hair, and you'll need some powder, for you look a sight without it."

Some might have thought that to be an insolent remark from a fourteen-year-old, but not I, for I knew it well meant, and in the blink of an eye Octavia had us all cleaned and at the ready.

"Why is everything so wet?" she asked, glancing at the floor.

No one replied, so she just rolled her eyes at the ceiling and said, "Lord preserve me from my family."

"Please do not blaspheme Dear, especially as we are in a vicarage."

Jacob was meek as a child as she adjusted his neck cloth for him, brushed specks from his high collar and handed him his gloves.

She scraped a bit of sleep from the corner of Martha Jane's eye, with the crook of her finger.

"What did I just say to you Sister?"

Martha Jane hesitated, then remembered, "bonnet and gloves?"

Octavia nodded, pointed to them and thus we were all ready to go downstairs for the light breakfast in the kitchen.

As we went in, Jacob touched his pocket, then tapped the side of his nose, to indicate that he had his brandy flask at the ready. For this I was glad, already my nerves were in absolute shreds and the day had barely begun.

Eliza looked very well in a plain dark blue dress with a white lace neckerchief spread over the shoulders.

"Am nervous as a kitten, and A dint think A would be, for there's no sense in nervousness is there?"

"Well come, it's not every day you get married Eliza, there's bound to be some nervousness," I said. "Now do tell us of your intended, what kind of a man is he?"

"He's a Godly and sober living man…"

"No, no, I meant what does he look like, is he a good catch?" I added coyly, "shall he make you happy?"

In a slightly girlish way, she looked down and said, "aye Mistress, A know he'll mek me happy, he's a good-looking man for his age. And he's well set up, for he's four cottages let out as well as his own, so we shall be living very comfortable like."

"Well, that does sound excellent," I said as Jacob discreetly poured a good shot of brandy into my half-drunk tea and then took a swig from the flask himself. "I cannot tell you how glad I was to hear you were to be married," I refrained from saying 'at last', but added, "for of course there is no greater happiness for a woman than marriage."

"And a man Darling, and a man," said Jacob gallantly, squeezing my waist.

"There's some as 'd say 'better late than nivver, eh?" replied Eliza.

She untied her apron, folded it neatly and from her pocket took a large black carved brooch, edged in gold. At once Octavia stepped forward to help her pin it straight.

"Why Eliza, that must be a lover's gift, for I have never seen you wear it afore," I said.

"Indeed it is, my Mr Thornton give it ter me when he asked ter wed me."

I finished my toast and wiped Martha Jane's face.

"What time is it my Love?" I asked my husband, desperately hoping there would be time to slip upstairs and relieve myself before the exodus to the church.

"Twenty to, my Lydia."

"Just time for yo two lasses ter get in t' garden and pick yerselves a couple of nosegays, though there'll not be much ter go at, for nowt grows well in t' bad air from t' dye works," said Eliza.

Indeed, the smell of the air was quite dreadful, and I was one who lived in Whitby and was well used to the smells of a busy town with the frequent stench from the boiling of the whale flesh.

Not many minutes later, I was hurrying across to the church with my daughters. Both looked so charming in sprigged muslins, summer bonnets trimmed with silk flowers and little posies of pink and white tied with toning ribbons.

I was surprised to find the church quite full, with a motley collection of parishioners. Elizabeth whatsit and the fat one who was her sister, were sitting half-way back. I slipped a couple of pennies to two ragged children at the end of one of the pews, poor mites, one of them blind. Jack stood at the front, so splendid in his ministers' robes and beside him a good-looking man, the aforementioned Mr Thornton. He was smartly dressed, though not of course as a gentleman and I was most surprised to see he was clearly a year or two younger than Eliza, not that there is any fault in that.

I sat in the pew next to my Belle, who was seated with that dear baby, held rather awkwardly in her arms. She was wearing quite an old silk dress and I was taken aback at how it hung off her shoulders, she must have lost a deal of weight since being married. I saw Jack look up and turned to see Jacob in the porchway, hugging Eliza, before giving her away, then the two them coming down the aisle and the wedding began. It was so lovely I had a lump in my throat, and I had to feel for my handkerchief. The couple were just 'plighting their troth' when the baby who had been rubbing his eyes, suddenly stiffened and let out a loud wail. Jack stopped speaking and looked across anxiously, Eliza and Mr Thornton exchanged glances, Jacob nudged me hard in the ribs and nodded towards the baby. Belle coloured up and her eyes filled with tears as she tried to hold him still. Of course, I did what any woman would; I took him in my arms, held him close and rocked him as he snuggled into sleep. There were sighs of relief all round and the wedding proceeded without further hitch, (apart from Martha Jane dropping her posy twice).

Afterwards, there was a little repast and quite a bit to drink in the vicarage dining room. This was followed by hugs and good wishes and the happy couple, plus a decent pile of presents, disappeared off to their new life together in a smart looking gig.

Now was my chance to speak to my firstborn. She was sitting alone in the parlour, knitting something or other in dark blue, I sat opposite to her.

"Belle dear, might we talk a little?"

"Yes, Mama." She did not look up, nor put down her work.

"Ben wrote to me some time since and told me you were not well… can you tell me of it?"

With a deep sigh she looked up at me. "Mama, it is hard for me to talk of, I am managing much better now, but I have found it difficult to be with my baby…"

"But he is such a dear thing, I cannot understand it."

"I knew you would not understand Mama, that is why Jack did not write to you of it. But Eliza has helped restore me, to get me back to things, she and Jack always had belief in my recovery and helped to put the darkness behind me...Margaret Ann cares for him so well too."

"But should a child not spend most time with his mother, in her tender care and not minded by some servant girl?"

"Perhaps Mama, but I am getting used to him now and Margaret Ann is so good with him."

"And were you not able to feed him at all yourself, for is it not a sacred duty and against nature to deny him his rightful nourishment?" (I had recently read this phrase in a medical book and thought it fitted the moment well).

"No Mama, I could not, I could not tolerate him near me at first, I am sorry Mama, but I can talk no more of it."

She turned back to her knitting. I knew not how I had grown so far apart from my own child, she could not tell me of her true feelings, and I could not understand her at all, I could not even reach for her hand, for I knew she would not take mine.

She looked up at me and added, "Ben came to stay at the first, and that helped me a deal, for he was much more understanding than you might think."

"I wish you would let me help you in some way Dear."

"I thank you for your concern, Mama."

And I saw that this was to be the end of our conversation.

A little later I spoke privately with Jack, but he was equally dismissive and said, "dearest Aunt Lydie, pray do not fear for Belle, she is over the worst now, for which I truly thank God."

With that he turned back to the sermon he was writing.

Did I feel tearful? Yes, I did, though unsure quite why. In the hall, I found my dear husband had packed our bags himself.

Seeing my face, he hugged me and said, "come on my Lydia, let's get ter t' inn now, coach's an hour off, but we could maybe ger a drink or two afore it starts, eh?" He whispered, "Can't wait ter get home and sleep in me own bloody bed."

So, we gathered together our daughters and with kisses and promises to visit again soon, we departed.

Never was I so glad to get home and lie in our comfortable bed, though there were many thoughts rattling around in my head. We lay in the dark with our arms around each other and his cheek against mine.

"So, what's tha mek of it all, my Lydia?"

"I cannot understand my own daughter, she seems so cold and distant."

"Talked a bit wi' our Jack, ter see what were what, he wunt say much but it seems our Eliza were t' one as helped Belle come round a bit, ter be more herself like. He said before she came, Belle just lay in bed all day a weeping."

"Dear God," I could have wept myself at the thought such a thing.

"Come now, my Lydia, all seems mended now." He wiped my cheek with the back of his finger. "And what's tha think of Mr Thornton then?"

Jacob always knew how to draw me from sadness.

"I thought him to be a fine figure of a man."

"Am A ter be jealous then?" He joked.

"Of course not," I smiled, "but goodness, he's clearly younger than Eliza."

"By a few years A'd say. And why not eh?"

We lay in the delicious warmth of love and intimacy and fell to our much-needed sleep.

(Though if anyone had told me that that fat, wet-nurse girl would be our daughter-in-law by Christmas, well I should have been more than astonished).

CHAPTER 9

Summer 1809.
In which Mr and Mrs Thornton make
an important decision.

Mr Thornton and I settled well to married life and we were comfortable with one another. Every morning we took a good breakfast and then he would go out walking and visiting for a couple of hours, which gave me time to get on with my housework. This was easy done, with a pump and our own privy near the front door; just a bit of sweeping, dusting and polishing and I was done.

Mr Thornton would return about eleven o clock and sit at the big table while I prepared the dinner, he said he liked to watch me cook and that. After our dinners, then the afternoons were our own. Sometimes we'd walk out and see which ships were in the harbour or go to the little market to buy knitting wools or notions. Mr Thornton always liked a look at the second-hand book stall. A time or two we'd been up all those steps to the abbey ruins and marvel at how that old tower was still standing there. Mr Thornton had a fascination for history and that. Some afternoons, we would stay at home so that he could work in our little garden, and I would bring a chair out and sit and do my knitting.

Thursdays, he went over the road to the cockpit to see the poor birds fight to the death and have a bet on them. I could not see any fun in that, but he assured me 'a man must have his sport.'

Our laundry was sent out and only needed checking and putting away when it was returned clean and ironed on a Wednesday, the greatest luxury to me. Mr Thornton said he didn't want me in the wash house or on the drying plat with the other yard lasses and he warned me about being too friendly with them in case they saw it as an excuse not to pay their rents. So, I confined myself to wishing them a good morning with perhaps a remark about the weather. They mostly had an outdoor kind of life, sitting mending nets, baiting fishing lines and scolding their children. He had a soft spot for those youngsters though, and if he thought they were spoken to too sharp, then he would glare at the women and say they were 'nobbut bairns.'

Friday afternoons, he went to the Grey Horse to take a drink and for myself, I went to take tea with Mary, (who had been a fellow servant with me at the farm) and Lizzie; they ran a sweet shop just around the corner. Of course, I always came back with some sweets for us in twists of thin pink paper and oftentimes a bit of gossip too.

And so, I was happier than I'd ever been in my whole life, save for that little idea which kept swimming around in my head and somehow, I could not rid myself of it. Thus, for good or bad, I had decided to speak out, this very night or forever hold my peace on it.

It was a Friday night; we were sitting side by side on the settle with our feet upon the fender, there being a chill in the air, even though it was still summer. Mr Thornton had one arm about my shoulders and his pipe in his other hand, I was at my knitting and there was a little paper of lemon drops between us.

"Husband, tha once said tha would have liked a bairn or two."

"Oh aye, A'd a liked nowt more."

"A've been thinking perhaps we could have…"

He wrenched his pipe from his mouth and turned to look at me in astonishment. "Eh Darling, surely tha's well past all that?"

I had to laugh out loud at the very idea; for although I had helped at the births of all of those Curzon children, I had never, ever wished myself upon the childbed.

"Nay, Husband, not I…I've told thee afore, of two bairns A came ter know at Cookby, a lass and her brother that were blinded, orphaned and without a real home."

"Aye, what of it?"

"Well, A've got ter thinking…" Then I said it outright, "A thought maybe we might tek 'em on and give 'em a home like."

"What ter have 'em here ter live, like our own bairns? Well, that's summat ter think on and no mestek…By God Wife, tha's a kindly lass thinking of that. That's thing A liked about thee when A first met thee; tha were that kindly caring for thy poorly mistress and then at party, A were a bit bored waiting wit' carriage like, so A took a peep in t' window and saw thee wi' two little lasses on thy knee, watching t' dancing and that. It touched me heart ter see thee so." He kissed my cheek. "And now tha's thinking of teking on two bairns, when tha could've had an easy life wi' nowt ter do but look after me."

"So, what's tha think?"

"A think…" and he paused only a moment, "let's do it. There'd be no relatives coming outer t' woodwork for 'em would there?"

I shook my head, "no, they've no-one in t' world, that A do know."

"Aye, so they'd grow up like our own?"

"A would not want ter burden thee Husband, for it may be that t' little lad could nivver earn his bread…"

"Nay, tha might be wrong there wife, for A'd a cousin as were born blind, and he could do all sorts. He learnt ter play t' fiddle and he went around all t' parties for rich folks and that, and he earned far more than any of us, who worked dawn ter dusk. Got himself a wife and a nice little cottage too. Course he's been dead long since… but A'm sure this here lad could turn his hand ter summat in time…So, shall we go termorrow and fetch 'em?"

"Termorrow?" I said, my voice rising in panic, "termorrow's too soon, there's so much ter do… preparations and that."

"Nay, Darling, that room upstairs is neat as a pin, there's only t' beds ter mek up, and tha can do that while A'm fetching t' gig…Aye, termorrow's best while it's fresh in our minds like."

Of course, I hardly slept a wink that night, thinking about this and that I had to do. But before I knew it, we were on our way, sitting side by side on our hired gig, just as we had on our wedding day.

Mr Thornton grinned at me, "reminds me of t' happiest day of my life…when A wed thee."

I squeezed his arm, thinking it was gallant of him to say this, because of course, he had been married before when he was a young man.

'The Black Bull' at Cookby was what I would call a rough type of tavern and I felt quite uncomfortable going in there. I heard a bit of swearing and lewd talk as we walked up to the bar.

But Mr Thornton confidently stated our purpose to the landlord, who said, "well A nivver, A'd best fetch our lass for this one."

She seemed quite a decent sort of person and asked us to come through, as the children were sweeping out the back yard.

She said, in a low voice, "ter be honest, this has come at t' right time, for summat men 'ave started looking at Annie improper like, and A cannot watch her all t' time."

I shuddered, for I knew Annie to be only twelve years old.

The two children were delighted to see us and did not need to be asked twice if they would like to come and live with us.

Mr Thornton said, "it'll not be all fun and games like, tha'll have ter go ter school Annie, shall tha like that?"

"Oh yes Sir, for A started ter learn reading and numbers when Mother were alive, A should like that very much."

"And thee Billy lad, does tha think tha'll be able ter help me in t' garden?"

"Oh aye Sir, tha'll not know how tha's managed wi' owt me when A get going."

Everyone laughed at this.

"All settled then, best get yer things and we'll get off."

In no time, Mr Thornton was lifting them on to the gig with their pathetic little bundle of possessions.

The landlady reached up and kissed them both, and said, "God Bless." And to me she said, "tha'll not find two bairns more willing and pleasant."

****

Annie was a great help to me in the house, scrubbing the floors for I could not bend as easy as I once could. A week later, in one of her new dresses and a fresh pinafore, she started at school and in the evenings, she would read aloud from her school-books or cut letter shapes out of paper so that Billy could feel them and learn them too. Mr Thornton suggested that I might learn to read, but I shook my head firmly, for it is my opinion, (I had seen it more than once) that when reading comes in at the door, common sense flies straight out of the window.

As for Billy, as predicted, he could do far more than you might think. He could make a decent job of polishing the fire irons and the grate, as well as digging in the garden.

"Save my poor old back," said Mr Thornton.

The following week, after much sawing of wood and hammering, the two of them went off to market and came back with a couple of baby brown rabbits.

"A'm ter fatten 'em for t' table," Billy said, with the greatest pride, putting them in the hutch by himself and bolting the little door firmly.

And so it was we became a rather happy family and none of us wanted for anything.

CHAPTER 10

August 1809.
In which there is a dramatic rescue and
a touching reunion.

The 'Olivia Belle' had made a prosperous voyage, the weather in the Northern Fisheries had been atrocious for weeks on end, with days of ice and snow, when one end of the ship could not be seen from the other and spittle froze when it touched the air. Nevertheless, six fin fish were caught, yielding two hundred and fifty butts of blubber, kreng and baleen too, as well as many seal pelts, white fox furs and a fierce wolf dog which Captain Curzon had traded for a bag of nails with one of the native Inuits.

The captain would let none but himself feed or touch the dog, knowing that it would become loyal to him alone. He had felt on many occasions to be in need of a good guard dog and had never known any other dog half as strong as this one. Several of the sailors were quite afraid of the great beast but Robert knew from the look in its eyes that it was a faithful and loving hound at heart.

Nearing English shores, the weather became bright and sunny and to show that their trip had been successful, the stripped whale jawbones were lashed high up on the mast. Three men set to this task, (Hugo being one of them); all experienced men who climbed the rigging on a daily basis, yet at any time a sailor could be at the edge of an accident. No one was ever sure what happened, but a light wind blew one of the jawbones out of line and it swung against Hugo. Unable to right himself, he slipped, and the dreaded cry was heard, 'man overboard'.

He fell many feet and hit the cold water with a hideous thwack, taking all breath from him, even before he had started to sink beneath the waves; it felt like a sack of stones had hit his chest. Like many seamen, he could not swim, gasping for air he came to the surface, flailing his arms and taking his last precious breath of air. Then, he disappeared under the water, desperately trying to hold his breath, his lungs felt as if they would burst, he could see a grey lightness above him but flounder as he might he could not break that surface again. Only blackness now and a bursting pain in his head, he knew, as all sailors do, that the long tentacles of the monstrous Remora would be reaching up to drag him to his watery grave. He did not see his past life before him though, as it was said the drowning did, all he felt was a thick tentacle tight about his neck. He could hold his breath no longer and opened his mouth just as he broke through the waves into air and light, and for a moment he lost consciousness. When he came to, he heard shouts of, "rope him, rope him under t' arms." and felt a rope pulled tight around him, against the burning pain in his chest and saw to his astonishment, the First Mate, Ged Stone with his arm around his neck to keep his head out of the water and at the same time securing a rope around him.

Spitting out water, Ged said, "tha bloody idiot," but he was laughing with triumph as he spoke. "Nah dunt struggle, for A've got thee firm."

Now he was hauled out of the freezing water banging against the sides of the ship and onto the deck, Ged pulled up after him.

Hugo lay face down, unable to move, and after cries of "ger him ovver t' barrel," he found himself being dragged onto the angled barrel and his back hammered to empty the water from his lungs. The black pounding in his head was draining away as he was roughly turned into a sitting position, a white froth was wiped from his mouth and he found he could take rasping, choking breaths.

Ged was on all fours opposite him, coughing and shaking his head like a wet dog.

Captain Curzon, ordered that they be taken to the warmth of the kitchen quarters, wrapped in blankets and given hot brandy. He gave these orders coldly and clearly and nothing showed in his face save the deepest bite mark on his lower lip.

Ged could walk well enough, but Hugo, battered and exhausted, had to be carried down by two of the sailors.

Propped by the stove, even though he was wrapped in blankets, Hugo began to shake uncontrollably with cold.

"Ger here."

Ged knelt beside him, rubbing him hard on the shoulders and back until the shivering stopped

Then he held a mug of liquid to his brother's lips, Hugo gulped and choked.

"Nah then, tek it steady, tha's too hasty, tek it steady."

With faltering hands, he took the mug himself, sipped the reviving brandy and looked at Ged.

Ged grinned at him, "tha dint know A could swim, eh? A learned ter swim years since; a were just a lad and saw some young gentlemen swimming strongly at t' edge of t' harbour and A were fascinated by it. They was all young lords and such, and they called ovver ter me ter join them. First off, they threw me in, and A were terrified for me life, sinking under and that. But then they pulled me up and taught me t' strokes and how ter breathe. And A practised a bit and got me confidence."

Hugo looked at him, self-consciously, "A cannot thank thee enough for saving me so, for A thought A were done for."

"A wunt throw meself in t' sea ter rescue just anyone…"

"Can it be that we are brothers?"

"A'm certain of it, A know it's been a shock ter thee but A'm sure tha's me lost brother. As tha thought… thought more of it?"

Hugo nodded. "Aye, A cannot get me head around it, but…"

"When we dock, w.. would tha come and see our sister? It'd mean t' world ter her, A allus promised A'd find thee one day, for she nivver got ovver losing thee…"

"Aye, A will. A thank thee again for saving me."

Hugo felt his words sounded shallow and flat for the very great bravery that Ged had shown in rescuing him from certain death by drowning.

He reached out his hand to him and the two brothers embraced, both turning their heads away in case an embarrassing tear slipped down their cheeks.

* * * *

A day later the 'Olivia Bell' had waited over an hour for her pilot, but at last she was rushing into Whitby Harbour. By hook or by crook her crew had managed to procure hot water to wash and shave, hair was slicked back, or plaited, clean shirts donned, and a wave of euphoria was obvious amongst the men. All were bursting to disembark, though some were allocated to stay behind to see to the derigging and bedding of the ship. Full of tales of their grand hunting trip, privations soon forgotten, adventures well remembered and exaggerated, but Captain Curzon never let any leave without a personal word from him, and thus a queue of jostling eager men formed near the gangplank.

As first mate, Ged was last to leave. He had stood in the line with a friendly arm around Hugo, as if he had half an idea that his new-found brother might try to escape at this final hour.

The captain shook Hugo's hand, "I wish you all the best in finding out more about yourself Cousin, and hope your little dip in the sea has not put you off sailing again?"

"Nivver Captain, A'll be signing for thy next trip no mestek," Hugo laughed and moved onto the gang plank.

"And you Ged Stone, my friend, a grand hunting trip we've had?"

"Aye Captain, the best."

With his hand on Ged's shoulder, he added, "and my especial thanks for your brave rescue of my cousin..."

"Nowt brave about it, A've spent twenty year looking for t' bugger, A wunt let him ger away now, me sister'd nivver forgive me."

"My best regards to Sarah and your mother, as always…When we've derigged, and all is in hand we shall meet up and discuss future sailings?"

"Look forward ter it, Captain."

Hugo was surprised that Robert seemed acquainted with Ged's family.

And thus, the two brothers disembarked and walked silently through the little streets. Hugo hardly knew the web of alleys behind the main streets of Whitby, having grown up in the countryside four miles away. The air smelt of cooking mixed with a strong stench from the overflowing gulleys, filled with all manner of human waste.

Dusk was already falling as the magnificent red sunset drained away, Ged led the way down a dark covered passage, through an ill paved yard, up a flight of twenty steps and along a balconied walkway. The balustrade was rickety under Hugo's hand, he suddenly felt an overwhelming nervousness of what was to come, as at last they went through a doorway. Before him was a shabby room, an older woman sat beside a thin smoky fire and did not look round at their entrance, there was a plain wood table with three more chairs at it and a single tallow candle burning there. Everything was clean, scrubbed to within an inch of its life and neatly set out, yet so down at heel and poor.

A curtain half concealed a box bed and sitting on it was a small fair-haired woman, who leapt up at once and said, "our Ged, A dint know tha'd docked."

She ran towards him delighted and then she caught sight of Hugo as Ged pushed him into the room. She clasped her hands to her chest and gasped with an almost animal noise.

"Aye tha knows him dunt tha," said Ged triumphantly, "it's our brother, our Hugo."

"Oh, oh…"

She held out her arms and Hugo clasped her dainty body against him. Her clothes were patched and worn, her body somewhat unwashed but Hugo only saw her beauty, her huge blue eyes, her soft blonde hair and her overwhelming loving kindness as she wept upon his chest.

"Dunt be crying Sister." Even Ged was suddenly moved, "tis a time fer celebrations, eh?"

Taking Hugo's hand, she led him towards the fireside, putting her arm around the old woman, she spoke loudly, "Mother, look, it's our Hugo come back ter us."

The woman looked round and stared at him with rheumy eyes, without emotion she said, "aye it is, A'd know him anywhere, spit of his father he is." With that she turned back to the fire and did not speak again for the rest of the evening.

Hugo could barely believe that this woman, old before her time was his natural mother, whatever could his father have found attractive in her to make him risk all, to have a love affair with such an old crone.

As if reading his thoughts, Sarah said quietly, "she's had a hard life has our mother and she's very deaf…" Her words faltered a little.

Ged elaborated, "aye, deaf because our father used ter knock her about and she hit her head on t' stone hearth, and he knocked out most of her teeth too, old bastard." And with those words he went to his mother, hugged her and kissed her cheek. She leaned against him affectionately for a moment and patted his arm.

Sarah reached for two large, chipped pot jugs from the mantle shelf.

"Shall A fetch some ale?"

"Aye good lass, and some port, and summat nice ter eat if they're still open."

Ged felt in his jacket and gave her a handful of coins and Sarah disappeared out of the door, pulling a thin shawl about her shoulders.

Soon enough they were sitting at the table with buttered bread and a cheap cut of boiled meat; a great deal was drunk, and Hugo began to feel more at ease with his most strange of situations. The old woman drank a mug of port wine and glanced over at Hugo a once or twice, but he could think of no words to say to her, though he saw that she held a handkerchief to her eyes a couple of times. As they were eating, Sarah shyly reached out to him, he took her tiny, calloused hand in his large strong one and smiled at her. He thought her a lovely, sweet woman and felt it only a pleasure to be her half-brother now.

"We looked everywhere for thee after Mother took thee away, honest we did."

"Can tha tell me a bit more of it?"

"Our father came back from sea, he'd been away nigh on eighteen month, for his ship were stuck in t' ice ovver Winter…his Captain had stayed too long, hoping for a bit more hunting and going too far North, where few ships went. Any road most at' men died of hunger, but our father were a strong man. He used ter tell us that he'd put a bit of snow in his tobacco tin every night and slept with it under his arm, so that he could tek a little drink of water each morning when he woke up, and somehow, he stayed alive. But he suffered and lost some of his toes in t' ice and he were on crutches when he got home, he could hardly walk…"

"Bloody good thing," went on Ged, "for he'd a tried ter kill thee if he could've got his hands on thee. He knew straight off tha weren't his. But our sister here, saved thee, for she grabbed thee and ran outer t' house and took thee up ter our grandmother's house fer safety."

Sarah spoke in a low voice, "then Mother came up and took thee. Grandmother locked t' door and held me back till she were on her way… We asked everyone we knew where tha was, but none knew."

"Or if they did, they wasn't saying," said Ged darkly.

She gazed up at Hugo, "we loved thee so much…"

"Aye, she cried fer weeks did Sarah."

"It weren't a good time after, our father were in a deal of pain, and it made him angry wi' everything."

"Aye, and he drank away every last penny we had…"

"But it were fer t' pain he were in, Ged."

Ged snorted; it would seem he would hear no good of their father, but he looked fondly at Hugo and said, "and now our little Chub has come back ter us," pinching his cheek at the same time.

Hugo grinned and knocked his hand away.

"That's what we used ter call thee, 'Little Chub' and we'd squeeze thy fat little cheeks ter mek thee smile, when tha were laid between us, for we'd ter look after thee when our mother were working."

The evening wore on and there was drinking till the small hours. Their mother lay down on the box bed, drew the curtains around her and soon seemed to be asleep.

Hugo was touched to see how much Ged and Sarah loved each other, but he had to laugh at their constant teasing and joking. Eventually, Sarah stretched and yawned, slipped off her dress and apron, released her stays without any self-consciousness and joined her mother in the bed.

Ged grinned at Hugo.

"All reet then?"

Hugo nodded with a mellow contentment, hesitantly he said, "we have a lovely sister, do we not?"

"Aye, means t' world ter me she does". Ged spoke awkwardly, "Am hoping after t' next trip ter ger 'em somewhere better ter live than this bloody hovel. A want things better now but A try ter save a good bit of me money each time we dock." With some pride, he went on, "A've started up a savings at a bank, A'm wanting ter get a share in a ship one day…then we can all have a bit better life."

Ged cared little for material goods, so long as he could have decent clothes and a few drinks for himself, yet he longed for money to help his family and most of all for the respect he knew it would bring him.

Later, the two brothers lay side by side on a hard bed in a tiny windowless room. There were no sheets only two thin blankets.

"Best have one each, dunt want thy arm round me int' middle at' night," joked Ged.

"Tha should be so lucky," grinned Hugo.

Like most seamen, Ged put his hands behind his head and instantly fell asleep. But Hugo lay awake for some time, with many thoughts; he had been welcomed with such warmth and kindliness, yet he could do naught but be thankful that he had not grown up in this home of abject poverty, hunger and casual violence. Instead, he had had a childhood of gentle love, plentiful food, warm clothes and a good education. That night, his prayers were long and grateful for everything in his life, both past and present, he begged God's forgiveness for his former anger and judgement when he first discovered he was not who he thought he was.

He resolved to walk out to Cookby the following day to see his brother Jack, perhaps calling in to see his Aunt Eliza on the way, then he closed his eyes and dreamt hardly at all.

CHAPTER 11

September 1809.
Lydia and her younger daughters
take tea at Mrs Thornton's.

I had been married three months and the children had been with us more than a couple of weeks. In all that time, I had never seen Lydia Curzon. I knew they had been away visiting various grandchildren, but I'd heard they were back, and I wondered if she would come to call. I was unsure of how we should address each other, for I could not call her Mistress, nor she call me Eliza now that I was married and no longer a servant.

But I did not wonder for long and it happened that the very next afternoon, the children and I were sitting at the table when there was a light tap at my door and without waiting, she swept into my little cottage. As usual she was a flurry of rustling silk, dangling feathers and strong perfume. Behind her were her two youngest, Octavia and Martha Jane.

"Now is this where one comes for a good pot of tea and the best cake in Whitby? My dear Mrs Thornton, how very good it is to see you." She looked around the room, "why I knew you would have the lovliest of homes, but it quite exceeds all my expectations, it is all so very charming."

"A thank thee, Mrs Curzon, and do A find yer all well?"

"Indeed we are at last recovered, for after we returned from our visiting, the four of us were all laid up with fevers and bad throats, though Martha Jane is still coughing a little, are you not dear?"

As if on cue, Martha Jane cleared her throat. Her mother sank into one of the elbow chairs and glanced at Annie and Billy.

"How thrilled I was to hear from Jacob, you had taken on these little ones…" Suddenly she stood up again, leaned across the table and peered at them. "Why, don't I know you two already, were you not sitting in the church at the wedding?"

"Yes Mistress," replied Annie. "And tha were kind enough to give us each a penny for which A thank thee."

She nudged Billy whereupon, he gave thanks as well.

"Well, goodness me, that was weeks ago, so it must surely be time for you to have another penny each, then you could all run along to Mary's sweetshop and get some sweeties."

Here, she fumbled in her velveteen reticule.

"Mrs Curzon, there is no need…" I smiled.

"There most certainly is," she laughed giving them each a coin.

I knew Lydia Curzon had given Mary and Lizzie money to set up the sweetshop in the first instance, in reward for their years of devoted service to her and her mama. Thus, Martha Jane piped up, "WE do not have to pay for our sweets."

"Well," I said maybe a bit too sharply, "WE do not like ter tek advantage of them as has less than ourselves, Martha Jane."

"Quite right Mrs Thornton very well said. You should not speak so Martha Jane, say you're sorry like a good girl," reprimanded her mama.

At once Martha Jane's eyes filled with tears at her mistake, and I had to put my arms around her and wipe her eyes with the corner of my apron. Though her only crime was to be too outspoken, taking after her mother in that one.

"Now Martha Jane, A've a fresh baked loaf here, why not tek that along as thanks, for A know Mary and Lizzie do not have their own oven. Come along now, off yer all go." I said, wrapping the loaf in a clean linen cloth.

Martha Jane took the bread. She stared hard at Billy as he felt for his stick and reached for Annie's arm, but she said not a word, for she was not an unkind girl, and it was only natural curiosity.

"Peace at last," sighed Mrs Curzon, as the four of them disappeared out of the door.

She leant back in her chair, spreading out her silken skirts, every inch the refined well-bred lady, yet I knew her to be of the bravest heart; she had once had a miscarriage, coping alone and telling none of it. I knew for a fact she always kept two loaded pistols in the cradle box under her bed and being a good shot she would not have hesitated to use them if the Frenchies had ever come anywhere near her children. She had even shot her beloved mare herself when the poor old horse's time had come.

I poured the tea and got a seed cake out of the tin. She looked longingly at the slivers of cone sugar, but did not drop one into her cup of tea, for I knew that she and Jacob were pledged not to touch sugar unless it was the expensive kind, harvested by free labour and not the enslaved.

"Really I seem to be tired all the time and now I'm hot," she was flushed and took a dainty lace fan out of her reticule even though the room was not all that warm.

"Ah," I said, "tis ter be expected, 'tis only natural at t' end of childbearing years."

She nodded, "if it is not one thing, then it is another. There is so much to do in the house, cooking, cleaning… of course we send our laundry out but there's always delicates to rinse at home and mending, well as you know, I do not sew…" I realised it must be hard for her now when she had been used to a lifetime of servants. "I could not manage at all but for Octavia, she can cook and sew like a dream…"

"And she has turned out quite a beauty A'd say," I said. For Octavia was one of those who had inherited all the best features of her parents; her mother's tall and graceful figure, her father's flashing dark eyes and cascade of curly hair and across her cheeks, that most fetching pink flush that all the Curzons had.

Lydia smiled and shook her head, "she does remind me so of her dear departed father, not just her colouring but the way she puts her head on one side and that half smile…"

I cut slices of the cake while she rattled on about her domestic arrangements. Just as the children were coming back in the door with their papers of sweets, she suddenly said, "one good thing that has happened, I now have a really excellent woman come in to do our scrubbing and polishing, she's only slight of build, but willing and stronger than she looks. In fact, our Sarah Stone is naught but a Godsend…"

Well, my jaw absolutely dropped at this, "why tha knows who she is dunt tha?"

I lowered my voice and glanced across at the children, who fortunately were not listening in and were chattering between themselves.

"No," she shook her head, "should I?"

As quiet as I could, I said, "she's our Hugo's sister, half-sister A should say."

In other circumstances, I would have laughed out loud, for her mouth fell open in a perfect 'O' as she gasped, her eyes wide with astonishment.

"Why I had no idea," she whispered, "I'm certain my Jacob knows naught of this, it was all so long ago; pray tell me, Hugo does not know of her?"

"Aye he does, he knows his half-brother and sister and met his natural mother only last week, when they docked."

"Dear God, I did not even know they had docked, wherever is he now?" She fanned herself vigorously and a little perspiration appeared on her upper lip.

"Gone to stay with our Jack, four days since. He called in to see us too, but only for half an hour." I did not want her to think he had favoured me over herself and his father. "He wanted to talk ter our Jack about it, for, of course he had no notion of it at all…"

"He should have been told of it years ago, but he was always such a happy child it never seemed the right time and I think Susannah did not want him told…"

I had to agree, and I suppose over the years none of them ever dreamed he would meet up with his original family, indeed it was what you might call a quirk of fate that it had happened so. As yet, I could not decide if it was for the good or the bad. When I had discussed it with my Mr Thornton, he had shaken his head and said, "Nemesis, aye Nemesis."

As I had no idea what that meant, I could not be guided by his opinion.

But one favourable thing that emerged that afternoon was friendship; for when the youngsters had finished their sweets, I saw Octavia whisper to Annie, Annie smiled and nodded and the two of them clambered upstairs to her bedroom. From then on, they were the firmest of friends and saw each other almost every day.

As for Martha Jane, she stuck out her lower lip and looked at the floor, until Billy turned towards her and said, "Martha Jane, A've two rabbits what A'm fattening for t' table. Would tha like ter see them?"

"Oh yes please Billy, I should like that more than anything." She grabbed his arm as he fumbled for his stick and the two of them were off outside. "Did you know Billy that I have a green parrot that talks?"

Mrs Curzon and I exchanged glances and had to smile.

"Has she a green parrot as talks?" I asked in surprise.

"Why yes, she does, it is the most darling thing and repeats everything that is said to it, both good and bad. Our dear Robert brought it back for her from his travels to Africa."

Then I made another pot of tea for us, thinking it probably best not to ask what Captain Robert Curzon had been up to in Africa, for sometimes Lydia Curzon could be a bit innocent about the ways of the world.

Just as they were getting ready to leave, my Mr Thornton returned, and was able to bid them good day. Octavia kissed myself and Annie on the cheek and once again I was struck by her prettiness. As they were all walking away down the little path, Mr Thornton put his arm about my shoulders, and I asked him if he did not think Octavia a beauty.

"Oh aye, she's certainly a good looking lass, none'd argue with that, but flighty A'd say, flighty aye."

I was most surprised at this, yet sadly, how very true those words came to be a few years later.

CHAPTER 12

Sept 1809.
In which Hugo visits the vicarage and
Margaret Ann receives an offer.

I had been working for the vicar and his young wife ten months now. They were as kindly as could be to me, and the baby I cared for was such a darling, I felt I loved him as my own; but he was not and I have not the words to tell how much I missed my own little boy, Tommy. Once a week I was allowed to visit him for an hour or so, every time I went, I felt him more distant from me than the previous, he even started calling my mother 'mammy' instead of me, and she never corrected him. Last time I visited, my little Tommy was fast asleep, and she refused to wake him, so I never got to see him at all save to kiss his sleeping head. I share a bedroom here at the vicarage with my sister Elizabeth Jane and every night I have waited till she sleeps and then shed my silent tears for missing my little Tommy so very much.

But now, I've another worry, I await being told that I am to be dismissed, for the dear little Jack is just about weaned and though naught has been said, I know I will not be required here much longer as wet-nurse. My father is sick and often misses his work, and my money is needed at home to help my parents, my mother only earns a few pence each week from mending and knitting, and, of course, she has to care for my Tommy and Father too. I have only one choice, when the vicar asks me to leave, and that is to get work in the local dyers' factory. The wage is not bad and there is always work going there, for so many die or get too ill to work after only a few years. Working there caused my father's present lung sickness and my husband's death from a horrible accident, which I can hardly let myself think of. He, my childhood sweetheart, never even got to his twenty-first birthday nor lived to see his son born.

All I could do was pray to God for guidance and help, and try my best to be a good and faithful servant. And so, I sat in the kitchen elbow chair with baby Jack fast asleep in my arms, feeling most sorry for myself.

Then, next thing, my sister Elizabeth Jane burst in, "Margaret, there's a handsome visitor come, tis t' master's younger brother, Hugo... Well first off, they were hugging and that, like tha'd expect, but now there's a bit of shouting."

"Where's t' mistress?"

"Resting upstairs, A'm pretty sure she's asleep."

Carefully I laid the baby in his basket, I did not cover him for it was a warm day and I crept into the hallway with my sister to find out what was happening, for in all my time of service, I had never heard the master raise his voice, after all he was a man of the church.

Elizabeth Jane had a cloth in her hand, in case she was caught listening, she could then pretend to be polishing the brasses on the front door.

We both stood close to the study door, and this is what we heard:

"Brother, I do beg of you to be calm and think of this matter with reason."

"Bloody reason? How can A? For A've grown up ter believe A were thy full brother and our Penelope me sister and all t' time, A'd another family that no one ivver took trouble ter mention. Nivver even give a hint of it. Sat at me mother's deathbed not knowing she weren't even me mother, wept me heart out for her, and A were nowt ter her."

Here the vicar raised his voice, "pray do not speak so of our mother, for she loved us all in equal part, as I think you know if you think quietly of it."

More calmly, Hugo asked, "does Penelope know of this?"

"Of course, for we were both there on the day the woman…your natural mother brought you to us."

Elizabeth Ann and I gasped with shock as this little tale was revealed, especially with our master and mistress being such very respectable, godly people.

I heard a chair scraping, so one of them must have sat down.

"Sit down brother and let me tell you of it as truthfully as I can, ask me anything and I shall answer as best I can and please know how I regret not speaking to you of it before, but the more time went on the more difficult it became to break our close family bond. On her deathbed, my mother asked me privately that you never be told of it, thinking you would not believe her great love for you if you knew from whence you came. Thus, you see how my hands were tied. Yet honesty and truth should always be our guide before God."

I exchanged glances with my sister. We heard another chair moving, so Hugo was obviously sitting down, voices were lowered but we could still hear pretty well. We heard the movement of glasses, and something being poured into them.

"Tell me Jack, how could it be that…that my mother as A thought, could tek in our father's bastard, was she not angry that he had been carrying on so?"

I heard a deep sigh from my master.

"Just before you were brought to us, Mother had lost a baby, a little girl they called Rebecca, even though she was stillborn, prior to that there had been several miscarriages. I know she longed for more children, as you know our mother had a very deep faith in God and when you arrived, she thought it God's will…"

"And how were Father wi' it?"

"Of course, there was some feelings of anger and betrayal from Mother, though they did their best to keep it concealed from us. Mother did not speak a word to Father for some good time, and I remember he slept downstairs in his chair till Mother let him back to her bed. But Penelope and I were thrilled to have a brother, no one ever said anything, but we always knew you were our brother, from that very first day. We were all young, we, nor our cousins ever questioned it, it was accepted, you were just another baby in the family."

There was a long silence and I clutched Elizabeth Jane's arm; we were both rather overcome with the emotion of it.

"Tha'll think me an idiot Jack, but when Mother died, A'd been told she were having a bairn, A'd no notion she were dying, no one told me. Next thing everyone were crying, and A dint understand she were dead, and A were wanting ter know where t' bairn had gone."

"I'm so sorry of that Hugo, I do believe we were all so engrossed in our own grief that we forgot to consider your childish innocence, you can only have been nine or ten then. Of course, it was another stillbirth and mother was taken with the childbed fever…"

"He is a bastard, the brother," whispered Elizabeth Jane with a look of shock.

"Ssh Sister, such things happen."

I heard him speak again.

"Ave met them all now, me mother's a bit of a strange one, but me new brother and sister, Ged and Sarah, they're both grand and seem ter have that much love for me. They've spent years looking for me…A felt a bond with them, though it were hard for me ter tek it all in first off."

"Then surely that is some good that has come from all this, that you have found a loving half-brother and sister?"

"Aye, it is."

There was a long silence.

We both went back to the kitchen and lucky we did, for next thing, the Master was calling my sister to bring them some tea and vittels. Fortunately, I had done some fresh baking that very morning while the baby slept.

Well, this was an opportunity not to be missed, I loaded up the tray and despite my sister's protestations, I carried it through myself. She was right to tell me that the master's brother was handsome, for I felt my cheeks flush a little when he was introduced to me. A good-looking lad and no mistake, tall and strong built with sandy hair and laughing grey eyes.

There was no hint of their previous conversation. Hugo just said, "A thank thee Margaret Ann, A'm fair famished, A've walked here from Whitby."

"Why indeed, that is a good long way Sir, please call me if tha needs owt else."

"Indeed, A shall, but this looks excellent, seed cake is me favourite."

"A baked it meself only this morning Sir," I ventured.

He caught my eye and smiled, "all t' better for t' touch of thy fair hand, eh?"

Now, I did feel myself blush, so I retreated to the kitchen with a quick bob and a "thank you Sir."

"Whatever's up with thee?" asked my sister.

Although she was fourteen now, I would say she was young for her age and I felt unable to explain, so I just attended to the baby.

Some while later, our Mistress came downstairs and there were exclamations of delight as she discovered Hugo's presence. I have to say our Mistress had been much better recently, almost her old self again. She had even started to care for the baby sometimes. Only yesterday she and the Master had bathed him together. I could not understand her at all, for months she had not touched her poor child, not even looked at him, stayed in bed half of the day weeping.

What did she want? She had a handsome husband (for he was good looking was the vicar, though too holy for my taste) and the most beautiful of babies and a nice home. I was fond enough of her for she was always fair and kindly with us but sometimes I felt something of a resentment that she did not appreciate what she had in life.

Later that afternoon, Hugo came into the kitchen. I was holding the baby, so I was able to hide something of my confusion by cuddling him. Hugo sat down opposite me and started talking to me in an easy comfortable way. First, he complimented me on my seed cake, saying it was better even than his Aunt Eliza's. So then of course I explained, it was she who had taught me how to bake seed cake and scones, when she had stayed at the vicarage earlier in the year.

Taking little Jack's hand in his, he asked if he would be tasting my scones anytime soon. He looked at me very directly with those laughing eyes, a strange grey with flecks of yellow. Then I was promising to bake scones the next day.

"Should tha care ter tek bairn Sir, thy nephew?"

"Aye, A should," he took the baby on to his lap, "but A should like thee ter call me Hugo."

"Aye Sir, A mean Hugo."

And we both laughed at my mistake. He kissed the baby's forehead, but he never took his eyes off me.

"Hugo's an unusual name," I said tentatively.

"Apparently me mother, me natural mother that is, had worked once for a fancy rich family and t' sons were called Gerald and Hugo and she liked t' names so me and me other brother got 'em. Tha must wonder what A'm on about," he laughed. "A've two mothers, and A've a step-mother too, two half-brothers, three half-sisters including Martha-Jane but just the one father. But A've only just found out about me other family and how A got me name…"

Then he went on about how he'd found his brother while sailing up to Greenland, and how he hadn't believed it until he fell into the sea and this other brother jumped in and saved his life. The whole thing must have been horrific, but he made it into an amusing story, and I was soon laughing, and little Jack joined in too with baby giggles, though he could not have understood one word of it.

Next morning, when baby Jack was having his nap and my sister was cleaning the parlour grate, Hugo came into the kitchen and sat with me while I did some mending. He leaned towards me and told me an amusing story about a great whale fish that had tossed all the sailors out of the little rowing boat, high up into the air and amazingly they all landed back in the boat, safe and sound and ready to carry on with the hunting. He gesticulated at the words "high up", and as he brought his hand down it touched mine for a moment. Now he was looking at me and smiling.

"Can A hold thy hand, Margaret Ann?"

I felt myself colour up when he looked at me that way, but I put down my sewing and gave him my hand, and before long he was kissing me, and I liked that feeling and I liked him too. I own I liked him very much and found myself thinking of his kisses for the rest of the day.

As for Hugo, he spent the day in the parlour with my mistress, making her laugh as they remembered the escapades of their childhood, (for the two of them were cousins and had grown up together). He spent a long time helping baby Jack to learn walking, and it was that day that the dear little soul took his very first steps. It must have tired him out, for he was ready for bed early that night and when I came down from settling him, Hugo was waiting for me in the kitchen. In his arms, he made me long for him a great deal. He told me how lovely I was; they were the same words that Ben Curzon had used when he tried to kiss me in this very room, last Christmas. Perhaps all the Curzons said the same thing when they wanted a woman. Indeed, I had had feelings for Ben Curzon too, but then I had known I would lose my place if anything came of it, and Eliza saw to it that most certainly nothing did come of it.

But this time I could not resist, and I let Hugo guide me into the privacy of the back porch with both doors shut. He kissed me over and over again, but when he began to loosen my clothes, I had to protest, for I was afraid of falling for a baby.

"A love thee Margaret Ann, do not fear, for A promise ter wed thee…if that happens."

Now here I was surprised, but I wanted him so much I thought I would trust him, I knew my mistress was resting upstairs, the baby settled, and my master rarely stirred from his study in the evenings, so my only fear of disturbance was from my sister who could be anywhere. But we were too far on to turn back, and Hugo was a fine man, he had a strong body and hands that could give such pleasure, I lost myself to him and it was all over far too soon, and praise God we were not discovered.

Yet, things were not over, for when we sat by the fire again, Hugo asked me to marry him, to my very greatest surprise. He wanted to wed soon, for he was off on a collier boat straight after Christmas and then in March he'd be away nearly six months with the whaling. He assured me we could get somewhere to live from his Aunt Eliza and her Mr Thornton who owned properties in Whitby. In truth I was unsure of being a sailor's wife, so much on my own, yet I asked myself, what choice did I have? I explained I had a little son, but he was not put off in the least by that and said he would come with me for my next afternoon visit, that he might meet him. So, I put my arms around his neck and agreed to marry him.

Bans were read for three Sunday's running, Hugo's father gave his consent, for Hugo was not yet of age, baby Jack was finally weaned with no trouble at all, for he now had a few good teeth for chewing and loved his milk from a little mug with the pattern of ducks and chickens upon it. My mistress seemed almost righted now and put her arm around me and said that she would miss me and thanked me for what she called my 'unfailing kindnesses' to her little son. Of course, that set me a thinking how I should miss them too. A new bride-to-be should be looking forward to nuptial happiness, in truth I was a little afraid of what was to come. Living in a strange town, for I had never left Cookby for a single day before and leaving my family behind too, but my first duty was to make a good home for my son and this I could do married to Hugo, for I supposed a sailor earned a decent enough wage.

Thus, I married Hugo Curzon a few weeks later and together, with my little Tommy, we boarded the stagecoach for Whitby and our new life in a two roomed tenement in Thornton's Yard.

CHAPTER 13

August 1810.
Margaret Ann has an impromptu family party.

And so, I lay a long and loving night with my husband Hugo, he had been away from me a full five months with the whaling. With his arms about me, whenever I half awoke, he was kissing me tenderly or stroking my hair and I did love him so. From first light, our new baby slept between us, and my little Tommy played in the blankets at our feet. He seemed so fond of Hugo and called him 'Father' from the first. As for Hugo, he reached out to stroke my cheek and then kissed our baby gently on her forehead, he touched her tiny hands with a kind of wonder. Though she was three weeks old, he had seen her for the first time, last night when he had docked. I was so happy to see him, feeling at ease now, for I admit, I had been desolate for the many months he had been away at sea. On my own with little Tommy, and then a new baby as well. The birth had been terrible, with only Hugo's Aunt Eliza and the midwife to help me; both of them kind enough in their way, but I hardly knew them. How I had longed for my mother, and my sister too. The last few months had been so very lonely, I had not made friends with any of the other lasses living in the yard, though they always wished me a good morning when I went to get water or use the privy. But I did not want my little Tommy playing with any of their children, they all seemed so dirty and low.

I stretched my arms above my head and smiled at Hugo. We had sat up talking well into the night before and now we had slept late, for next thing, the clock was striking ten o-clock.

Hugo smiled back at me, "best be getting up now Darling, for they'll be here at half-past."

"What? Who'll be here? Is someone coming round?"

"Aye, dint A tell thee? All t' family's coming round... ter see our new little one of course."

Here he kissed her again.

Horrified, I sat up, "tha nivver said, A've nowt in or got ready or owt."

"No worries, A'll go out now and get tha owt tha wants, it's only me family, they dunt expect things fancy."

He put his arms about my neck and tried to kiss me, but I shook him off and jumped out of bed, pulling on yesterday's clothes as quickly as I could. With so little time, I then grabbed Tommy who was playing quietly, he hated to be rushed and I usually made a game of getting him dressed but no time for that today and I had to slap his leg for being difficult. At once he started to cry.

"Eh dunt strike him Meggie, he dunt need that."

Now I was astonished, "how can he know right from wrong if A dunt teach him?"

Hugo shrugged, "we were nivver hit when we were bairns, and we seemed ter know right from wrong pretty much. Dunt cry Tommy lad, be a good lad for Mammy eh." He ruffled his hair. "Nah then beloved wife, tell me what's wanted for our little party, and it'll be fetched at once."

He put his arms about me again, and I felt a bit better, but I was still anxious, being uncomfortable with all of his family, I hardly knew them and every one of them seemed so strange to me.

"Please hurry then Hugo, for A dunt want ter be here on me own when they come, and A dunt want them ter find me wanting for owt."

"At once my Angel."

He quickly pulled on his breeches, stockings and shoes and off he went, still in his shirtsleeves, while I set out our few mugs and plates, we only had two glasses, so they would have to be saved for his haughty stepmother and cousin Octavia, for I felt pretty sure they would have been invited along, though I could hardly imagine them in our humble little two roomed tenement. While worrying that I had no idea what manners would be expected from me, I raked the ashes into life and put a kettle on to boil to make some tea for myself and Tommy. I had no taste for the spirits, that Hugo's family seemed to take at every possible opportunity, in large quantities; my own parents had recently followed Methodism, which forbade the taking of strong drink.

As luck would have it, Hugo was speedily returned with two jugs of ale and two bottles of brandy tucked under his arm.

"See my heart's angel, all at the ready and non yet..."

His pretty speech was cut short by a knock at the door, and without waiting, his stepmother Lydia Curzon, swept in, followed by his father Jacob, his half-sister Martha Jane a girl of about ten years old and lastly his cousin Octavia. Octavia was most prettily dressed in apricot silk, trimmed with yellow, her fine wove straw bonnet wreathed in a cascade of velvet flowers in yellows and soft greens. I would much have liked such a costume myself, though I could not have worn it with one half of her elegance. I knew her to be only fifteen, but she looked at least twenty.

"Now where is she, our darling new granddaughter?" gushed the stepmother.

His father Jacob laid his two walking sticks against the table and took me in his arms, kissing me fondly on both cheeks.

"Nah then Margaret Ann, tha's looking reet well."

Of all of them, I liked him the best, he was just a bit too much for me, hugging and kissing everyone all the time; my own parents rarely showed affection and I was more comfortable with that. I felt lost and lonely within the warmth and joviality of this close affectionate family.

Before I could fetch the baby through from the bedroom, Hugo's brother Ged, and sister Sarah arrived. I had met them only once before and forgive me, did not like either very much. Ged was a rough type, always making stupid jokes in a loud voice and drawing attention to himself, he had the same yellowish grey eyes as my Hugo but was not one half as handsome. As for sister Sarah, she would stare adoringly at Hugo all the time, wringing her hands in a humble way as if she hardly dared to be there. Although well past thirty, she had not married, I suppose she just devoted her life to worshipping her brothers. At one time she had been a servant to his father's family and had come out this day with two patches sewn on the hem of her skirt and wisps of hair escaping from her shabby bonnet.

Drinks were poured for everyone, and Jacob completed his circuit of hugging, kissing and back slapping as appropriate. I knew from the way Cousin Octavia stared at Hugo's every move, that she was quite in love with him, I wondered if Hugo knew this, if he did, he had never mentioned it.

As soon as I brought my baby through, Sarah clasped her hands and gasped, "oh, it's t' bairn."

"Quick as thought, our Sarah," joked Ged.

Sarah looked at her with such adoration, she might have been looking upon the infant Christ.

Almost at once, my baby started to fuss, much to my relief, as I thought I could now escape into the bedroom to feed her. But not so, next thing stepmother Lydia and Cousin Octavia were following me in. Hurriedly I kicked some soiled clothes under the bed and sat down on it to nurse. We had no bedroom chairs, but the two of them perched happily on either end of our clothes trunk.

Lydia said, "how good it is to see you and the little one looking so well and healthy, er... Margaret."

Then she launched into her favourite subject, her nine children, of course they had all been born as easily as shelling peas, and she had nursed them herself, without a minute's trouble from any of them. She made no mention of Belle, my former mistress, but she went down in order from Ben, the skilled farmer who had inherited the family estate, perfect father and husband, (here I could not help but smirk, remembering him with his hand on my breast, telling me how lovely I was in the vicarage kitchen two Christmases ago). Then there was his twin, Robert, a successful seafarer, made a captain when aged only twenty-three. Next Olivia, who seemed to be married to the richest man in Yorkshire and lived in the most beautiful house ever seen. George and Frederic, away bravely fighting in the war, Francis, the clever son, at Cambridge following in his dead father's footsteps by taking holy orders. She then asked me most earnestly if I thought Jack would be able to take him on as Curate. Of course, I said I had no notion at all.

She went on, "then comes my dear Octavia, such a talented girl, are you not dear?"

Octavia smiled at that, and her mother continued, "she can sew like a dream, I would say she could make anything at all, can you not dear?"

"Certainly, I would try Mama."

"Of course, I can barely sew a stitch myself. And cook too, we can always rely on a good dinner when Octavia is in the kitchen."

"Mama, you make me sound quite the drudge."

"Indeed not, Octavia, for you are quite the beauty, what think you, Margaret?"

I had been brought up not to fish for compliments, but I said I thought Octavia most elegant. She looked at me strangely and I could not tell of what she might be thinking.

"And last but not least, our darling Martha Jane, such a gift when a second marriage is blessed with a child. And of course, I remember your dear husband Hugo as a baby for I visited almost every day, always smiling, his dear fat little pink cheeks, always smiling whatever was going on... Oh, now that darling babe has finished, may I take her?"

Without waiting for a reply, she snatched my baby into her arms, cradling and cooing. Then Octavia took a turn, walking up and down rocking her to sleep. I did not want her sleeping yet as I had not had chance to change her clout and I felt cross at their intrusion, after all she was my baby, not theirs.

To cap it all, the door creaked open, and that Sarah peeped in, wringing her hands.

"Why now Aunty Sarah, is here. Come along now you must take a turn with this darling babe."

Octavia handed her over. They all carried on as if I was not even there.

Sarah clutched my baby to her as if she would never let her go. Her eyes were absolutely full of wonder as if she had never seen a baby before and I just hoped her patched dress was cleaner than it looked.

I felt sick of the lot of them, so I took my little girl firmly in my arms and carried her back into our living room just in time for the arrival of our final visitor.

And an impressive visitor it was, in his captain's hat and jacket, I knew at once who it must be.

Lydia rushed to him, "dearest son."

But he only brushed her cheek with a brief, "Mama," and strode across the room, capturing me in his steely gaze.

Hugo introduced me, "Meggie, this is me Cousin Robert."

He took my hand to his cool lips and gave me a slight bow.

"Pleased to meet you at last Margaret Ann," he said in his quiet, educated voice.

"And A'm pleased ter meet thee Captain Curzon."

"Robert please."

"Robert...this is our little Susannah."

I turned back her shawl that he might see her better.

He nodded and said, "And what a fine name you have chosen; for Hugo's mother, our Aunty Susannah was the very dearest person to us all."

"A very angel amongst us," interrupted Lydia, looking at her husband because of course, that Susannah had been his first wife.

"Aye, both of yer angels," Jacob replied gallantly, "both of yer."

I marvelled at how easily and often they all talked of this first wife Susannah, for my first husband was never mentioned by anyone, though I own I thought of him still in my heart.

I liked Captain Robert Curzon at once, a good-looking man of middling height, his face and hands decorated with strange bluish dots and swirls which I later found a lot of the sailors had. Tattoos, they were called.

Hugo stepped forward, "Robert, we'd be that honoured if tha'd stand as godfather to our bairn?"

Of course, with Hugo being away and her being a strong, healthy baby, she'd not been baptized yet.

"The honour would be entirely mine, know that I will take my duties seriously as such. We sail in two weeks' time, and I have much to do, but this will be my priority, so let me know when the christening is to be, and I shall put all else aside to be there."

He took my hand again and begged that I might excuse him as he needed to talk business with Ged.

I have to say, I took to Robert Curzon with his gentle good manners. I watched him carefully as he crossed our little room to talk to Ged, who was at once serious and stopped his silly fooling about. For some time, they were deep in a quiet, intense conversation, Ged mainly nodding in agreement. The two of them sat upon the windowsill, as of course we had not enough chairs, both of them pointing at a small map, which Robert held up to the light. I wanted to know something of this discussion, for Hugo had mentioned nothing about sailing in two weeks' time, for goodness sake he had only been back for one day. Everyone seemed engrossed chatting and drinking and playing a peepy game with my Tommy, so I slipped back into the bedroom, prepared little Susannah, as she was to be called, for sleep and tucked her up in her cradle. Then I went back, took up the ale jug and approached them, they spoke in low voices, and looked across at my Hugo every now and again.

"So, let's hope fortune favours the brave eh Ged? We shall sail to Cadiz and find a crew experienced in dealing with such cargo, register under another name and make for the Western Coast…"

Robert had his back to me, but Ged saw my approach and nodded to him.

At once Robert stopped talking, turning to me he said pleasantly, "yes, Margaret Ann?"

I held up the jug, he smiled and gave me his mug. "I thank you kindly, Margaret Ann."

"Ged?"

Ged glanced at me, with nothing but disdain in his look. I knew he disliked me, though I knew not why. But he let me top up his ale mug and thanked me curtly. And that was all I managed to overhear and none of it meant anything to me. Then to my surprise, I saw Octavia slap Martha Jane on the arm, quite hard, in exasperation about something or other; but instead of running to her mama for comfort, Martha Jane went to Robert to shed her tears. He put a consoling arm around her, and she buried her head in his jacket, though when she tried to speak, he put his finger to his lips and carried on talking to Ged.

Next thing, Hugo told me that Cousin Octavia and Sister Sarah had agreed to be the other godparents; of course, I had not been consulted about any of this, not even the naming of my baby. I should have liked to have called her Elizabeth, after my mother and my sister, with Lizzie for short. I knew it would be no good talking of this to Hugo, he would just hug me, kiss me and laugh it off, anyway the whole thing was arranged now, and clearly my opinion stood for nothing. Worse was yet to come, when Lydia Curzon insisted that I visit them with my baby, every Thursday afternoon to take tea, I would certainly come to dread that each week. This was followed by her thrusting a small, wrapped present into my hands, to my disappointment it contained two little books, one for Tommy and one for the baby.

"Never too soon to start with books and reading to little ones, I find," she said firmly.

Well, that was all very good, but as I could not read myself, it was not going to happen; though I supposed Hugo could read to them if he was ever at home for more than two minutes together. To be fair Tommy seemed thrilled with his book, which had a picture of an old woman and a cat on the front of it. Octavia presented me with an exquisitely embroidered baby bonnet and Sarah an indifferently knitted white shawl. Robert discreetly put a small leather pouch of money on the mantlepiece as he left. For, to my relief, the giving of gifts, seemed to herald the end of the visit. The whole stay had lasted little more than an hour, though to me it seemed more like ten and it was with the greatest relief I thanked them and bade them goodbye despite the flurry of embarrassing hugging and kissing.

As the front door finally closed behind them, I sat down with such a sigh.

"See Meggie, it was a great success, they all had a marvellous time."

"Shall tha really be going away in a fortnight?"

He took me in his arms, "Meggie, I shall, it will be for almost a year, it's a bit of a secret expedition, but A've been promised some reet good money, more than A've ivver had in me whole life and when A get back, A'll have enough fer a decent cottage fer us all and we can live very comfortable then."

I had not the words to tell him how I dreaded the months of loneliness and cared little for the promise of a cottage, for I would rather have lived in a lean-to shed with him than be alone so long.

My heart sank as there was another knock at the door, but it was only Hugo's Aunt Eliza, who lived a few doors down and owned all of Thornton's Yard with her husband. She carried a cooking dish wrapped in a towel, with a fresh baked loaf balanced atop and set it upon the table.

"Thought yer might need a bit of dinner after yer entertaining."

A delicious smell emerged as she unwrapped a steaming pot of meat and potatoes in thick gravy. I was so grateful, for now I was suddenly very hungry and poor little Tommy had had nothing but a crust of bread since we rose.

She winked at me, "sometimes they can be a bit of a whirlwind them Curzons, when they visit."

And so it was, Hugo sailed away two weeks later; their voyage did seem to be a bit of a mystery, for I knew not which country they were going to, having never heard of this Cadiz but all I cared about was that he was to be away for the best part of a year. I could think of naught but the grinding loneliness awaiting me in those long months to come. He promised to write letters, but how was that of any use to me?

CHAPTER 14

A year later, August 1811.
Hugo returns from his long voyage
and takes on a cottage.

The 'Olivia Belle' rocked comfortably into the harbour a year later, as if she recognised Whitby as her home. Heavy laden with a desirable cargo of rum, tobacco, timber and many hogsheads of dark raw sugar, as well as some exceptionally strong sugar-spirit of the finest quality for the personal use of Captain Curzon, his First Mate Ged, soon to qualify as a captain himself, and his Cousin Hugo. All had prospered greatly from this voyage.

Hugo was involved with five others in the roping up of the sails, as the ship docked. A straightforward enough task which allowed his mind and his eyes to wander to the fast-approaching quayside. He could not see his wife anywhere amongst the great crowd there, for there were three other ships docking at the same time and wives and children waited and waved in great number, some holding up babies. He longed to see her and his little girl, a year old now; he wondered if she could walk yet or speak a few words. He had received no letters from Margaret Ann, but she could hardly read and could only just write her name, so he had not expected them. He had written to her a number of times, in the hopes that she would find someone to read them to her; in case she had not, he had filled the margins with little drawings of all his doings.

At long last he was dismissed by his captain, Robert Curzon, and he ran through the narrow streets up to Thornton's Yard and home. Pushing open the heavy old door, his heart leapt to see Margaret Ann sitting by the fire with little Susannah and Tommy playing together on the rug beside her. At once Tommy ran to him.

"Father, Father…"

"Eh Tommy lad, tha's a reet big lad now…" he laughed, dropping his bag to the floor and picking him up.

Of course, little Susannah had no memory of her father and stared at this stranger quite anxiously and as for Margaret Ann she remained seated with only the slightest of smiles.

Hugo put Tommy on the floor again and held out his arms to her.

"Has tha no kiss fer me Sweetheart?"

She stood up slowly and he took her in his arms. At once he reeled back in disgust, for as he had drawn her into his embrace, he had felt her swollen belly against him, a belly well on in a pregnancy.

"Well that can't be mine…" He stood away from her with his arms folded, he felt he could hardly breathe with the shock of it.

"A'm that sorry Hugo, A dint mean it ter happen… A were that lonely wi' owt thee."

"Lonely?" His voice grated with anger, "dunt tha think A were bloody lonely at sea all of them months? Working me guts out, in all that foulness, so as we could get a better life here, all A'd ter think about were thee and t' bairns, longing ter see yer and planning for us all ter get a summat of a nice cottage now. And all t' time tha were whoring wi' someone else. Tha bloody slut."

"Please Hugo, A dint mean it ter happen…" She reached out to him, "A've allus loved thee…could we not bring it up as our own, no one would know otherwise…please."

"Tha's mad, course they'd know, any as could bloody count would know and A'd know, tha bloody whore, how could tha do this ter me?"

"Bairns were being difficult, and A were missing thee and so lonely, A'm so sorry, forgive me, please forgive me. A tried ter be rid of it but nowt worked."

He glanced at her with such disgust now that she wished she had not spoken. She clutched at his arm, but he knocked her away, and started to look about him. He went to the clothes press and took out a bundle of little clothes and stuffed them into his sailor's bag. Grabbing Margaret Ann's heavy check shawl from the back of a chair, he picked up his little girl, wrapped her in it, slung his canvas bag over his shoulder and opened the door.

The baby cried loudly with fear and struggled to free herself, Tommy tried to grab his leg saying, "please Father, please stay with us."

"A'm sorry Tommy lad, A cannot, A would if A could, but A cannot." He delved in his pocket and threw some coins on the table, "A'll not see thee go short Margaret Ann…"

"Please dunt tek me bairn, A'll do owt but dunt tek me bairn from me Hugo." She sobbed with a kind of desolation that wrung his heart, but his anger was the stronger feeling and he walked out of his home and briskly on to his own father's house not ten minutes away. The baby sobbed miserably all the way and though he tried his best to comfort her, she did not stop until they turned into the house on Baxtergate, which she clearly recognized.

His father and stepmother did not seem in the least surprised to see him and obviously knew of the situation.

"What little girl cries when she comes to Grandmama's house?" Lydia wrapped the baby in her arms.

Jacob took Hugo in a comforting embrace, "a hard thing ter bear son..."

"A knew nowt of it, none of yer wrote and told me of it."

"Hugo dear, we only knew of it for certain very recently, for we used to see Margaret every week but of late she made excuses not to come. How could we write to you with such a blow as this, when there was naught could be done? Besides, we have hardly known where you were for most of the past year."

Lydia took his arm and guided him gently into the parlour. Octavia's heart turned to see Hugo so distressed and longed to hug away his hurt but instead she was summoned into action.

"Octavia dear, would you warm some milk with a teaspoon of brandy and plenty of sugar for little Sukey."

"Yes Mama."

Moments later she returned from the kitchen, took Sukey upon her lap and tenderly helped her to hold the little cup. Hugo looked at Octavia thoughtfully but when she glanced up, he did not say anything, only giving her the smallest of smiles. It was nothing but Octavia hung onto that moment for many months to come.

Hugo was not one to brood and after a couple of drinks, he was outlining his plans to take on a decent sized cottage with Ged, and as it happened Jacob had heard of a property, recently vacated and suitable to the purpose on Church Street. So, the next day Hugo was up early and off to see the agent, for a decent cottage went so quickly in an overcrowded and prosperous place such as Whitby.

It was in fact ideal being quite newly built, the floors were well scrubbed, the walls freshly limewashed, fireplaces blacked and the furniture basic but adequate. There were two rooms downstairs as well as a scullery, another two above and upstairs again a spacious high garret which Ged, at once, marked out for himself, being the only room with a sea view. They had their own privy in the outside yard and a shared pump alongside.

"What about thy bloody whore?" he asked Hugo, clearly having full knowledge of the situation, for there was little gossip that escaped his mother and sister.

Hugo shook his head, "nay she'll be stopping right where she is, only t' bairn'll be living here with me."

Ged nodded, "our Sarah'll be glad enough ter help with all that, seems she knows about her carryings on already."

Later that morning their sister and mother were brought to look at the commodious little house, and both were much delighted by the prospect of living there, and almost in disbelief in their change in fortune, in that the very next day they would be leaving the miserable tenement in Nicholson's Yard for ever, along with its flooded privy shared by eighteen families.

Their mother sat in the front room, which was to be hers and stared about her in a silent contentment, while her children made plans.

Both Ged and Hugo had considerable amounts of money in their pockets as a result of the recent long voyage. Ged had also finally completed his tests to become a captain now.

"Ger owt that's wanted Sarah, linens and blankets and china and what not, vittels and that, but no drink for we've a crate of finest sugar spirit still on t' ship," said Ged pushing notes into her hands.

"A'll ger all that's wanted but A'll be careful and not waste thy money Ged."

"A know that, but don't stint, for we want it set out nice, eh Hugo?"

"Oh aye." Here Hugo made his contribution and produced more money. "Get thyself some dresses and bonnets or such; and for our mother too, will that be enough?"

Sarah smiled, "A think so, but A've nivver had a new dress afore, so A'm not sure of t' cost. That'll be such a treat"

He rubbed her arm affectionately. She went on, "and might Ar ask, what of thy wife? A've seen her a few times recent but she's looked t' other way and not spoke."

Hugo spoke bitterly now, having spent so many months imagining a loving home with his wife. "She'll not be living in any house of mine. She can do as she bloody pleases but t' bairn'll be living here with us. A'm off today ter see me other brother and sister, it'll maybe be five or six days afore A'm back, our Sukey'll be with me father and Aunt Lydie till then…"

"And then here wi' us." Sarah smiled with happiness, "so we'll all be together again, like we should be."

****

Hugo returned a week later, on an impulse he first went into a jeweller's shop and bought two thin gold chains with single pearls on them; he stuffed them in his pocket and went on to their new little house on Church Street.

He was well pleased with what he saw there. Everything neatly and practically arranged throughout. The spacious kitchen was to be a family living room as well, with elbow chairs at the fireside and six highbacked chairs around the large table which was covered by the whitest of cloths. The built-in dresser shelves creaked with blue and white crockery, a wooden tray of cutlery and various cooking pots and pans.

Sarah was neatly dressed in a fresh print dress, white apron and cap. She rushed to hug Hugo tight, to welcome him home.

"Hugo, shall tha go in ter see our mother? She wants ter thank thee, but tha knows how awkward she can be sometimes…"

He stepped across the passage and into his mother's room. For a second he was taken aback, for she looked so different, yet exactly how a mother should look. Sitting beside the fireplace, she was dressed in a plain brown dress with a neat white neckerchief at her throat and an extravagantly frilled and starched cap, she held out her hands to him.

"Come here son."

She had never called him 'son' before, he sat down opposite her and let her take his hands.

"A want ter thank thee, son, for thee and our Ged giving me this beautiful room, A've nivver had owt so nice in me whole life." She looked at him intently, and after a pause said, "broke me heart ter give thee away…"

She spoke so softly that he did not catch what she had said and leaned forward, "what?"

She repeated the words with tears in her eyes.

He squeezed her hands, "shall tha tell me more of it?"

"It were a bad day for me, but A could do nowt else, A walked out ovver t' moors, A knew roughly where he lived, thy father that is. A were that tired wi' me head hurting so bad and dizzy too, but two children told me which way ter go." She looked at him sorrowfully, "me last words ter thee were sharp, A'm so sorry for it, tha were crying and that, but of course tha were crying, for A were giving thee away ter strangers… anyways, at last A got ter t' cottage and…and his wife opened t' door and A can remember it all as clear as if it were yesterday. A beautiful cottage it were, A could see behind her, a good fire burning in a shining grate, with all clean washing hanging ovver it, everything were so neat and bright. Little coloured curtains and cushions everywhere and fresh baking on t' table. She'd a lovely dog at her side, there were everything that A couldn't give thee. A put thee in her arms and she took thee lovingly. She could easy of dashed thy head on t' step, but when she took thee so kind A knew it were ter be a good home for thee…"

Hugo nodded, "it were a good home." He spoke loudly and looked at her directly so that she could read his lips. "A were allus happy there though A nivver knew owt about yer all."

"Maybe that were for t' best then. Tis everything ter me that we're all together now, shall tha bring thy wife here?"

He shook his head ruefully, "na, tis ovver between us but t' bairn'll be coming later today."

"Eh that'll gladden me heart, for A've hardly seen t' little lass fer weeks."

Hugo smiled, he looked around the room with its unadorned white walls, wooden bed covered by a white quilt, a chest of drawers with jug, basin and candlestick standing on it, and the two chairs by the fireplace.

It seemed too plain and empty to him, "Mother, should tha like owt else in here? Maybe some pictures for t' walls?"

She shook her head, "A like things simple."

"How about some ornaments and that for t' mantle shelf?"

"Nay, nowt fussy."

"A can get thee owt tha wants, tha's only ter say."

"Well…"

"Is there summat tha'd like, A can get thee owt tha wants."

She was hesitant. "There's summat A would like, but a dunt want ter be a trouble…When A were a lass, A had a dog called Bran, he were that loving and faithful… he'd sit up and beg and he were so comical."

"Mother, tha wants a dog?"

"If it's not a trouble…"

"No, me Aunt Lydie breeds spaniels, and reet good ones they are too, there's many a hunting gentleman comes ter buy them from her. A'll get thee one of her pups, then tha can tek it out fer walks and that. A've seen collars and dog leads in t' Cordwainers in different colours… what colour should tha like?"

"Oh red," she said at once, "Our Bran had a red collar."

"Red collar then and a spaniel pup. Shall tha call it Bran too?"

"Aye, A think A will."

At that moment Sarah came in with three cups of tea on a flowered tin tray and at once Hugo remembered the gifts in his pocket.

"Mother A got thee this."

He handed her a small leather box.

"Eh it's beautiful, A've nivver had owt so lovely." There was the glisten of a tear in her eye. She touched it carefully with her fingertips, almost afraid to take the pearl and chain out of its leather box.

"Shall A do it for thee Mother?" Sarah stepped forward and fastened it around her mother's neck. "There that looks reet bonny on thee."

"And for thee Sarah," Hugo gave her the other box.

Sarah smiled up at him, "why brother A thank thee."

She handed it to him, turned round and held her hair up so that he could put it on for her. He looked at the prettiness of her neck, and when he had secured the necklace, he kissed that soft nape, even though he knew at once that that was not the way to behave with a sister. But the moment quickly passed and the three of them settled to drink their tea.

"Our Mother wants a dog, is that all right for thee Sarah?"

"Oh aye, a dog meks a happy home dunt it, though A'll tell thee, our Ged cannot abide a dog. We'll tek no notice of him, eh Mother?"

Their mother smiled and nodded. The following week she was the proud owner of a twelve-week old, liver and white spaniel, who was kissed and petted to the highest degree.

"Why's she called bloody thing Bran when it's not brown?" asked Ged.

Sarah shrugged her shoulders, but Hugo replied, "she had a dog called Bran when she were young, and she's named it after that one."

They both stared at him in amazement and Ged said, "bloody hell tha's only bin int' family five minutes and tha knows more about Mother than we do."

Hugo grinned and felt wonderfully at home.

CHAPTER 15

September 1811.
In which Ged meets the Faichneys.

Idina Faichney had had a trying morning at the dressmaker's; she had felt it necessary to go there as she was in need of two autumn gowns and some new underwear. She used the same dressmaker that her mother had always used when she was alive and did not have the means of changing to another, as Idina had no money of her own and accounts were paid at the end of each quarter by her elderly father. He would have thought it a nonsense to go to another dressmaker when this one had been quite good enough for his dear departed wife.

Idina was a tall, well-built young lady, and for some reason best known to herself, the dressmaker found this something of an annoyance, thus the visit had been punctuated by a series of caustic remarks.

"Yours, a difficult figure to flatter Miss Faichney," or, with shaking head, "there will be quite a bit of extra cloth needed here," or to Idina's disappointment she had said, "I think these pretty new prints would not do for the larger figure, best stick to something plain and dark, Miss Faichney."

Her apprentice, well under five foot in height and with a waist no larger than seventeen inches, quietly simpered throughout the measuring.

Thus, rather humiliated and with, what was, she told herself an unreasonable hatred of her dressmaker, Idina walked straight home, and had a tray of tea brought up to the quiet of the parlour. She poured herself a cup and gazed out of the window at the simply magnificent sea view. Her father had had the house built high up so that the main rooms overlooked the harbour entrance, in order that he could see ships arriving from a distance and watch them dock. Now he spent most of the days of his old age gazing at the waves from his bed or sitting at the parlour window reminiscing about his life as a sea captain and then his trials as a ship-owner, when he had to employ others to take the 'Fortitude' out.

Although Idina had heard every one of his stories many times, she always dutifully expressed surprise or interest as required. But right now she thought she had a little time of peace before her father would be ready to come downstairs, for he always arose late.

But not so, for she had hardly drained her cup, when there was a bold knock at the front door, and she suddenly did remember that a new captain was due to visit, with a view to taking out the 'Fortitude' on her next voyage.

The little maid servant showed him in, "Captain Stone ter see t' master."

Idina had imagined the new captain would be a stout middle-aged man of the lower orders, but in fact she saw a tall, good looking, nay handsome man in a captain's jacket enter the room.

"Thank you, Jane… Good morning Captain Stone, I am Captain Faichney's daughter. My father is not downstairs yet but will be shortly."

Her voice trailed away as their eyes met, but the moment was quickly broken by a booming voice from upstairs calling her.

"Please do excuse me Captain Stone, I have to help my father downstairs."

"Might A be of assistance, Miss Faichney?"

"I thank you, no. My father will not accept help from any but myself."

With that she swept from the room.

Ged Stone was taken aback; he had known that the Fortitude's owner had an older unmarried daughter. He had expected some dry spinster, not a statuesque beauty of around his own age with clouds of magnificent red hair on her shoulders, wide green eyes and the softest of sweet voices.

Captain Faichney's entrance was preceded by grunts of, "hold steady lassie," and "for God's sake lassie, ye'll be the death of me."

At last he came in the room, a frail elderly man on two sticks wearing an old-fashioned white wig. Idina settled him in a chair at the table in the window. She plumped his cushions and draped a small tartan shawl about his shoulders, her only thanks being a snappish, "by God, leave me be woman."

"Yes Father."

Whereupon she sat at the fireside and opened a book.

"Captain Stone, at thy service Sir."

Papers and charts were at once spread over the table and the men talked intently for some time aided by two large whiskies. The drinking was preceded by a call of 'Slange Var', which the old man managed to make sound more like a battle cry than good wishes between two sea captains. Ged quickly saw that although frail in body, the old captain's mind was sharp as a knife, as he outlined a proposed route, calling at Newcastle, Leith, Prestonpans, Bo'ness and Dundee; with diverse cargoes of edge tools, coal and oil to be delivered and vitriol, linen, flax, whisky and other sundries to be brought back to Whitby. The whole circuit to be completed in around eight weeks, depending on weather conditions.

As Captain Faichney fumbled in a drawer for some certificates. Ged took the opportunity to glance across at Idina and found her to be staring at him. Before he could smile at her, she attended to her book and quickly turned a page, her lovely hair falling forward to cover her face and concealing the smallest twitch upon her lips; then he found he had not heard what the captain had just said to him. The old man looked at him expectantly, so hoping for the best, Ged said, "Aye, indeed Sir."

"Good, now let us be signing, and ye can be on yer way Captain Stone, ye've been highly recommended to me by Captain Curzon and I hope for this to be a prosperous voyage for both of us."

All cargoes and routes confirmed, with signatures duly placed, he stood up to shake the old man's claw like hand.

At once Idina leapt up, "do not ring for Jane, Father. I shall show Captain Stone out myself."

Ged then twisted awkwardly around her to open the parlour door for her and their eyes met again for the briefest of seconds.

He took his hat and gloves from the hall stand, as Idina unfastened the front door.

"A bid thee a good day, Miss Faichney."

"Good day, Captain Stone."

She felt strangely emotional, as she watched his long loping strides take him away from her. He grasped the top of the garden gate and paused for what seemed an age to Idina but was perhaps only three seconds. Then he turned on his heel and walked back up the path.

"Miss Faichney, would tha care ter walk out wi' me, termorrow?"

"Captain Stone, I should indeed, I would find that most pleasant." He hesitated, so she went on, "I usually walk out about two o'clock, if that is convenient for you?" He nodded.

"Then I shall meet you at the corner of the road at two, tomorrow."

With that she closed the front door, leaned against it and hugged herself in delight.

Both had arranged the meeting most successfully considering that Ged had never asked a lady to walk with him before, indeed Ged had hardly ever met a young lady before, having only taken his pleasures with the paid for lasses of the dockside in his various ports of call.

As for Idina, no man had ever asked to walk with her, and she had generally found herself overlooked at the few excruciating balls and parties she had attended.

* * * *

Around twelve thirty, the following day, at the house on Church Street, Hugo and Sarah stood outside their bedrooms, when there was a thundering step upon the stairs. Ged climbed up, two at a time and shoved his way past them, a clean shirt and a pile of starched neck bands over one arm and a can of hot water in his other hand.

"Out of me way yo two."

"What the hell is happening?" asked a puzzled Hugo.

Sarah burst into giggles and put her finger to her lips, looking upwards till they heard Ged's footsteps above them in his garret bedroom.

Then she pushed Hugo into her bedroom, closed the door and said, "Our brother goes a courting."

"Nivver."

She nodded triumphantly, "he does."

Overhead, something was dropped upon the floor, followed by a barrage of swearing.

"Why, whoever is t' unfortunate lass?" asked Hugo, laughing himself now.

Sarah paused to give full dramatic effect, "Miss Faichney, Miss Idina Faichney."

But her words fell upon stony ground, for Hugo frowned and merely said, "who?"

"Come, Brother, tha must know of them. Her father owns t' 'Fortitude', old Captain Faichney, and she, his only child. A say only child, so who else will inherit that great ship, with him quite an old man?"

"Bloody Hell," said Hugo, clearly impressed, "so Ged's ter captain on t' 'Fortitude' in two weeks' time and now he's courting t' daughter. Sly dog," he grinned.

Eventually, Ged appeared; shaved, washed, starched, brushed, and cologned to the highest degree.

At once Sarah was serious, "tha looks most fine Brother, what's tha think Hugo?"

"Impressed," he replied, "has tha gor a clean handkerchief?" For when Hugo's mother had lain upon her deathbed, she made him promise to always say his prayers, scrub his nails and ensure he had a clean handkerchief.

"No…thanks Bro."

Ged ran upstairs again and reappeared a moment later with one.

Sarah reached up to brush a speck from his collar.

"Sister, A'm that nervous, about not knowing proper manners and that, at end ut' day A'm just an ignorant pig."

"Come Ged, tha's a captain now, and a good match for any lass. A'd be that proud ter walk out wi' a man such as thee," she said loyally.

Ged patted her arm and turned to go.

Hugo called out, "good luck".

Laughing, Ged turned and put two fingers up at his brother, opened the front door and was gone on his adventure.

****

Idina felt a little frumpish in a plain sombre dress and shawl, untrimmed bonnet and sensible outdoor shoes, as she walked towards Ged. Not knowing, that when he caught sight of her, he saw a beautiful woman, long flaming hair enhanced by her dark dress, soft white skin and green eyes framed to advantage by her lack of feathers and ribbons.

"Miss Faichney."

"Captain Stone."

He wanted to compliment her, but somehow in his nervousness, words failed him, and he feared he might stutter which he had not done since he was a small child. Instead, he offered her his arm; as she slipped hers through his, Idina felt weak with the happiness of it.

They did not discuss where to go, but simply walked up the back road to the ancient abbey in silence, save for a couple of remarks about the fine weather.

As they approached, there was a row of benches and Idina said, "shall we sit awhile?"

She removed her arm from his and turned to look at him. "Tell me something of your family, Captain."

She expressed great delight to hear of his mother, sister, brother and little niece, all living together in the house on Church Street. She expressed even more delight on hearing that a spaniel pup now completed the family.

"Oh, how I should love a dog myself, but my father never would allow it. Now he is old and frail, I would fear him tripping on it and when I was younger, I often went to sea with him for the whaling, and a dog would have been left too long at home with just the servants."

Ged was astonished now, for he had not heard of a lady going to sea on a whaler.

"Tha's been ter sea then, wi' thy father?"

"Oh yes, probably a dozen times or so, when I was a girl. Of course, when he got too old to captain himself, and others worked the ship, I could no longer go."

"And did tha like it then, life at sea."

"No, I did not 'like' it, I loved it, more than anything. It was the only time I've felt truly alive, out at sea and I think that I know most things about sailing too, mainly by watching but I have read a great many books on shipping as well."

Ged looked into her eyes in sheer wonder, as she went on, "so have you not known of a woman going to sea afore, Captain Stone?"

"Only t' once."

Here, he proceeded to tell the story of some years before when he had been in the Americas on a whaler. Robert Curzon (his brother's cousin) had been First Mate then and he the second. It happened that they had stopped to take on extra crew at New London. Black men were supposed to have papers that showed them to be free men and not escaped slaves. One of the black youths had no such papers, but the captain waved him on anyway as he was anxious to set sail with a full crew as soon as possible. Just as they were drawing away from the quayside, two bounty hunters jumped aboard ship looking for a slave woman who had absconded and, with the help of their Swamp Hounds, had tracked her down to the New London quayside. An annoyed captain quickly showed them an entire crew of men and boys. Satisfied, the bounty hunters disembarked, even though the dogs were still barking furiously from where they had been tied up on the quayside. Several days passed until after some minor misdemeanour, the black lad was to be flogged; Robert had procured the rope tail whip in readiness and Ged had pushed the lad forward onto the barrel and pulled up his shirt, both got the shock of their lives, to find him to be a woman.

Ged paused in the telling of the tale, suddenly fearing it had been too vulgar to be told to a lady, but Idina merely asked what happened next.

"Why, we covered her up as best we could and took her to t' captain, thinking he'd be reet angry, but not so, he put her into t' guest cabin and she kept us all entertained for t' next three month wi' tales of how she had escaped and passed through six states to get to Connecticut, and all of her other adventures."

"And then what."

"Quite a happy ending A think, for when we got back ter port, our captain married her, good and proper and they sailed away for t' Canadas."

Idina smiled and looked impressed. She wondered for a moment if this Robert Curzon was the son of one of her friends, for she knew Lydia Curzon quite well from their charity work.

"You said Robert Curzon was your brother's cousin, so is he not your cousin too?"

Ged's heart sank, he had dropped himself in it, for now he could either lie or confess the tangled tale of his mother's infidelity, an abandoned baby and its rediscovery twenty years later. However, fate intervened, for the mild weather suddenly turned to splashing rain.

"Oh no," gasped Idina fumbling in her little reticule for a tiny, folding umbrella.

"Ad we best get back then?"

She hesitated and then said, "Captain Stone, there is a cottage just over there, the second one along, that sells tea and cakes. It is not very refined, but the baking is excellent…"

He grinned with relief that their meeting was not yet over.

"Let's get there then."

The smallness of the umbrella meant that a degree of intimacy was required in order for it to shelter them both. So, with his arm boldly about her waist, they ran across the damp grass to the cottage.

It was dark inside; crammed into the room were four rough wood tables and a dozen chairs, mainly taken up by other wet walkers. Idina and Ged squeezed into the last table, and at once a woman with a walnut face and a none too clean apron, wiped their table half-heartedly with a grimy rag and shoved teapot and cups in front of them.

"Sconesercakeerboth?"

"Both if tha please," said Ged.

"Buttererjamandcreamerboth."

"Both," Ged bit his lip to suppress his laughter and caught Idina's eye.

She had strands of wet hair across her forehead, he longed to stroke them back for her, but did not dare. He thought her so lovely and ladylike, that it made him hesitant, though he had never been so before, in any other female presence.

She smiled, showing off two rows of pearly white teeth. "I told you it was a bit rough and ready here, though really very good."

"Bit like me then." His eyes crinkled attractively at the corners.

Before she could answer, plates of scones and cake were slammed down in front of them with a dish of soft butter and one of thick yellow cream. Some of the jam slopped over the side of its saucer, whereupon the old woman wiped it on the corner of her grubby apron and said, "beg pardon."

Idina put her hand over her mouth to supress a giggle and then said, "Captain Stone, may I butter a scone for you?"

"If tha please, Miss Faichney."

The captain had never before had a scone buttered for him, he was charmed and waited quietly like a child, while she heaped jam and cream on the two halves.

"There now, tell me if that does not absolutely melt in your mouth."

"Indeed it does, Miss Faichney," he said a moment later, as she was pouring his tea.

By now she was rather sticky and said, "they never have napkins here."

"Shall Ar ask?"

Ged was anxious to do the right thing, even though he had rarely in his whole life, felt the need of a napkin himself, the back of his hand generally being sufficient to the purpose.

She shook her head, her mouth being too full to speak and pulled a tiny handkerchief out of her reticule.

Whereupon Ged was able to produce his own more substantial one, neatly starched and ironed by his devoted sister. He handed it to her, and she flashed that lovely smile at him.

"Why thank you so much, this is much more suitable than my own."

Now they were onto the cakes, and having drunk all the tea, each feared the other suggesting an end to the afternoon. As if on cue, the old woman banged a jug of hot water onto the table, some of it slopped onto Ged's hand, but he made no mention of it.

"Owt else?"

"A thank thee no, it were all reet good though," said Ged.

"Tha'll get nowt better in these parts," she said confidently and retreated behind a tattered curtain into her kitchen.

He stared at Idina, she looked up and caught his gaze and they smiled at each other, not turning away until she felt a blush creeping up onto her cheeks.

"Miss Faichney, may A ask of thy name? 'Idina,' A've not heard it afore?"

"I was named after my mother, who died shortly after my birth, Idina means 'from Edinburgh' which my mother was. My father came from much farther north, in the Highlands and our name Faichney is Gaelic for wolf."

"Wolf," he repeated, having not the least idea what Gaelic was, though without realising, he had often heard it spoken by sailors picked up on the Scottish islands.

"Some may think a wolf a nasty animal to be feared, but in truth the she-wolf is loving and devoted to her family and will fight to the death to protect them. Faithful to her mate, they pair for life." He looked amazed, so she went on, "of course I could not tell you my middle name, for you would laugh too much at its inappropriateness…"

"Oh, please do, A'm sure A'll not laugh."

Her mouth twitched and hesitantly, she said, "Aphrodite."

Puzzled he said, "Afro what?"

"Aphrodite, the goddess of beauty and love."

"Oh," he smiled, at once seeing his chance, "why surely that is a most suitable name for one as lovely as thee."

She flushed slightly and looked downwards, "Captain Stone, I think you do flatter."

"Indeed, A do not, for A make a most particular point nivver ter flatter, A only spek t' truth of it."

Here they looked at each other for a moment, each with the smallest of smiles. Ged had never seen anyone with true green eyes before and was transfixed.

The rain had stopped, the customers started to leave, and the old woman pointedly appeared with a broom.

"Ave we ter go then?"

"I fear we must."

Ged paid and hardly thinking of it one way or the other, he gave a generous tip.

The old woman's face lit up at once and she said what a pleasure it was to serve a real gentleman and his lady, and she hoped to serve them again soon at their leisure.

They walked back as slowly as they reasonably could. Ged had no idea how the encounter was to be finished. When he departed his ladies of the night, a peck on the cheek, a 'thanks Love,' and maybe a friendly pat on the bottom had seemed quite adequate.

They stood at the end of Idina's road, and she looked up at him expectantly.

His words tumbled out badly, he remembered being hit as a child for stammering as he said, "c could, might we a again."

Without the slightest flinch, she said, "is tomorrow too soon, Captain Stone?"

"Tis hardly soon enough Miss Faichney."

"Then I shall meet you here, at two of the-clock tomorrow."

CHAPTER 16

That same day.
In which Idina and Ged think about their encounter.

When Ged reached home, tea, bread and cheese was set out, with his family sitting around the kitchen table.

"Shall tha tek some tea, Brother?" said Sarah, lining up the cups.

"No, A took me tea wi' Miss Faichney."

"Ooh ooh er," said Hugo and Sarah, in one voice.

"And what were it?" his sister asked, "a silver cake upon a golden plate?"

Ged looked at the floor and shook his head, in full preparation for being teased mercilessly, though he was grinning too at the memory of his afternoon.

His mother looked across from the fireside, where she sat with the spaniel pup upon her lap. "Tis time tha settled down our Ged, me and thy father were wed at twenty," she said piously.

Under his breath he muttered, "well, them two are enough ter put anyone off gerring wed ivver."

Though she could not hear him, she caught his meaning and shook her head, "nay Ged, thy father were a good man when A wed him."

"Blink once and tha'd bloody miss that," he muttered darkly.

"So how were Miss Faichney?" asked Sarah, to change the subject.

"Wondrous," he sighed, "she knows how to sail a ship and A intend ter marry her."

Taking advantage of the stunned silence that followed, he disappeared upstairs to hang up his good coat before it got dog hairs on it.

* * * *

When Idina reached home, she ran straight up to her bedroom, took off her bonnet and shawl and threw herself onto the bed. She lay upon her side, hugging two pillows she burst into tears, suddenly realising how lonely she had always been.

Cook came up a few minutes later with some clean linens. "Eh dear Miss, whatever ails?"

Cook was the nearest thing Idina had known to a mother, having been with them nearly thirty years.

"Was thy young man not what tha expected Lovie?"

Idina wondered how she knew she had met a young man, but then, as a general rule, servants seemed to know everything that was going on, without being told.

"He was wondrous," she wept.

"Did he not behave as a gentleman then, for he's from a rough family is Captain Stone?"

"He did, and he was so kind to me." Idina pushed away the pillows, feeling it was quite silly to be hugging them.

Cook put her arms around Idina, but her comfort only made Idina sob even more.

"Perhaps he has not asked ter see thee again, Hun?"

"We are to meet again tomorrow, Cook."

"Then, whatever has made thee cry so, dear Miss Idina?"

"Nothing at all Cook, only that he was so very, very lovely."

Cook sighed and put the whole thing down to Idina's monthlies, which always seemed more troublesome to ladies than they were to lasses of the lower orders.

"Cook, do you know of his family then?" Suddenly, Idina sat up, wiped her eyes and was ready to listen. It did not take much to get Cook to launch into a story.

"Oh aye, A do Miss, A've known his mam, Sally Stone all her life, for her family lived in t' same yard as me, though she's probably ten year younger than me. Poor as could be, none of her lot ever kept work for more than five minutes but any road when she were about twenty, she wed one o' t' whalers, a handsome enough lad, but eh, he used ter knock her about, 'specially after t' drink. So, one Spring, off he goes ter t' fisheries and nivver comes back, news comes that ship's lost. Well that's disaster for t' sailors and masters, and worse still for t' wives and bairns who's left wi' nowt. But A will say Sally pulled herself together fine well quick, for she'd two little ones by then, thy young man and his sister, and she got herself work behind t' bar at 'Grey Horse,' for she were still a good-looking lass. And a lass as were a bit too friendly like." Here Cook shook her head, "next thing she were throwing herself at a Mr Curzon, a Mr Jacob Curzon…"

"Oh," said Idina, "Captain Stone mentioned a Curzon."

"Why whatever did he say?" asked Cook, surprised.

"He said something about his brother's cousin, Robert Curzon, and I asked was he not his cousin too and before he could answer, it started to rain, and we had to run to the tea cottage…"

"Well A'll tell thee truth of it, shocking though it is, probably best tha knows, now tha's courting wi' him."

Idina wondered if she really was courting with him, as Cook went on.

"So afore tha knows it, she were with child, and he were a married man too, should ha' known better. She nivver seemed that bothered, perhaps she hoped ter catch Mr Curzon wi' it, for A will say he were a bonny lad, and as even tempered and as amiable as any could wish."

"So, what became of them?"

"Well, when t' bairn were only a few week old, her husband comes back, turns out t' ship weren't lost but only stuck in t' ice and he'd ter wait a year afore he were rescued, most o' t' crew were dead, but not he, he'd come back like t' bad penny he were."

"Did he know the baby wasn't his?"

"Course he did, for he'd been gone ovver a year."

"And?"

"A don't know if A should go on, A wunt want ter shock thee Miss wi' tha being a lady …"

For what great storyteller does not know when to pause for dramatic effect.

"Please do go on, tell me the baby was not hurt."

"So, he were mad as can be, knocked poor Sally ter t' floor and ter this day she's deaf from hitting her head on t' hearth. But sister Sarah, little lass were quick of t' mark and ran owter t' house with t' bairn and took him up ter her grandmother's for safety. And he could not run after 'em, for he were on crutches, having lost his toes in t' frost ovver t' Winter…Next thing tha knows,

Sally's running up there too, and teks bairn ter live wi' his real father, this Jacob Curzon. A didn't see her that day, for A were working here by then, but A've heard tell she were in a bad way and she'd ter walk four mile and give up her bairn. Soon after, husband died anyway and she and Sarah had ter tek in washing and that, and young Ged were sent ter sea, and he could only have been eight or nine, poor lad."

"So, was that how it ended?"

"Dear me no, Miss. Twenty year passed and by chance thy Captain Stone and his lost brother were signed up on t' same ship. A don't know details of how they found each other or even knew each other, but A do know they're sharing a house on Church Street now, and Sally and t' sister Sarah live there too, so they must all ger on well together…"

Idina hardly knew what to say, so she said, "fancy that, perhaps I shall hear more of this from Captain Stone tomorrow."

And next day she certainly did hear more of Ged's life, for he gained in confidence and barely stopped talking, pausing only for her to laugh at his endless jokes, which she quite happily did. He spoke of how extremely poor he had been as a child, yet how much he was loved by his mother and sister, who had made something of a happy home despite their poverty which had occasionally tumbled into destitution. She told him of her motherless lonely childhood, without siblings or cousins to play with; though she had never wanted for anything, her father having made a great deal of money in the early days of the whale fishing.

Ged worked long into the nights, preparing the 'Fortitude' for her voyage, so that he could spend every afternoon arm in arm with Idina walking about, talking about every subject under the sun. Every night he imagined holding her soft yielding flesh against his body and running his fingers through her beautiful hair.

She longed for him to kiss her, yet she had no idea how such a thing would come about; in the novels that she read, it only happened after a firm proposal of marriage had been secured, yet she had seen sailors openly kiss girls they hardly knew, quite passionately. With no close friends to ask, she felt it would be inappropriate to question Cook. She would stare at the captain's strong profile with its dark shadows, wanting to feel their roughness on her cheek, she loved his roman nose, slightly off centre after some sailor's brawl and longed to know his chiselled mouth against her own. On their third afternoon together, he felt able to take her hand in his, watching her face intently as he did, fearful of making a mistake. For he was determined to marry her whether she came with her father's blessing or as a penniless bride to share his garret bedroom. He loved her intense gaze; he had never before seen eyes that were a true green in colour. He loved her long red hair which was never worn pinned up and he longed to touch it. Her modest kindly way of speaking enthralled him. Sometimes it took him a moment to realise that she had said something amusing when she spoke so seriously with only the smallest of smiles. It was on one such occasion that he suddenly threw back his head with laughter, snatched her hand and slapped it against his leg. She felt the warmth and power of his hand, he turned towards her, and she thought they might kiss but he only took her fingers to his lips. Then he laid their two hands upon his muscled thigh and carried on talking. Thrilled by this, she shifted in her seat and felt a flush creep up her neck, as he whispered in her ear, and she felt his warm breath upon her. Now, he launched into a shocking tale about how their house had fallen down one Christmas Eve when he was only seven years old. Idina gasped with the full horror of such a thing. Apparently, they had lived in one room of a cottage built against the East Cliff, and due to wet weather, there was a great landslide resulting in the destruction of the entire street. All were forced to run from their houses with only seconds to spare.

"Aye, there were hundreds running from their homes, carrying bairns and t' sickly ones in their arms. Tha'd have laughed though…"

"Oh, I do not think I should, for how terrible to lose everything one owned with no warning."

"Aye, but it were late at night, and some were abed and forced ter run out inter t' street wi' out a stitch on 'em. Well, me and our Sarah were nobbut bairns, and we had ter giggle a bit ter see t' neighbours so." His eyes creased at the corners, as he grinned at the memory of it. "Course we was that cold in our house, we'd gone ter bed wearing ivvery scrap of clothes we had, just for t' warmth, so we was fine, had iverything we owned on our backs. Anyroad our mother were on her way home from working and she saw whole street fall down from a distance and thought us dead, so we had a reet big hug when she saw us, reet as rain." He smiled at her and she had to smile back, for somehow there seemed to be something of a happy ending to this awful story. "So wi' it being Christmas Eve, Mother had a big bag of sweets and oranges and such for us what she'd been given at her work, so she wrapped us up in her big shawl and we just sat on t' harbourside, reet away from t' buildings and rubble and ate them all. A loved t' oranges, so A thought A'd try a lemon then, eh A thought A'd been poisoned wi t' sourness of it." He laughed, "Mother and Sarah nivver forgot me face and whenever A were in a strop or owt, they'd tease me and say A'd got me 'lemon face on'. Then we slept out in t' open as best we could and next day, we went ter stop with one of me uncles on t' West side, but not for long though, for they'd six inch of water in rooms when ivver it were a high tide. Mother said she could put up wi' bugs and mice but no way were she going ter tek her tea wi' her feet in six inch o' water."

Idina gazed into his eyes with the most adoring of expressions.

It came to the last afternoon before sailing, and Ged was nervous again, for he knew that serious words needed to be spoken between them. They sat close upon the usual bench, overlooking a rather tumultuous sea. He took her hand in his.

"Miss Faichney, A wish ter ask thee summat, but A cannot until A have completed this voyage successful like, afore A can speak with thy father…"

She smiled at him sweetly and waited.

"Can A… might A think that we have summat of an understanding?"

"Why Captain Stone, I think perhaps we have always had an understanding since our first meeting, have we not?"

He grinned and nodded. He put his arm tightly around her, pushed back her bonnet, snapping its ribbons and at last he kissed her. Softly at first, their lips gently touching and as he felt her leaning into him, he clasped her firmly and kissed her with all his truest feeling.

They walked back slowly, stopping only once in a little private alley way. He took both her hands in his and laid them against his shirt, she could feel his heart beating against her fingers. With his other hand he pulled back her hair, moving her head from side to side, that he might kiss the golden studs in her ears, both her cheeks and a final long kiss upon her mouth, with his fingers wrapped in her hair.

At their parting place, Idina took his hand in hers, "will you write to me Captain Stone, while you are away? It will much comfort me to know how your voyage fares. And I should like to write to you, if I may."

Here she showed her good knowledge of sailing, by listing the various ports from which letters could be sent or collected.

He nodded, charmed by the notion of receiving letters from her. "Can A use thy name, or would Miss Faichney be more proper in a letter?"

"No, for a love letter it should be Idina, will they be love letters?"

"Oh aye, they will that," he said embracing her, even though they were in clear sight of the house now.

"Tha gaol agam ort," she whispered in is ear.

"What?" He smiled, puzzled by her words.

"I shall say it again in English, when you come back to me."

He grinned, for he was sure she had said something nice from the look on her face. Then he took her gloved hand to his lips and turned to walk away, looking back only once to blow her a final kiss.

He strode towards home, the happiest man alive; about to go on his first voyage as captain on a splendid mizzen ship, and with the love of a fine woman in his heart. However, as he neared the bridge, doubts suddenly engulfed him, for he had no idea of what to say in a love letter, never having written or seen one before. He feared making a fool of himself, with his lack of education and breeding. His pace slowed and he leant pensively against the harbour rail. He felt neither his brother nor his sister would be of any help in this matter, and it would only be another excuse for merciless teasing. His best friend Robert Curzon, who would have known just what to say in such an epistle, was currently away at sea. But he quite suddenly had an idea; he would have to admit to his ignorance but there was one person he knew who would know exactly how to go about such a thing, and instead of walking straight home, he turned left over the bridge and onto Baxtergate.

CHAPTER 17

Five minutes later.
In which Lydia Curzon receives an unexpected caller.

Lydia Curzon was in the parlour reading a book, her daughter Octavia was sitting in the window sewing. Lydia thought she might ring for some more tea when her thoughts were quite interrupted by a loud knock at the front door.

"Whoever can this be?"

The maid showed the visitor into the parlour.

"Why my dear Captain Stone, what a surprise, but a very pleasant one, do please be seated."

She indicated a comfortable padded chair opposite her own and seeing at once that the captain was not a 'dog person', she ordered the two fussing spaniels, one of them heavy with pups, back to their bed which was an old blanket, incongruous in that most elegant of rooms.

"Mistress Curzon, Miss Curzon."

Octavia looked at him with some interest, for though only sixteen, she considered any handsome man under the age of thirty-five, to be fair game. "Captain Stone," she said sweetly.

Ged hesitated, whereupon Lydia said, "Octavia dear, would you go to your bedroom to finish your sewing, the light is so much better up there."

He stood up, as he had seen Robert Curzon do, when in the presence of ladies, politely waiting till Miss Curzon had left the room before sitting down again.

Octavia did not in the least mind her dismissal, for she knew from past experience that if she lay flat on her bedroom floor, just above where the parlour chandelier was fitted, then she could hear quite as well as if she were still in the room below.

"Mistress Curzon, A'm hoping tha dunt mind me calling unexpected but A'm in need of some advice, and we are family now, A'm thinking."

"We most certainly are, my dear Captain Stone, you being brother to my very dearest stepson. But before you tell me of your quest, I shall ring for some tea. I generally take a glass of brandy about now, perhaps you would care to join me and do the honours?" Here she indicated a little gilt table with blue spirit decanters and glasses. "The larger glasses I think."

So, with brandies poured and the tea tray settled upon another dainty table, Lydia looked directly at him and said, "so tell me what brings you here, dear Captain Stone."

"It's summat of a personal nature, and A dint know who else A could ask…"

"Please do speak freely Sir and know that your words will go no further than these four walls."

Here Lydia leaned forward greatly intrigued and up above, Octavia pressed her ear to the floor.

He swallowed, "A've been courting a lady and A'm sailing on t' first tide termorrow and A'm wanting ter be writing ter her, but A've not least notion of what ter say, what words of love is proper ter write. For she is a lady and for meself, A've no education at all, A've nivver had call ter write such a thing before." He looked at her desperately.

"Ah, I see," she said thoughtfully, "a love letter is a very special communication between two people. My first husband wrote me a great number of such letters during our long courtship, I read them many times over and treasure them to this day in his very dearest memory."

She poured two tiny bowls of tea and offered the captain a little pink cake, which years later, he found out was called a macaroon.

"Please take two or three, for they are only small. So, let us take our tea and then I shall write out a list of phrases which you might use. You can take it with you and have it to hand as you write your letters."

"A do thank thee Mistress." He spoke humbly, with gratitude and enormous relief too.

"I am only too pleased to help, though I will say that the words that will mean the most to your beloved are those that come truly from your own heart."

She sat to an elegant writing table and wrote out ten phrases that might be incorporated into an amorous epistle. Wafting it dry, she folded it neatly and handed it to him saying, "do not feel obliged to tell, but who is this most fortunate of ladies?"

"Tis a Miss Faichney."

"Why, not Idina Faichney?"

"Aye, does tha know of her?"

"Indeed, I do, she and I are on a committee to promote the sale of needlework to raise funds to help the poor widows of seamen. Of course, I do not sew myself, but dear Idina is the most talented of needlewomen and quite the sweetest person I know… Why, what an excellent choice you have made Captain

Stone." She paused and leaned forward confidentially, "I do not suggest for one moment, that you will have even thought of this, but it is a fact, that her father is a very old man now, and she his only child to inherit that fine big ship. Do you know Captain, the 'Fortitude' was the first ship my son sailed on when he ran away from home at only fifteen?" She paused and smiled in fond maternal memory.

"Aye well that were how A met him like, a good few year since, 'Fortitude' docked in Dundee, and we was both signed up on t' 'Clara Mae' and was off to t' Americas together and got ter be reet good friends. Am ashamed ter say A couldn't read nor write then, A had no schooling for A went ter sea at eight year old. It were thy son Robert as taught me ter read, for rough as A were, he saw it in me that A could get ter be a master and get me papers if A could study books and that…"

Here Lydia gasped with shock, "surely you did not go to sea when you were only eight years old my dear Captain, why you must have been hardly out of your cradle."

Ged laughed out loud at the notion of him ever having had a cradle, when in truth, a pile of sacks stuffed with straw on the floor had been all any of them had had as a bed for many years, but he refrained from saying this. Instead, he said that it had soon made a man of him, going to sea so early in life and when they met, how much Robert had taught him, even though, Robert was the younger of the two.

Lydia refilled his brandy glass liberally, "how interesting, I do not think my son Robert has ever spoken to me of this time, we never saw him for seven years, and upon his return, well he was a captain himself by then…"

Here Ged laughed out loud, "A were a reet hot head then, allus in a fight with any as crossed me and of course when yer on-board ship tha allus gets a blood…a good flogging for fighting."

Here Lydia shuddered, always horrified by the casual brutality of life at sea.

"But A saw how calm and controlled he were, dint matter what 'appened, thy Robert just bit his lip and took it. He used ter say he'd be better than all of them one day, and that's what he were aiming for. 'Aim high Ged,' he used ter say, many a time, 'hold back and don't waste time brawling.' And it were good advice, eh?"

"Certainly, for look at you now."

"Am not just saying this, Mistress Curzon, but every sailor, high or low, has greatest respect for thy son, even though he were so young ter be a captain. He has taught me that an ordered, clean ship with strict rules and decent food can conquer t' world if guided by knowledge and good seamanship."

Lydia smiled, "why that is good to hear, for with all the worries of wrecked ships and disease, one hears of mutiny too. Indeed, I am a worrier for I'm always fearing for my two middle sons as well, in the army, both tied up in this endless French war." Here she sighed, for it was a few years since she had last seen her middle sons, though they wrote from time to time.

Above their heads, light footsteps could be heard. Little Martha Jane came into the bedroom to find her sister flat on the floor, her ear pressed hard upon the boards.

"Octavia, have you fainted?"

"No, of course not," she said crossly, "I dropped a pin and I'm looking for it."

"Shall I help?" Martha Jane crouched down beside her.

Octavia scrambled to her feet, wondering if her younger sister was quite as stupid as she always seemed.

"Did you find the pin?" she asked innocently.

"No, but I found lots of other interesting things."

For Octavia felt she had had a most fruitful eavesdropping session. She liked Captain Stone's deep rolling voice and his strange yellow grey eyes. In fact, she found him altogether attractive, his rough speech only adding to his charm. She put him on her mental list of her top five most handsome men, though her cousin Hugo remained always her number one, despite the fact that he was still married, for Octavia had loved him from being a little girl. She brushed the dust from her dress and was just in time to peep out of the window to witness Captain Stone's departure.

"A do thank thee Mistress Curzon for thy kindness and help."

Lydia gave him her hand, "it was a pleasure to see you Captain and not the least trouble. But I must ask one thing of you." She had let her hand stay rather too long in his. "When things come to their proper fruition, as I am most sure they will, I would be honoured to help Idina choose her bridal dress and trousseau, for I know she has no mother or older sisters to aid her. We have a marvellous draper in Guisborough who gives us ridiculous discounts on account of him being married to one of my cousins. And fabrics can be made up there now. Of course, it's quite a traipse to get there, but so very well worth it…"

Ged, knowing of Idina's tribulations at her own dressmaker's, felt confident in saying that she would appreciate this and thanked her again. (Though he had no idea what a trousseau was).

He raised her hand to his lips, took his leave and also her good wishes for a safe and prosperous voyage.

As for Lydia, she closed the door and thought to herself, not for the first time, that one never quite knew where life was to take one next.

On his way home, the captain passed two young ladies with whom he had had financial and intimate arrangements, in the past.

He grinned at them and touched his hat.

"Eh Mr Stone we han't seen thee in a while," said the dark haired one.

"Captain if tha please," he said.

"Ooh, so sorry, Captain Stone," she replied with mock emphasis, tossing her curls.

"So, shall tha be visiting soon?" asked the fair-haired one.

"Nay, sorry Ladies, for A sail termorrow."

"We shall await thy return," she said flirtatiously.

He shook his head. "Nay, for on my return A'm ter be wed. A bid yer good afternoon Ladies."

He was past them now. The fair-haired girl took the other's arm and said quietly, "A should give me left leg ter be wed ter him."

Her companion snorted, "he wun't want likes of thee with two legs, he'd certain not look at thee with only the one."

She cackled at her own joke and then whispered in her friend's ear, upon which they both shrieked out loud and arm in arm, laughed their way back to their place of business.

CHAPTER 18

November 1811.
In which Captain Stone returns from his voyage.

Two months passed; the 'Fortitude' made good passage, cargoes were delivered and without mishap, letters were posted and collected by the lovers, to the delight of both. Words of love had been freely exchanged, but also Ged's long descriptions of the weather, the temperature readings, the measurings and needing to unbend the topsail from its spar even though it was quite a short voyage. Idina had expressed the greatest interest and enquired about ballast weights and whether the lastage had been sufficient.

And now the ship stood at the harbour mouth awaiting the pilot, Ged's heart was full, he had not heard from Idina for three weeks, and though not anxious about it, he had wondered if anything were amiss. He stood high on the bow, he could see a crowded harbour, but he could not pick her out, even with the aid of the telescope.

At last, the pilot signalled, and the great three masted ship was guided into safety. It was not until he was giving orders for the unloading and movement of the final parts of the cargo when he suddenly caught sight of her. His heart leapt. Furiously waving with both arms to attract his attention, she was dressed from head to toe in black, even to her bonnet and gloves. Ged raised his hand to acknowledge her, she blew him a kiss, which, after checking that none of the crew were looking his way, he returned. He could hardly keep from grinning now and before he could stop her, Idina was coming up the boarding ramp and with a discreet little wave of her fingers, she waited patiently at the rails until all was unloaded and the crew were dismissed, save for the First Mate.

"A bid thee good day Captain. Methinks tha's a fine lady waiting for thee, eh?" He nodded towards Idina. "And if A might say so Cap'n, about time too." He passed her and touched his cap, "good day Miss Faichney."

Ged hugged her, as if he could never let her go, and when at last he did, he said, "tha's all in black Darling?" (He had never called her Darling to her face before).

She nodded, "it is my father, he passed two weeks since and was very poorly for some time afore that." Her lip quivered.

He hugged her again, "Darling, A'm that sorry, so sorry."

She nodded, tears trickled down her cheeks, she said, "twas what they call a blessing, for he struggled so hard to breathe for days afore he passed and was in more pain than any laudanum nor whisky could help."

"And today A were ter ask him if we could marry," sighed Ged. "Aye, he were a grand old man and a fine captain too."

But inside his head, his mind was racing; now he could marry Idina without having to negotiate, that difficult old man, freely and without impediment. As to the 'Fortitude', well he could hardly dare to hope, he feared that her father might have forgotten his daughter and dredged up some distant relative to leave it to. But even Ged, with his rough direct ways, knew that this was not the time to ask about inheritances.

Without discussing it, both of them wanted to go back to Idina's house. They walked silently through the darkening streets as little lamps and candles started to be lit, the air was crisp and wintery and there were enticing cooking smells wafting. Ged had his arm firmly around her, whether this was a proper way to walk, neither cared. He had his leather case of papers and logbook under his other arm and his canvas sailors' bag over his shoulder.

Idina pushed open the front door into the quiet of her house, a quiet, broken only by the ticking of the hallway grandfather clock. No cheap whale oil lamps here, only beeswax candles with their pleasant warm smell and soft glowing light.

A cosy fire burned in the parlour grate and tea things were set upon the table. At once Cook bustled in with two hot pies, one of beef and the other apple. She set them on the table beside a dish of potatoes, some cheese, bread, butter, a jug of cream and crystal decanters of wine and brandy.

"Miss. Welcome Captain Stone, good voyage A hope?"

"A thank thee, yes."

"Shall tha need owt else Miss?"

"Thank you no, and please would you leave the dish clearing until morning, we have everything we need."

"Very well Miss, A'll tek Captain's things up ter t' best guest room. May A say how good it is ter ave a man in t' house again."

Ged nodded his thanks and the door had hardly closed when Idina threw herself into his arms.

"We are alone now, Jane sleeps in the kitchen, and we'll hear Cook going upstairs to bed quite soon I think."

They sat at the table and drank a good deal of the red wine, eating was awkward as they held hands throughout, and between flirtatious giggles Idina kept putting morsels of food into the captain's mouth.

They talked of the voyage, Ged saying how he had thought the 'Fortitude' a bit slow at first but with time, realised what a powerful ship she was, reckoning she'd be strong and steady in the ice of the Greenland seas.

"Shall you take her up for the whale fishing in March?" asked Idina.

"Aye, A shall." A simple answer, yet it thrilled Ged's heart to think of it, his wildest dreams fulfilled by taking this finest of ships on the most exciting of expeditions. "And steady as she is, she can move that well and fast in a contrary wind."

"Always a mizzen ship moves best in a contrary wind," smiled Idina, who understood sailing as well as any.

Every time she laughed, which was often, Ged saw her little pearly white teeth. When they had eaten almost everything on the table, Ged kissed her hands and looked into her eyes.

"The letters you wrote to me were wonderful," she said, "you have such a way of expressing feelings of love, I was quite… quite overwhelmed reading them and I read them again and again every night afore I went to sleep." Smiling at him she quoted, "All hours not spent with thee, are blanks between the stars… Those are such beautiful words…"

Ged grinned sheepishly, thinking Lydia Curzon had done him proud with her list of amorous phrases. "And A loved every word tha wrote ter me, knowing tha'd touched paper of it and then A were holding it in me own hands, what tha'd touched." He did not want to dwell upon the subject of letters in case she questioned the source of his words of love, so he stood up and said, "Darling, would tha show me round t' house a bit, would that be all reet?"

"Of course, my Love."

Taking his hand, she led him into the dining room at the back of the house. It was a dark panelled room with heavy old chairs set around a long table.

"This room is hardly used, Papa and I always ate at the big parlour table, just as we have done tonight."

"Why 'tis like being on board a ship," laughed Ged.

"Well 'tis from an old, wrecked ship; my father bought it up and used every bit of it. As you see, none of the panels are the same width, but Father would have none wasted, so they're just nailed up as they were in the cabin. There's more of it up in his bedroom, but I think that was just to make him feel at home, for he only felt content when he was at sea, and he wanted his bedroom to look like a part of his ship. When I was a little girl, he had a hammock up there too and slept in it on warm nights, with the windows open so he could hear the sea."

"A grand old man, eh?"

She smiled up at him and he kissed her tenderly; she thought with some satisfaction, that now she might be kissed whenever she wanted and for as often as she wanted. They went into the next room, which was the old Captain's study. Here Ged was mesmerized, half a century of logbooks, charts, accounts, invoices and recordings filled the shelves, which went around three of the walls. There were half written papers, pens and inkstand on his desk as if Captain Faichney had just left the room minutes before. Ged longed to look at everything closely, and to make it all a part of himself.

"I've not had the heart to touch anything in here yet, but it all needs to be sorted," she sighed.

"A'll help thee," his arm about her waist, he pulled her to him. "Maybe mek a start termorrow, after A've dry docked ship?" He tried not to sound too eager.

"Mmm, I feel I can cope with things now you're here; I've felt a bit lost since the funeral." Leaning against him, she felt a wonderful sense of warmth, knowing he would, in fact, always be there, to help her in life's troubles. "Downstairs is just the kitchen and two pantries and the tradesmen's entrance," she said dismissively, taking him through the hall and up the stairway, lit only by a tall narrow window.

There were four doors leading off the square landing.

"Father's room, old room I should say, and my room," she said indicating the two doors facing the front of the house. "And this is the guest room." She opened a door to show a neat but sparse bedroom, they did not go into it, and she then opened the fourth door. "And this is to be your room, that is if it suits."

Ged stood in the doorway of a comfortably furnished room, with a lamp burning, books and a water flask on the bedside, soap and towels on the washstand. He saw that his bag had been brought up, his outer coat and hat had been hung up and the bed covers had been turned back at the ready.

"I did not think you would need a fire, my Love, but things are there if you want them."

He saw logs and kindling in buckets on the hearth, he was unsure now as to where things were to go from here. "Darling…"

He held her to him, breathed in the clean smell of her hair and waited.

"So, should you like to see my bedroom now?" She asked hesitantly, drawing away from him a little.

Together, his arm about her shoulders and a lock of her hair twisted around his finger, they moved across the landing. Ged had never seen a lady's bedroom before, nor had he ever seen a lovelier room. A blazing fire in the little grate, a high four poster with floaty muslin drapes, piled with cushions of satin and lace in softest shades of pink and lavender and a white arctic fox rug covering the foot of the bed. The walls were a mass of pictures in gilded frames, flowers, dogs, pretty girls and many seascapes with ships. Every surface was covered with books, writing things, sewing bits, ribbons, perfume bottles and scented powders. On the night table burned two candles, a tiny brass clock, a pile of letters resting on a handkerchief which he recognized as his own and a small, framed drawing. The smell of the violet perfume she always wore filled the room. He felt intoxicated now, not with the large quantity of wine he had drunk but by the sensual loveliness of Idina, and her very obvious desire for him.

She led him to the large, uncurtained window overlooking the sea, black now with only dots of light to mark out the anchored ships against a moonless charcoal sky. He stood behind her, put his arms about her waist and kissed the side of her neck.

"Tha gaol agam ort," she murmured into his cheek.

He drew away from her a little, "what does it mean, tha said tha'd tell on my return and here I am."

"Tis only 'I love you,' in the Gaelic."

"Dunt say 'only', them words is everything ter me."

Gently he unfastened the back of her dress and put his lips between her shoulder blades. Feeling his fingers run lightly down her back, she gasped with the pleasure of it.

She turned in his arms and looked at him, "my Love, this has been the happiest night of my life."

"But Darling, our night together is only just beginning."

And with that he led her gently to the bed.

****

Cook had wondered, in the preceding weeks, whether she should speak to Miss Idina about the expectations of the marriage bed and outline the rudiments of it. Idina, she feared, having no mother nor sisters might be quite ignorant of such things. But what with the old captain dying and one thing and another, there had been no opportunity for such a sensitive conversation, and now she was fearing it might be too late.

The following morning, she took cans of hot water upstairs. Into Captain Stone's own room first, he having returned there in the early hours of the morning and there he was sitting up in bed, naked to the waist, flicking through a book, quite as proper as could be. She could not but help thinking what an exceptionally fine figure of a man he was, as she bid him a 'good morning'.

Then she knocked lightly at Idina's door and went straight in. Her mistress was still asleep, curled up and warm, but Cook knew from the flush on her cheek, the soft smile on her lips and the sight of one of the captain's stockings which had rolled under the bed, that the little 'conversation' was no longer necessary.

CHAPTER 19

Still 1811.
In which wedding plans are made.

Bans were read and Captain Stone and Idina Faichney were to be married shortly before Christmas. The few weeks before the wedding were filled with the usual whirl of preparations. Several visits to the Faichney solicitor on Grape Lane were required, though he refused to allow any final signings until the wedding was over.

He regarded Ged with deep suspicion, looking over the top of his spectacles he said, "many a slip twixt cup and lip."

Ged had merely shrugged and said it was of no matter to him as he did not plan on sailing before the following March. Though he had to hold back his immense surprise when he heard of the considerable amount of money that was settled upon Idina and thereby himself when he became her husband, as well as the fine house and the 'Fortitude' itself.

The solicitor asked to speak with Idina on her own, while Ged waited outside the offices.

When she came out, she was flushed and cross, Ged saw for the first and only time her temper.

"What is it Darling? Did he speak ter thee improper like? If he did A'll brek his bloody neck."

Shaking her head, she said, "no, naught of that kind. But an insolent man he is."

She took his arm and deftly steered him towards the jewellers to choose a wedding ring before he could question her further.

Years later she told him what the solicitor had said to her in private. He had suggested that Idina being well past 'the first flush of youth' was marrying a man only interested in her fortune and advised her to remain a spinster.

She tossed her head, she went on, "but as soon as all is signed and settled, we shall be choosing ourselves another lawyer; and now I have some money of my own, I shall be finding another dressmaker too. Horrid old woman."

This jogged Ged's memory. "Darling, A forgot ter tell thee, Lydia Curzon said she would tek thee to her own dressmaker and help thee choose thy bride dress…"

"Oh, how very kind, for she and those daughters always look so fashionably dressed. But when did you see her my Love?"

"Oh, er, A bumped into her afore A sailed last." He spoke as casually as he could, "She said summat about a 'true' summat or other?"

"True what?"

He shrugged, "A dun't know, summat ter do with clothes and that."

Idina thought for a second and then laughed out loud, "why my own Love, I think you mean a trousseau do you not?

"Aye that were it… A think." He felt mildly hurt at her laughter. "Tha knows A know nowt."

"Well no man would know that," she said soothingly, "for it is the French for special wedding clothes."

The buying of the wedding dress took place a few days later, involving an overnight trip to Guisborough with Lydia and Jacob Curzon, and Octavia too.

Of course, the dress had to be black as Idina was still in mourning, but with Octavia's help, she picked out a heavy silk which draped exquisitely and was discreetly embroidered all over with the tiniest silver stars. The cross over bodice and elbow sleeves edged in a narrow silver lace, would be most flattering, yet still appropriate for her bereaved state. All agreed she would look stunning, as the fabric was held to her face, her pale skin and red hair being most enhanced by it. The finished dress was to be delivered to Whitby in two weeks' time, along with bonnet, gloves, merino shawl, a pile of exquisite undergarments and one of the latest short bridal corsets in a black figured silk, trimmed with ropes of embroidered rosebuds and picot edged ribbon.

After the shopping they all adjourned to the 'Fox Inn'. Idina had never been in an inn before and found it quite exciting to be visiting there with such a pleasant and jolly family as the Curzons. She was to share a room with Octavia, and as they climbed into bed together, Octavia produced a bottle of brandy that she had sneaked into her traveling bag. Much giggling ensued and eventually after half a bottle and some questioning from Octavia, she had to confess that she and Ged had already sampled the pleasures of the marriage bed. Octavia was gripped by the scant details that Idina revealed, her modest nature making her reticent about telling too much even though Octavia promised faithfully never to tell, and much fun was had as they chatted and giggled long into the small hours. It was a genuine friendship between them and no-one who saw them would have thought otherwise, but Octavia had a deep ulterior motive for replacing Annie as her best friend and moving onto Idina, for Octavia was determined, by hook or by crook to become Idina's sister-in-law one day.

※ ※ ※ ※

"It's reet awkward," sighed Ged, "and A don't know what ter do for t' best. Hugo's me brother and he should stand by me as me groom's man; but no one ivver 'ad such a good friend as Robert Curzon, we've been all ovver t' world together…"

"Well, you cannot choose both, that is certain," said Idina. "Which of them would be the most disappointed by not being chosen?"

"Why Robert definite, for our Hugo dun't mind owt, he just laughs and jokes his way through life wi' out a care… So, is that me answer? Choose Robert? Darling tha's that clever, for A've been puzzling ovver it for weeks, all t' time A were at sea, and tha's solved it in a minute."

Idina smiled her sweetest of smiles and felt triumphant.

For the first time she saw her betrothed to be a worrier, for next thing he was fussing that his family were not good enough for her to meet and were bound to embarrass him.

"Come my Love," she laughed, "if only you knew how much of my life I have longed to have a brother and a sister, and as for a mother, well I have never known one, so I'm sure yours shall be quite good enough."

In truth, Idina was most excited about the meeting, having heard a few lurid tales about them all from Cook, over the preceding weeks.

On the appointed afternoon they entered the little house on Church Street, and what a welcoming sight met her eyes. A good fire burned in an open brick fireplace, hung about with shining kettles and pans. The big table was laden with three kinds of cake, currant scones and cherry scones, buttered bread and a little dish of boiled eggs, with pots of jams, jellies and pastes, alongside the large blue and white cups and plates.

A small slight woman with pale hair and large eyes and an even larger smile, rushed forward and took Idina's hands in hers.

"Miss Faichney, A'm Sarah."

"Idina, please call me Idina. I am most pleased to meet you, Sarah."

"And A'm pleased ter know thee. And this is Sukey, our Hugo's bairn."

A dainty little girl in a print frock clung shyly to Sarah's skirts.

And still holding her hand she led Idina to the fireside where a woman, old beyond her years sat with a young, liver and white spaniel upon her lap.

Sarah put her arm about her mother's shoulders and loudly said, "Mother, this is Idina, Miss Faichney."

The old woman turned her head to look at her. Idina held out her hand, but it was not taken, so instead she fussed the dog while she was looked up and down.

At last she spoke, "tha wants a bloody medal teking on our Ged, for he's a difficult man, aye he is that." She shook her head, "not like our Hugo, now he's a man as could mek any woman happy, favours his father our Hugo does."

Anxious to steer the conversation away from its dangerous ground, Sarah said, "shall we sit ter t' table and get tea."

"Aye grand," said Ged briskly, hanging his coat and hat on the back of the door.

Sarah took Idina's outer things, but before anyone had sat down, the aforementioned Hugo burst in.

At once he hugged Idina warmly and kissed her on the cheek. She was fascinated to see how like Ged he was in looks and yet somehow, so different at the same time.

He held her at arm's length and said, "Nah then, what's a beauty like thee doing weddin' our Ged, for he's a cantankerous old bugger?"

She had to laugh and felt a flush creeping up her cheeks, as like a true gentleman, he held the chair for her to sit down.

Then he took his own seat and put Sukey onto his lap to help her with her food for she was only a few months past her first birthday.

Idina had never known family life like this before, they were all quite rude to each other, with constant teasing and laughing, yet never seeming to be in the least offended by anything.

Short work was made of the stupendous tea, and no sooner had the last cup been put down, than Ged jumped up, and grabbed his coat.

"Best be off now, eh Darling? Wedding's Thursday week, up at church, ten o clock, so see yer all then."

"Oh, A'm that excited for it," said Sarah clasping her hands, "me and Mother's got new bonnets too." She lifted Sukey into her arms. "Nah then, 'as tha a kiss for Aunty Idina?"

Thrilled by her new title, Idina kissed the little girl's soft warm cheek.

Unsure of how to take her leave of the old woman, she stood before her. The spaniel was put to the floor, and she held out her arms to Idina.

"Tek care of tha self Hun, and please ter call me Mother as t' others do from now on. A see tha's a good lass and tha'll need ter be wi' our Ged, for he'll tek some settling down will that one."

She let out a cackling toothless laugh.

With that Ged grabbed Idina and firmly guided her out into the street.

As she took his arm, he said, "tha nivver knows what me mother'll come out with next."

"They were all so kindly and welcoming, my Love."

"A just hope she dunt bring that bloody dog up tut' church."

"Surely not? Not to a church, though it is a lovely dog, just the sort of dog I should like myself."

"There's no telling what me mother'll do, she's obsessed wi' that bloody dog. Cannot stand thing meself."

Here Idina sighed, somewhat defeated on the dog issue.

****

Thus, Miss Idina Aphrodite Faichney and Captain Gerald Stone were bound in holy wedlock at St Mary's Church on Thursday December 19th, 1811. Only close family, Idina's Cook and Captain Robert Curzon attended the ceremony, (Bran the dog remaining at home).

As they walked out of the church together, Ged grasped her hand tightly and turned to her, with a note of jubilation in his voice.

"We did it, Darling, we did it, we are married!"

"We did indeed, my Love."

There was an equal feeling of jubilation in her heart as she spoke the words, still hardly believing that she was bound for life to such a handsome and clever husband.

"Thy turn next, eh Robert, man."

But Captain Curzon only smiled his usual mysterious smile.

These nuptials brought the couple the very greatest of happiness for many years.

CHAPTER 20

March 1812.
In which Idina makes a bold decision.

We had been married less than four months when, it seemed we were to be parted, for the whale fishing season was fast approaching.

The nearer the time came the more I felt I could not bear this parting; I could not tell how my husband felt about it, for he was stressed by the preparations and was subject to various delays through no fault of his own.

I tried to help as best I could, I hoped he would ask me to go on the voyage with him for I had sailed to the fisheries many times when I was a girl, with my father, but Ged seemed to hardly to notice me in the daytime now. Yet when night came, I was always assured of his most tender and kindly love, and afterwards as we fell asleep in each other's arms, I knew only the most perfect happiness as he murmured intimate words of devotion. That is, until we awoke on the morn when I felt sick with dread at our separation as it neared. I hardly saw him from dawn to dusk as he prepared the ship and signed up the officers and crew.

On his last day I awoke, nauseous with fear, I could take no breakfast and when he looked across the table at me, tears rolled down my cheeks.

"Eh Darling, what ails? Tha's not sickening or owt?" He leapt up from the table and took me in his arms. I shook my head too upset to speak. "Darling, parting with thee is t' hardest thing A've ivver done, generally A can't wait ter be sailing but now hours are passing way too fast." He pressed his face into my hair. "Dun't let me last sight of thee be of weeping, for it'll cut me for all ut' voyage."

It was then that I made my decision, it had been to the back of my mind since we had married, and now I had decided upon it, definite.

I wiped my tears, kissed him and smiled a bright smile that I did not feel.

Minutes later he put on his captain's jacket and hat, we stood in the hall and embraced for that last time.

"Stand at parlour window and watch us sail from t' harbour; it'll be a comfort ter know tha's there even though A'll be too far away ter see thee. A'll look up this way any road."

"Of course, my Love," I lied.

"Allus in me heart, Darling."

And with a short hug he was gone.

I stood still for a moment staring at the closed door and on hearing the final click of the gate, I gathered myself, for I knew I had little more then an hour to execute my plan and ran upstairs.

In my bedroom I took out a small canvas bag, not risking taking anything larger in case it would seem too conspicuous. My winter beaver bonnet just fitted inside, and I put six bars of scented soap into the bonnet, my perfume bottle wrapped in a good pile of rags for I could not remember when I had last had my 'flowers', so that must be due very soon. I folded my sewing things into a shirt I was making for Ged and that left room for my indoor shoes, with five pairs of new stockings slipped around the underside of my bonnet. The bag only just closed. Then, I took off my dress and put another three chemises on and three more cotton petticoats and two of flannel, then my warmest wool dress and on top of that my light print dress, my winter boots, spring bonnet, gloves and shawl. Fortunately, it was a cool day, otherwise I might have boiled to death, dressed thus. I looked around my bedroom, dropped my toothbrush, tweezers and four clean handkerchiefs into my pocket, picked up my little bag and concealed it by carrying my heaviest plaid shawl over my arm. With the household keys looped around my finger, I carefully descended the stairs, to be met by Cook in the hallway.

She looked up at me and caught my plan at once.

"Eh Mistress, tha nivver is?"

"Yes, Cook I am. I know I can trust you to keep house for the captain and myself. It is the usual routine; we shall be away until the end of August." As I handed her the keys, I added, "unless I get sent back later today."

"God go with thee Mistress."

Cook wiped away a tear and kissed me.

I walked as briskly as I could, though I knew I still had plenty of time. It was easy to walk along the staith unnoticed, for there were crowds of busy people and great piles of cargo and supplies waiting to be loaded onto the line of ships there. At the 'Fortitude', I hardly knew how I could board her without being noticed by at least one of the crew of around forty men. Yet, incredible luck was with me, for as I walked up that gangplank, the only person looking in my direction was my brother-in-law, Hugo. At once he waved, but before he could shout out, I put my finger to my lips and pointed to the captain's cabin. He grinned broadly, gave me the thumbs up sign and turned back to his work. I slipped quietly down the narrow open stairs to that cabin I knew so well and looked around me in triumph.

No time to lose, I stripped off all my extra clothes, folded them and put them with my bag into the built-in cupboard at the end of the wide box bed. Then I sat on it, drew my knees up, unlaced my boots and shut the curtains around me so that I was quite concealed from any who should enter the cabin.

I was there some time, but it did not seem much to me for I was filled with excitement at that so familiar sequence of cries and sounds of reeling and hauling that preceded 'stand by to make sail,' and at long last, my husband's loud, booming voice, 'make sail' and then I felt the steady rocking as the ship moved away and the sudden jolt as she left the harbour for the waves of the open sea. I was as much thrilled by it now as ever I had been as a child and could not help my smile.

A little time later, I heard my husband coming down the steps, muttering "fucking idiots" under his breath, heard him drag out his chair and the rustle of papers on his table. Then there was a long pause, a "what the …" and the bed curtains were wrenched open to reveal me.

"Bloody hell," he laughed and laughed. "Darling A'm that glad ter see thee, that glad…"

I put my arms around him, "you'll not send me back then?"

"Nivver will. By God A wanted thee ter come that much."

"But you never said…?"

"How could A? Ask thee ter spend five month in frozen cold and stinking mess, wi' them bloody animals up on deck and thee such a lady?"

"Am I really such a lady?"

"Oh aye, a lady through and through," he grinned kissing me.

I had to smile a little, knowing that, as a boy my own father, a humble cowhand, in fear of his life after the terrible, humiliating defeat at the battle of Culloden, had walked from Kiltarlity to Glasgow, barefoot, with only the clothes on his back and despite hardly knowing a word of English and being only fourteen years old, found himself a working passage to the Americas. Of course there he made himself a good fortune, sailing back many years later in his own whaling ship and settling in Whitby.

"But how did you know I was here, for I sat really quiet and still on the bed?"

"A could smell thy scent o' violets couldn't A? First off A thought A were imagining it 'cos A were missing thee, but when A could smell thee for real, why A knew tha must be hid on t' bed."

Our conversation was cut short by the entrance of Mr Briggs, the ship's cook, who also doubled as ship's surgeon as required. I knew him well from my childhood sailings, for he had served on the 'Fortitude' for many years.

"Eh Mrs Stone, what a surprise, A dint know tha were ter sail with us. It gladdens me heart ter see thee in this cabin again, indeed it does."

"Mr Briggs, tell me are you keeping well?"

"Indeed, A am that, A 'ave ter dunt A?"

"And all your family, do they keep well?" I never could quite remember how many children he had, though I knew it to be a prodigious number.

"Oh, aye Mrs Stone, well enough. My good lady 'as recent give me another lad, so that's our twelfth, though we've only the nine living."

"My congratulations Mr Briggs, you must be quite a houseful now, I think?"

"Not so bad as it were Mrs Stone, for we've the three rooms and family's not all at home now. A've me two eldest lad's at sea, next one down's on t' colliers and A've three daughters married and they've…"

I could see my husband twitching, thinking we were to be there indefinitely as Briggs got onto his grandchildren.

"We'll tek our dinner soon as tha's ready Mr Briggs."

"Aye, aye Cap'n, Mrs Stone."

After he had gone back to the kitchen, I put my arms around my husband's neck again.

"My Love, we shall never know of Mr Briggs' grandchildren."

"Believe me we shall, we shall hear of little else A warrant, who's married who, who's their cousin and so on… why 'tis a story as nivver ends, Mr Briggs and his family."

He moved his papers and charts to the far end of the table to make room for the dinner, which Mr Briggs was ready to serve.

We ate off those oh so familiar plates in Chinese blue, which I remembered from my childhood sailings. As always Mr Briggs served a well-cooked dinner. Today, roasted pork with green beans and rice, cheese and a wide dish of fresh fruits. Port wine and brandy were in plenty for us.

But we did not sit long to dinner and soon my husband was up and pulling on his jacket, he held out his hand to me and I followed him up on to the upper deck. Quite the innocent I might add, for I had no clue as to what would happen next.

No sooner had I appeared on deck, than a rough looking sailor stopped in his work and stared blatantly at me and still looking at me whispered to his two workmates. He stepped in front of my husband.

"Scuse me Cap'n is yon lass sailing wi' us ter t' fisheries?"

"What's it ter thee Mr Sanders? Get back ter yer reeling man."

The man made a grumbling sort of noise and said, "nay it'll bring bad luck ter us all, a woman sailing and a red-haired one at that, worst of all."

My husband turned upon him, his fists clenched and for a horrific moment I thought his anger might kill Sanders, there and then.

The man reached for his rigging knife, he already had his marlin spike in his other hand, though he was shaking badly in his agitation. My husband was quite unarmed, yet he turned to Sanders without one shred of fear.

"Dunt reach for yer knife Mr Sanders for A'll fucking kill yer first off. And speak of me wife so again and A'll have yer thrown ovver t' side."

Sanders looked downwards and muttered something.

"Speak up man," roared my husband, "if yer's summat ter say, speak out loud for all ter hear."

"Tis bad luck Cap'n, a red-haired woman and all knows it, A'll not sail wi' a woman aboard."

His voice trembled as he turned to his workmates for support, but none spoke up.

My husband looked across to two of the younger boys.

"Lower a boat lads, our Mr Sanders wants ter try his luck elsewhere."

And one of the six little rowing boats that were taken out when the whales were sighted, was lifted from the davits and lowered into the water.

"Nah then Mr Sanders, since yer so keen on luck, yer can row ter Shields and try yer luck, for A hear t' Press Gang's there this week. These two lads'll go with yer there and bring t' boat back. Quick as yer can lads."

"Tis too far ter row Cap'n," mumbled Sanders.

"Maybes thought of that afore, eh? Nah, any of yer mates want ter go with ye, for A cannot spare t' time ter be waiting about later in t' voyage? Any that's unhappy then on'll be ovver t' side. For A'll remind yer all, this is my ship and if A want ter bring a whistling curly tail on her, A bloody will. So, if any of yer want ter go, speak up now." He looked around at his crew, but all were turning back to their work. "Right Mr Sanders get down inter t' boat afore A mek yer jump, and one of these lads'll fetch yer bag." Here he nodded to the older lad, who disappeared below to fetch Mr Sander's possessions. "And any other man that speaks disrespectful of my wife shall be flogged until he cannot stand and then some."

Thus, Mr Sanders picked up his jacket and his canvas bag, and he climbed down the rope ladder on the side of the ship into the rowboat and was gone.

Of course, I was mortified, I should have thought that this might happen, for I well knew sailor's superstitions. Though I had sailed many times before, I had been much younger then and, of course, 'a maiden'. I turned as if to descend into our cabin, but at once my husband grabbed my arm quite roughly.

"Sit down here with me wife, A might need thee ter tek wheel in a bit, when them two lads bring t' boat back. Show this pack of dogs who's who."

I sat down meekly and waited, knowing he had not meant to hurt my arm, it only being his anger and heightened emotion. When we were alone, I asked him if he had not feared Sanders with his spike and knife, when he was unarmed himself.

"Fear?" he replied puzzled. "Nay, a weren't afeared, for he's a left hander, so as he raised t' spike A'd 'ave snatched his wrist wi' me right, twisted it afore me so he couldn't reach me wit' knife. Any road A could hear Briggs coming up behind me from below, and he's a man as can think on his feet if any can." He laughed, "A've been in worse situations than this in me time, A've had three or four come at me at once, but if tha can think fast tha's ahead of them, for men like Sanders dunt think or plan at all, just blunder about through life, like a chicken wi' its head off."

As the afternoon wore on, and the little rowing boat was safely returned, several of the older sailors who remembered me from past voyages, spoke kindly to me, offering condolences for my late father's passing. It saddened me to see how much some of them had aged, a sailor is old before any other man for reason of the work being so very hard.

At the four o-clock bell, Hugo came from below to start his watch, it being the second watch, grinning broadly.

"Eh sister, A've missed all t' fun, eh?"

"Not much fun Hugo, I was a bit upset by it all, for I had not expected it…"

"Aye well sailors are allus superstitious, for sometimes at sea it seems that God has forgotten us, so omens and that are looked for. Meself, A just say me prayers and if God teks me, so be it."

He shrugged, rubbed my back affectionately and looked up at the ratlines on the rigging he was about to climb.

Later, as the first cast of the sunset came, I steered our ship, myself, my Love behind me, his arm about my waist. I always remembered this moment in time as one of perfect happiness. When troubles came in later life, I would try to put myself in mind of this, at one with the beautiful sea, at one with all of my life.

When I awoke next morning, I felt strange, I washed and dressed as quickly as I could, for it was obvious breakfast was about to be served. My husband had been up some time and we sat to the table together. Mr Briggs waddled in (for the ship was reeling quite a lot), carrying hot plates of smoked fish.

"There tha goes, Mrs Stone, A remembered tha likes a bit of fish, at breakfast."

"Thank you, Mr Briggs," I said weakly, taking the smallest sip of tea and trying to avoid looking at it.

My husband cleared his plate in seconds, gulped his tea and stood up to leave.

"What ails wife? Not sea-sick is tha?"

Laughing at his own joke, he kissed my cheek and disappeared.

I stared at my fish, and the congealed butter as it cooled, and I felt queasy and strange.

"I am so sorry Mr Briggs, I cannot eat, it must be sea-sickness, though I have never felt so before…"

"Aye Mrs Stone there's choppy waters out there today indeed, but A think it's not that. Tha'll not mind if A speak plain like?" Clearly, he was going to speak plain, whether I minded or no. "A thought it afore when A saw thee yesterday. A'm eldest of eight and as tha knows, A've a big family meself and A can allus see it in a woman's face, there's a kind of softening, that many would not notice, but A can allus see it. Mrs Stone, A'm certain tha's with child."

"Oh," I had truly not thought of this. "Oh, do you think so Mr Briggs?"

"And with tha feeling sickly in t' morning as well, A'm sure of it… Captain'll be pleased eh?"

I answered hesitantly, "umm, I think he will…"

"Aye, well A'll let thee get on Mrs Stone."

Adeptly he piled up all the plates, balancing the cups and cream jug and teapot on top.

"A'll bring thee a bit of lemon water and some dry toast, that generally does t' trick."

Later that morning, the waters became more tranquil, a warm sun came out and I felt so much better. Mr Briggs carried an elbow chair up on to the deck for me and I sat there with my sewing, trying to keep calm, for I was no longer feeling sickly, and I wanted to jump up and down with delight at my very special state. At long last, my husband came to me, with one hand on my shoulder, he looked into the far distance through his telescope. Then he retracted it and put it carefully into its special case and looked down at me. He touched my sewing with his fingertips, for just as I always took an interest in his sailings and tradings, he was always interested in what I was reading or making.

"What's tha sewing?"

"Tis a shirt for you," I fastened off and bit my thread. "Of course, it is the last thing I shall sew for you for some time…from now on I shall only be sewing little things, very small things…"

He gasped and I took his hand to lay on my stomach.

"Eh Darling, A'm that pleased."

He knelt beside me and took me in his arms.

A nearby sailor smiled across at us and spoke quite boldly.

"Good news is it Cap'n?"

On his feet in one swift feline movement, he replied with a rare smile, "aye it is, and there'll be double rum rations for all today ter celebrate."

A little self-conscious, I wondered if the entire crew would now know of my condition when I was still getting used to it myself. Clearly news spread fast, for at tea-time, Hugo burst into our cabin, shut the door firmly, kissed me on the cheek.

"Congratulations, Sister, 'tis good news, the best." Then he clasped Ged in a great bear hug, "By God brother, A dint know thar had it in thee." He thumped Ged on the back as hard as he could.

"Ger off me tha bugger, tha's winded me now," but he was laughing as he spoke.

Then Hugo went back on deck and all due formality was resumed between Captain Stone and crew member Hugo Curzon. And a jolly evening was passed with double rum rations for all later on, though I knew this was not only to celebrate my husband's forthcoming fatherhood but also a deliberate ploy to soothe any doubts and rumbling discontent amongst the crew after the incident with Sanders the previous day.

****

So, we sailed towards the Greenland Fisheries, stopping at Lerwick to take in supplies, and engage eight more crew. I took the opportunity to buy another heavy plaid shawl, woven by the local women. My husband teased me because I paid them more than they asked for it, feeling so sorry for their very obvious poverty. Their children barefoot and in rags and not one of the women having a decent shawl themselves.

"Call tha self a businesswoman, eh", he laughed.

The sun shone most days, refreshing rains came only at night and the steady winds were, on the whole kind. Already I had put on my woollen dress, beaver bonnet and my heavy tartan shawls, as the first of the ice bergs came into sight. I saw that the ice was already melting at its edges, a good sign, though we were held up two full days by blinding snowstorms, when we could barely tell night from day and could only anchor ship and wait. We had seen many dolphins and they were replaced now by groups of gentle seals with their pups. As soon as the weather cleared and they were sighted those rowing boats were dropped and the innocent creatures were clubbed and bagged up, the babies too.

Of course, as a woman and in my condition, I was bid to stay down in my cabin and not witness this bloodshed. Once, years ago I had asked my father about the cruelty of it, but he just said it was a sin to deny God's bounty and asked me whether I expected food on the table or not. At once, I was silenced, never daring to argue with my father.

The whole slaughter over, I went up on the deck again.

"Grand eh, we've thirty seal pelts on t' first day of hunting, A'll be bound we'll see a whale fish in a day or two."

"Mmm, poor things, do you think they feel pain as we do?"

"Oh aye, judging by t' squealing, course they do but it's ovver quick for em."

"And their young wrenched from them?"

"Dunt think on it Darling, they've no reason only instincts."

I put my frozen hands under my shawl again, for of course I had forgotten my fur gloves when I had packed my little bag.

"Cap'n," called one of the sailors from the stern.

"Aye," he walked over to him and a couple of others.

I saw them talking and looking across at me, my husband smiled, nodded and most unusually patted the sailor on the arm approvingly.

"What was that about my Love?"

"Lads is worried about thy hands being cold; 'as tha no gloves?"

"No, I forgot them."

He took my hands in his, "by God A've touched ice flows warmer than that, any road they've a summat of a plan ter mek thee a bit warmer."

Before I could ask more of this he had disappeared off to the far side of the ship. So, I assumed that one of the sailors was going to knit me a pair of gloves, for I well knew that many seamen were adept at the plain sewing, needed to keep their clothes in good order and some could knit as well. Years ago, a few of them had made me a fine set of doll's clothes, while on board, but that is a story for another time.

A couple of days later, there was a light knock at the cabin door, and I opened it to find two sailors standing there.

"We was worried for thy hands being cold Mistress, for thar had no gloves."

The other man shyly handed me a little muff they had made from one of the sealskins.

Charmed, I thanked them for their thoughtfulness. It was neatly made and had been sewed with the sealskin inside as well as out, for of course they had no access to lining silk. The neck ribbon being made from thin ship's cord it was a practical rather than fashionable item; but how very warm it was, being double thickness.

My husband took my hand from my new muff that day and laid it against the ice crystals on his frozen cheek, for he had not shaved for a couple of days.

"Bloody hell," he laughed, "tha could cook an egg on t' heat of that."

I much treasured my sealskin muff, for its warmth, for the true kindness with which it had been made and as a souvenir of my last and best trip on the 'Fortitude'.

That same night, the speksioneers and other office holders were invited to take dinner in our cabin, as they always were the night before the whale fishing began in earnest. As usual, an excellent dinner was served; roasted beef, dripping pudding, a selection of fresh vegetables followed by a number of dainties and cheesecakes. Of course, a great deal of wine and spirits were drunk, yet all the men behaved in a polite and respectful manner throughout, due I believe to my presence. My husband said afterwards that these dinners usually ended raucously without the company of the fairer sex. Though the meal went on late, of course it was still light when they all left for their beds. I put on my heavy shawls and we both went up on deck looking at the pale sky as the ship rocked and creaked gently.

"I miss the darkness," I said, for I had not seen a dark sky for several days now.

"Aye, know what A'd like reet now?" I shook my head. "A'd like ter be at home sitting by our fire on a winter afternoon when it's dark by teatime, with you toasting some of Cook's best teacakes and having them wi' lots of butter."

This we had done on many cosy afternoons when we had first married. I had to smile at the pleasant picture it made. "So, by the time we can do that again, you'll be holding our son in your arms."

"Aye," he said thoughtfully and let his hand caress my stomach.

Next day there was a feverish excitement as we waited for the sighting of a whale, the men were tense, relieving their tension with joking and whittling on bits of bone and wood. The ship was still, and we were surrounded by floating ice. I marvelled at the beauty of the icebergs caught in a pinkish light, always hearing the soothing creaking of the larger ones.

"The light is so beautiful on them, it is one of God's wonders I think, this magical ice scape."

"Aye, maybes, but dangerous too, we can nivver master t' sea nor them icebergs, we sail only at their grace."

I nodded in agreement, remembering how my father had often said, that we were always only one large wave or one turn of the wind away from disaster and God's mercy.

We waited until that first whale was glimpsed in the distance and then the chase began, the greatest game hunt in the world, every man working to his bravest and best. For men seem to feel so fulfilled by that dangerous pursuit and then a successful kill. Part of their preparations included donning themselves in some very strange attire, oiled coats, sealskin parkas, knitted caps that covered most of the face, reindeer mittens and boots purchased on previous voyages; in fact, anything that would keep out that grinding cold and icy water was welcomed. Those not out pursuing the prey, were occupied for all their waking moments in cutting the whale flesh from the huge carcass lashed to the side of the ship, it had to be cut into small pieces and stored in barrels, and as always, the stench was terrible, and there was no escaping it. Though I washed most carefully every day there was no ridding of it. At night as I lay in bed, I watched my husband clean every inch of his fine body as he stood before the washstand and then climbed into bed. But still there was a reek of fish as he reached out to kiss me. He slept naked now, for in the early part of the voyage he rested fully clothed with loaded pistols on the shelf above our pillows. But once the hunting began, there was no fear of mutiny or riot among the men for none would risk the loss of pay or a share of the much coveted Government bounty paid out after a successful voyage.

"My Love," I said, "do I smell of fish?

"Only a little," he laughed, but clearly he did not mind, for he added, "but of course, it does not detract from thy loveliness." He caressed me and moved onto me and said, "let us pretend this bed's sea and we're two whale fish that's fallen in love."

I gasped with pleasure, lifting my body to him, "do you think they feel love for each other?"

"Oh aye, when tha kills one, its mate cries terrible and tries ter help it and nivver leaves its side, so yer can get that one easy too."

"I'd be like that with you, if someone hurt you, my Love." I kissed him.

"A wunt, any as came near thee, A'd kill t' bastards straight off."

I smiled with happiness and then we both concentrated fully upon our loving task.

****

We came back in late August with a magnificent haul of twelve whale fish, all neatly flensed and stored in barrels, the seal skins, ten white fox furs and a couple of polar bear skins. I packed our clothes carefully in two bags and a small trunk, I also had a little collection of animals modelled in walrus ivory which I had bought myself, from a pair of native women who had paddled out to us in a boat made of seal pelts. One of them had a baby swaddled up in animal skin; she had pointed to it and then pointed to my stomach, and we had all laughed. I gave them a packet of steel needles in exchange for the carvings which I thought would be nice for my baby's small hands to hold. One of the carvings was a whale fish and I could not understand what they were trying to tell me. They kept holding the little fish near their baby's mouth and then indicating my protruding stomach. Eventually, Mr Davis, the ship's carpenter had come to my aid; he spoke a few words to the women in their own language and they had nodded vigorously, pointing to me again.

"What they're trying to tell thee, Mrs Stone is that if tha holds that toy fish in thy baby's mouth, when it's new-born, then he'll grow up ter be a fine hunter like."

"Why thank you Mr Davis."

He had nodded and turned back to his repairing of a split brail. I thanked the ladies kindly and shook hands with them, which they seemed to find immensely amusing and then they had climbed back down the side of the ship into their little canoe, waved their sealskin mittens goodbye and swiftly paddled away.

Later, I asked of my husband how it came to be that Mr Davis could speak the language of the local people.

"Oh, aye, he can, our Mr Davis got himself shipwrecked near here a few year back, well he were rescued bit' natives and lived wi' em for a couple of year…A've heard it said he had a bairn ter one of 'em."

Now I was quite astonished, and for a moment was lost for words, for I could imagine nothing more strange than living day to day with these people.

As soon as we had docked, Ged said, "leave everything here, A'll have them two young lads tek it all up home fer us." He grinned, "A want ter get round and tell our Sarah and me mother t' news."

"I think they need not be told my Love, one glance at me and they'll see for themselves."

Indeed, I was feeling large now and had had to let down the hems at the front of my two dresses to make them hang evenly. Mr Briggs had helped me with this, because of course we had no long mirror on board ship.

"He's a reet old woman is Briggs," laughed my husband affectionately, when I explained why the dinner was served late on that particular day, because I had had Mr Briggs on all fours pinning up my hems. In fact, it seemed to me that Mr Briggs could do pretty much anything. Not only had he kept us served with decent food every day of the voyage, even when we were eating his polar bear stews and the dark meat of the seals, he made them tasty and filling. He had also set two broken bones, extracted more than a few teeth, made up poultices, dealt with hernias as well as the other various sicknesses of the crew in his duties as ship's surgeon, and all were returning alive and reasonably well. He had had great success with a new medication called Dover's Powder, to relieve fevers and quieten agitation, for the sailors greatly feared illness, and this so relieved their anxieties as well as their actual fevers. On top of this he had knitted twelve pairs of children's stockings in his spare time, for his little ones at home.

As he prepared to disembark, he thrust two pairs of neatly made baby socks into my hands. "Not made 'em too small, Mrs Stone, for it's a big bairn tha's having. A wish thee all t' best wi' it."

I thanked him kindly, though I was rather taken aback at the prospect of 'a big bairn.' And rather more alarmed when we reached the cottage on Church Street, where my mother-in-law regaled me with tales of how big Ged had been, how she had been three days in labour, thought herself ripped in half and all had thought her near death for many days after. She then told me that when Ged was born, his father was so proud of his fine son, that he carried him, all wrapped up in his swaddling, to the local tavern to show him off to everyone there. I was quite touched to hear a good story for once about this most treacherous of parents.

But there was no turning back now, 'big bairn or not' and my heart was much touched when Sarah took my hands in hers and said, "Sister we do not know each other well yet, but if tha'll let me, A shall be with thee ter help when thy time comes, however long that may last. A've helped with quite a few births with our neighbours when we lived in Nicholson's Yard, so A know what's ter be done."

"I would be so glad of it, dear Sister."

And Sarah was as good as her word.

CHAPTER 21

October 1812.
Idina is brought to bed.

In October Idina was brought to bed, Dr Myers was sent for, as was Sarah. Cook sat with Idina and set out all the necessaries, in between the pains. The maid Jane was much occupied heating water and making trays of tea. Ged stood about awkwardly until Dr Myers told him the childbed was no place for a man and sent him down to the parlour to wait. And wait he did, hours dragged from that day into the next punctuated by cold meals being brought to him by Jane and dozing with cushions in the padded chair. He well knew the sounds of a labouring woman; he had grown up in a yard of eight houses, into which seventeen families crammed into every semi-habitable space. Hardly a month had passed but one of these women was giving birth, sometimes a tiny white covered bundle was brought out amidst tears from the helpers, occasionally a midwife was in charge but generally this could not be afforded, and the women just relied upon each other for aid. Sometimes the unfortunate mother was carried away in the community coffin, a box with a hinged base, so that the corpse could be tipped into a pauper's grave and the coffin reused. But more often the proceedings ended in the lusty cries of a new little life arriving in the world and yet another mouth to be fed in an already large family. Ged had never thought much about any of this process one way or the other, he would always offer a sympathetic nod to the bereaved but to him it was just life as it was. But now his heart was rent by the groans, and as time wore on, the agonized cries of his beloved wife. As the third day dawned and he was brought his breakfast, he saw Jane's eyes were quite red with weeping. Cook came down and said the mistress was very weak now and shook her head. Then Dr Myers himself appeared in his shirt sleeves; Ged noticed a bloodstain on one of his rolled-up cuffs.

"Well?"

"Captain Stone, I fear we are in God's hands now. There is little more I can do for your dear wife. She is bearing a very large child and the progress is not good. We must pray for God's mercy..."

Ged leapt at the good doctor, grabbing his waistcoat lapels, he threw him against the wall.

"What kind of crap is that? Help my wife, help her, do anything but for God's sake help her..."

In despair, he let go of the doctor and turned and put his fist right through the upper panel of the parlour door, drawing blood on his knuckles as he did so.

The doctor had been attacked in this way before now, by desperate fathers and distressed brothers, and without protest had calmly turned his head to one side.

"Please know Captain Stone, all that is possible has been done for your dear wife, now we can only wait."

Ged sucked his knuckles and nodded.

"My apologies Dr Myers, but A could not bear to lose my beloved wife..."

"No, no of course not, but we are not there yet, by no means. Where there is life, there is always hope in God's infinite goodness."

With that he went back upstairs, and Ged heard yet another heart-rending scream. He sat at the table, pushing away his breakfast tray, he stared out at the grey sea, remembering Idina sailing with him on the Fortitude and her delight in knowing she was with child. He thought of her laughing eyes and her most tender love for him and her always very obvious desire when they satisfied each other, afterwards she would tell him how much she loved him and call him 'mo Ghradh', the Gaelic for 'my Love.' Those nights she had lain on the bed, when he had pulled up her shift and together, they had watched the baby moving about, thrilled by every strong kick. Never before this day had Ged thought for one moment that he would not soon be holding his son in his arms. Never until now, had he thought of living without his wife. With tears stinging his eyes he remembered how much she had wanted a dog, which he has always refused her. Now, he spoke with God for the first time in his life; even in his most trying and near-death experiences at sea, he had never thought to call upon God before, relying always on his own abilities. He made the faithful promise that if Idina could live, he would get her a dog, in fact any number of dogs. It seemed a shallow bargain but suddenly Ged realised that there was no longer any sound at all coming from upstairs, he waited in absolute silence for many minutes, hardly daring to breathe, so profound was his fear. And still he waited, now wondering which of them would come down to tell him the worst news. Then he gasped, for that oppressive silence was abruptly broken by the loud rhythmic cries of the new-born. He was up the stairs two at a time and Sarah caught him at the bedroom door, she held him back with the palm of her hand.

"Not yet brother, for we are just finishing up." There were tears on her cheeks, but she was smiling broadly too. "Tha's got the lovliest son, a big healthy bairn."

"And, a a and Idina?"

"Fine, tired but fine honestly...now A must go ter her; but wait a few minutes more while we get them both ready."

Ged leaned against the wall and looked up to thank God with all his heart. Mysterious buckets and basins were brought out, but both Cook and Jane were beaming.

"Congratulations Sir."

"A more splendid lad A've nivver seen, Sir."

At long last Dr Myers opened the door wide to usher him in, he put his hand on Ged's shoulder and spoke in a low voice, "all is well with mother and child, but I should caution you Captain, there should be no more children after this one, for we may not be so lucky next time."

Hardly listening Ged pushed past him, and took Idina in his arms, almost weeping with the relief of it all.

She was pale and worn, her lips cracked and dry, her voice a little croaky, but her green eyes were laughing as she looked up at him.

"Shall you take your son?"

Too choked to speak for a moment, he nodded and took the baby. Grinning in delight, he kissed the little wrinkled forehead.

"Well, I have carried our son most carefully to the Greenland Fisheries and back and devoted three days to bringing him into this world, so what do you think to him?"

"He's grand, just grand…" He frowned staring into the little face. "Idina is our bairn a bit ugly?"

"Only a little my Love, but we still like him, do we not?"

"Oh aye, he's grand." And he kissed him again. "Does he favour thy father?"

"You mean fat, red and bald?"

Cook snorted with laughter at this, as she set down the tea tray.

"And irascible too?" smiled Idina, for the little face had started to redden and crumple.

Ged watched fascinated as she took the baby and pushed a large dark nipple into his soft wet mouth.

Cook poured tea for everyone.

"There now Mrs Stone, tell me if that is not best cup of tea tha's ivver tasted."

Sarah held the cup to Idina's lips, and she drank it all in one go.

"How right you are Cook, how did you know?"

"Had a bairn or two meself tha knows, though it were a long time since."

The doctor drained his cup, rolled down his shirtsleeves and reached for his coat.

"I must thank you especially for your help Miss Stone, your sister is a born nurse, Captain Stone, I would take her with me if I could, to all the confinements I attend." Sarah smiled at his compliment as he went on, "there are few who know as well as she when to comfort, when to encourage, when to wait quietly and all with such efficient calmness, a true gift."

He packed his medical bag, bid his farewell and promised to return in the morning to check on matters.

He could hardly remember a time when he had longed more for a hot meal, a good drink, a warm bed and the comfort of his wife.

The Captain and Idina were at last alone, they curled up together and slept exhausted with their new-born son between them. In that first night they awoke a time or two to look with wonder at the baby, hardly able to believe that they had made this most perfect of beings. Tiny toes were tweaked, plump cheeks kissed, his soft red hair stroked, and fingers were put into the strong clutch of his little fists. Idina wept openly with the emotion of it.

"Dunt cry Darling, 'tis ovver now and all's well."

He stroked her hair anxiously and wiped away tears with the back of his finger as she smiled explaining they were the tears of true happiness. Remembering his words on their wedding day, she whispered, "we have done it, we have done it, made our most wondrous son."

****

Three weeks after the birth, Idina finally had the strength to hobble downstairs with her baby under her arm. At once she saw the panel in the parlour door.

"Goodness, whatever has happened to the door?"

Sheepishly, Ged explained that he had thought she was going to die and could not bear it.

"A wanted ter punch that bloody doctor, but A held meself back and punched t' door instead."

"The better choice I think, my Love."

She seated herself carefully in a cushioned chair and stared at the door with a little smile upon her lips. Secretly she felt curiously flattered, and though every few months she would say, "we really must get that door repaired," somehow it never happened, and it remained for some years as an outward symbol of her husband's abiding love and passion.

When young Gerald was one-month old, Idina felt well enough to invite the ladies of her sewing group (who worked to raise funds for the aid of sailors' widows), to take tea with her and see her new baby.

Mrs Hawker, Mrs Pybus, Mrs Walker, Mrs Lydia Curzon and Miss Octavia Curzon all sat decorously on the high-backed chairs in the parlour. Of course, Mrs Curzon had taken the baby as soon as she arrived and was presently marvelling at his size, his obvious intelligence and his likeness to his dear papa as she cradled him in her arms.

Mrs Pybus caught Mrs Walker's eye and nodded towards the shattered door panel, but Idina saw their glances and said brightly, "oh the door? My husband smashed it in a moment of anger, we really must get it repaired."

"I expect the dear Captain is a very passionate man is he not?" said Mrs Curzon, rather admiringly.

Mrs Hawker shifted uncomfortably in her seat, Mrs Walker gasped with shock and Mrs Pybus looked at the floor. All of them knew that Mrs Curzon was somehow related to Captain Stone, although none could remember exactly how, they remembered, however, that it was in some way very shocking and something to do with her present husband having fathered a bastard years ago.

Octavia bowed her head but only to conceal her overwhelming desire to giggle.

Fortunately, all were quickly diverted by the entrance of Cook with the tea tray, followed by Jane precariously balancing several plates of buttered bread, cakes and scones.

"Thank you Cook, you need not pour for us, I'm sure that Miss Curzon will oblige."

Octavia had hardly passed everything out when the captain himself burst into the room; although he had been told several times of it, he had entirely forgotten it was the ladies' tea-party, hence he appeared in his shirt sleeves. Mrs Hawker hardly knew where to look, for he certainly cut a very fine figure, Octavia stared at him with admiration, but her face was largely concealed by her fashionable deep bonnet brim, so her stares went unnoticed.

Quickly, Idina introduced him to her friends, he nodded to them, then begged to be excused.

"No, no, my dear Captain, please do stay to take tea," gushed Mrs Curzon, "for a ladies' tea-party is so enhanced by a gentleman's presence, if they can but be procured."

Thus, Ged sat down somewhat self-consciously, and Octavia served him a cup of tea, ensuring that she touched his hand as she gave it to him, along with her most charming smile.

Gulping his tea as quickly as he decently could, he said, "Mrs Curzon, might A have a private word wi' thee, concerning a surprise for me wife?"

"Why of course, my dear Captain."

She handed the now sleeping baby to Octavia and followed the captain into the hall.

None could hear his words, but all heard Lydia's squeal of delight as she said, "why my dear Captain, what a romantic you are, as luck would have it, I have the very thing, ready in about two weeks-time, if that suits."

And with that, Captain Stone bid the ladies good afternoon and Mrs Curzon returned to the parlour, saying again what a very romantic man the captain was, though on no account could she reveal their little secret.

Idina smiled to herself and exchanged a friendly glance with Octavia.

Two weeks later Idina was the proud owner of a brown spaniel puppy, the progeny of Lydia Curzon's finest breeding bitch and sired by her eldest son's favourite shooting dog.

Ged said, "keep t' bloody thing away from me, that's all Ar ask."

Cook said, "eh, we've got us work cut out now."

Jane said she had better fetch a soapy cloth.

But Idina and baby Gerald loved that pup to bits and named her Bella.

CHAPTER 22

March 1813.
In which Octavia turns her ankle and
there are far reaching consequences.

I was just getting used to things again, baby Gerald was now a large plump baby of five months, the apple of his father's eye, and mine of course. I thought my insides would never heal up, but they had, and I was so glad that Ged and I could be husband and wife again, albeit he had to be very slow and gentle with me. It was as if we had to take the time to get to know each other all over again. So, I was really feeling reasonably well now, though I had barely been out of the house for months, when Octavia Curzon decided to visit.

At once, I could see that she was quite agitated, not her usual composed self at all, despite looking most elegant in a striped lavender silk dress and a short jacket in a purple with a matching bonnet trimmed with an extravagance of violets, dark green leaves and toning ribbon.

"Sit down, Octavia. A tray of tea Jane, please close the door as you go out."

I did not want the servants listening in to whatever it was that she was going to say.

She leaned forward, took my hands and looked at me anxiously, "please Idina you have to help me, I'm in the most desperate plight and there is only you that I can turn to."

"Why whatever has happened?"

"Naught, naught has happened yet, and that is my problem, you must help me before anything does happen…"

I waited, having no idea what she was talking about, I suppose I had not really been keeping up with things having been so busy with the baby and the puppy who was going through a very lively phase and was currently chewing the leg of Octavia's chair.

"It is my cousin, my cousin Hugo, as you know, I have always been in love with him, I love him more than I've words to say…I cannot live without him."

I saw tears on the edge of her long dark lashes, and I own, although she had told me before, on several occasions, that she loved Hugo, I had not quite realised its intensity. Perhaps she had not spoken of it so openly before, as until recently Hugo had been a married man, however, two months ago poor Margaret Ann had died of a horrid growth which she had had since the birth of her last child, a stillborn. Hugo had taken in her little boy Tommy, as of course, the poor mite was an orphan now.

She went on, "I could not marry him before, for I was only fourteen when he married Margaret Ann and then I thought I had lost him forever. I tried to put him from my mind and look at other gentlemen, as my mama was always wanting me to, but I could never, never love anyone else."

Here she burst into a full flood of weeping, just as Jane brought in the tea.

"Come, my dear Octavia." I offered her my handkerchief. I had never seen anyone else manage to look so pretty when they cried. Usually, the face becomes an ugly red, has a puffed look and the nose runs; but Octavia managed to weep most elegantly, oozing out large tears which hung on the ends of her long dark eyelashes and tumbled down her cheeks. "Perhaps in the fullness of time, as Hugo overcomes his grief, you may have your chance with him?"

For even though he and Margaret Ann had lived separately for well over a year, I had heard that he had wept openly at her funeral.

"You don't understand Idina, I fear it is already too late."

"Goodness, but why?"

"You don't understand, I have not explained my plight properly." She took a deep breath and wiped her eyes. "I think you know my good friend Annie, do you not?"

"Hugo's Aunt's ward? Of course, I know who she is, but I know little of her."

"Well, she and I are close, best friends until now, though I have never told her that I love Hugo, for I think she would have been shocked with him being married; she's quite a moral sort of a person, you know. Anyway, when we were talking in private in her bedroom yesterday, she was terribly excited because Hugo had been to see her several times over the last few days, they'd been out walking, and he had kissed her many times and told her she was lovely and all that…"

"Goodness, poor Margaret Ann's hardly cold in her grave, it cannot be more than two months since he buried her."

In truth I was quite taken aback, I knew for a fact that after the funeral, Hugo had gone straight to his mother, sat at her feet and sobbed into her lap for over an hour. Ged had told me this, as he had accompanied his brother to the funeral, though only to support him, for Ged could not have thought less of Margaret Ann if she had been the whore of Babylon.

Octavia's voice shook now, "she's sitting there asking me what I think, and do I think she is too young to marry…Idina, I could barely keep my composure, but I did not want her to suspect my true feelings so I stuck it out as long as I could, before making an excuse to leave. But I just ran home and wept my heart out, wept as long as I could before I'd got Martha Jane and Mama, poking their noses in." She looked up at me, "Idina, you are the only one who can help me now, with Hugo being your brother-in-law…"

I had no idea that I was expected to do something, I had thought it was just a case of showing sympathy. "But whatever can I do?"

"I have not seen him in some time, would you take me to visit him? It would seem odd if I called in on my own but you being married could take me…"

"Oh yes I see, I could, I have not been out properly yet, but I'm really feeling quite well now."

"Could we go today, please Idina."

"But what of little Gerald? I have never left him for a moment before."

Indeed, I was quite aghast at the idea, but I was moved by Octavia's sad face before me, so I sent for Cook.

"Cook, Miss Curzon and myself, have to go out unexpectedly. Would you look after Gerald for a little while, we shall not be long I think…I have just fed him, so he should sleep but if he wakes, do not let him cry… would you…"

"Yes, yes Mistress, A know how ter look after a bairn. Tek as long as tha needs, Master Gerald'll be as fine as can be with me."

So, I put on my bonnet, shawl and gloves and off we set.

"Is there a plan Octavia? Why shall we say we have called? Perhaps just a social call?" I thought of the value my husband always put on careful planning in any difficult situation.

She shook her head, "we'll think of something, as we walk."

And just as we were nearly at the little house on Church Street, I suddenly thought of a plan, and quite a good one as it happened.

We were arm in arm, so it was easy done. I pushed Octavia into the wall, causing her to stumble.

"Oh dear, Octavia, have you hurt your ankle?"

Catching on at once, she said, "oh no, I think my ankle quite badly turned."

She clutched my arm dramatically and at once, a burly fisherman stepped forward. He must have seen the whole thing and he looked at me rather suspiciously.

"Might A be of assistance? As t' young lady hurt herself?"

"I do thank you Sir for your kindness, but no assistance is required, for my brother-in-law lives just two doors down and my friend may rest there."

The man looked doubtful and watched us as we knocked and walked into the house.

Inside we had the full audience of mother-in-law, Sarah and Hugo (and the two children).

Octavia limped convincingly and crumpled her pretty face in imagined pain.

Sarah rushed forward, "dear Miss Curzon, whatever has happened?"

"I fear she has turned her ankle, but I think it not broken," I said.

At once Hugo grasped her about the waist and helped her to a chair; most carefully, Sarah lifted her foot onto another chair. Fortunately, she remembered to wince even though Hugo still had his arm around her and kissed her cheek.

"Poor old Cousin."

I sat opposite my mother-in-law and smiled at her, I actually felt quite tired with it being the first time I had been out since my confinement.

She put her head on one side and looked at me quizzically but said nothing. Meanwhile Sarah fussed around with cold bandages and serving us all with hot cups of tea, with some brandy to brace the invalid.

Hugo held her hand while Sarah bandaged her foot and ankle. "Fortunate, there is little swelling…"

Mother-in-law glanced at me again and raised an eyebrow. Octavia drained her tea and thanked Sarah for her help and kindness, she looked up at Hugo, "I must trouble you further Cousin, would you be able to help me home? If I could lean upon your arm, I think I could manage to walk a little."

He laughed, "bloody hell, tha can't walk, A'll carry thee, tha's only light and it's no distance."

She took off her bonnet, so that when Hugo lifted her up, she put her arms around his neck and laid her head upon his shoulder.

After they had gone, Sarah cleared away the tea things and disappeared into the scullery.

"A may be deaf, but A'm not bloody daft, what's going on Idina?" asked mother-in-law.

I leaned forward and spoke loudly, "that is Octavia, Hugo's cousin."

Her lips twitched, "Aye well cousins may marry as well as any, as well as any." She nodded to herself, then looked up and wagged her finger at me, "but if that lass has turned her ankle, then A'm t' bloody virgin Mary." Cackling at her own joke, she repeated, "bloody virgin Mary."

Sarah reappeared, wiping her hands, "what is it Mother?"

She shook with laughter and said, "by she's a rum 'un is our Idina, a rum 'un... So, when's tha bringing me grandson round ter see me? Our Ged says he's biggest bairn in Whitby."

I smiled with maternal pride, "yes I believe he is, I shall bring him round very soon, now the Spring weather is coming."

"Eh, bless him," said Sarah.

Talking of my darling baby made me want to get home at once, though of course, he had been absolutely fine and slept soundly throughout the whole of my absence.

When Ged came home, he was tired having had much to do in preparation for sailing in two weeks' time, and also still being in some pain from having had two teeth pulled earlier that day at the barbers. Usually he went to Mr Briggs, our ship's surgeon for extractions, swearing he 'nivver felt no pain wi' Briggs,' but unfortunately Mr Briggs was currently unavailable due to a bereavement in his vast family. So, for some reason, I never mentioned the day's adventures and we just went straight to bed with our darling baby sleeping between us. Goodness though, I came to wish I had told him of it, when he was quite cross with me, the next day.

So, that following day when he returned for his dinner, he was clearly angry.

"By God, me brother's a bloody idiot."

"My Love?"

He sat down, his fists clenched and a vein sticking out on his forehead. "A bloody idiot, he'd got a nice little thing going wi' Thornton's lass, she'll come in ter all t' houses in Thornton's Yard in time. Not two days since he told me he were thinking of weddin' 'er, now, NOW, A find he's eloped wi' his cousin, Miss Curzon." He paused and looked at me, he narrowed his eyes and leaned forward, "tha dunt seem much surprised at this, does tha know owt of it already?"

I felt so deceitful, for I had never lied to him, and he had only ever been truthful with me.

"I…I knew them to love each other," I said weakly.

"Love," he roared, as if he had never heard of such an outrage, "what good is that? Our Hugo's no ambition, he'll never mek t' effort ter be a captain, he could have set himself up good and proper with that Annie and them houses, he can't be a seaman all 'is life, he'll be dead bit' time he's forty, there's no life harder on a man than going ter sea."

Well that was true enough. I took his hand to soothe him, but he still ranted on, "trouble wi' our Hugo is, he's hasty, any woman as gives him a nod, then he marries 'em. Look at that bloody whore Margaret Ann, only knew her two minutes and he'd got ring on her finger…"

"My Love, don't call her that, not now she's passed…"

"Well, she were a bloody whore, A nivver took ter her at all, even afore she showed her true colours like. He musta liked Thornton's lass well enough, for A caught 'em a couple of days since in our side passage and he looked like he were swallowing her up and she weren't minding neither."

Sometimes my husband had a very coarse turn of phrase.

"Please my Love, have your dinner, and then you can tell me more of it. Please don't shout so, for I think little Gerald is getting upset."

Throughout this tirade, Gerald had stared wide-eyed at his father, though some might have thought he gazed at his parent more in admiration than in fear, impressed by the tremendous noise his father could make by banging his fist on the table and raising his voice. Myself, I suddenly felt like a child again, when my father would sit in that same chair and shout in quite an irrational way, and I would tremble in his presence. Though it is said that women are happiest if they marry a man like their father.

"Sorry, Darling, A just want ter see our Hugo happy in himself. That last 'un he had, cut him up good and proper. A'm t' elder and A feel responsible fer him now…"

He pulled me towards him, held me close to him and pressed his aching head against me. Then he drew back holding out my skirts as I stood beside him.

"By God Wife, tha's looking particularly beautiful today, what is this gown?" He moved the fabric in his hands to catch the light. "But what is it's colour? It's green and another shade…"

"Tis a shot silk of green and light gold, my Love."

Indeed, I was very pleased with this dress, made quite full, of this gorgeous stuff, it had no sleeves and under it I wore a blouse of the thinnest silk gauze in white, frilled at the neck and cuffs.

He kissed me and then turned away to take his dinner. He ate a large plateful of food, in spite of his toothache and seemed to calm down somewhat. He sat Gerald upon his lap, made blowing noises into his little neck to make him giggle and told me about his morning.

It seemed he had been at the Golden Lion to meet Robert Curzon, when a message came to say Robert would be late due to a family trouble.

"A saw Jacob Curzon sitting on his own, (or so A thought), so A just nodded ter him, friendly like, next thing old man Thornton storms in, grabs Jacob bit' collar and has him up against t' wall, calling him all t' names under t' sun, which A'll not repeat for thy sake. Well, Jacob were a sitting duck like, for he's on two sticks now for walking. So, A thought A'd best intervene wi' t' Curzons being like family…"

He paused and looked at me.

"Yes, my Love, they are, as well as our very kind friends."

"Well, A'd hardly stood up when a great tall heavy man rushed in from t' privy at back, clapped his hand on Thornton's shoulder and says, 'unhand my brother Sir, else I shall be forced to make you." Here my husband imitated his upper class, educated accent. "Turns out it were Jacob's brother-in-law…"

"Oh, Louis Franklin, Lydia's brother…"

"Tha knows him?" he asked in surprise.

"Yes, though not well, for he's an army captain and always away fighting in our dreadful war. He's married to one of Lydia's cousins."

In truth, many years ago, Louis Franklin had partnered me for two of the dances at an Assembly Ball and I own I had thought him very amusing and charming; he had filled my dreams for quite some time after even though he was already married, but I certainly would never mention such a thing as that to my husband.

"Aye well, tha wunt want ter mess wi' a man like that, for he did have summat of a military bearing. So next off, old man Thornton skulks away, a beaten man, saying his lass Annie is worth better than any bloody deceiver like Hugo Curzon and that were first A'd heard our Hugo mentioned. Then Robert arrives and t' four of us sat down together, and bit by bit A got ter bottom of it. Seems previous evening, late on, our Hugo and Miss 'fancy' Curzon had eloped, and her note weren't found till this morning, by which time they was well on their way ter Gretna Green…"

"Oh, how romantic."

My husband looked at me as if I were completely mad.

"They told me her mama had took ter her bed wi' a bottle of brandy and a drop of laudanum too and can't give ovver weeping. Robert and Jacob's fearing for 'em on dangerous roads up North, but they cannot go after 'em now, they'd nivver catch 'em up."

I had not thought of this, and it set me off in a fluster of anxiety, thinking of highway robberies and murders.

"So, turns out that Octavia one, had sent a note to Annie, Thornton's ward, before she went, and she's been weeping as well ever since. Old man Thornton said our Hugo had broken her heart wi' his philandering and false promises. Next off, A thought A'd best get on and see what our Sarah knew of it, so when A gets there, she's out wi' t' bairns and there's only me mother there. Well A can get no sense out of her, she kept laughing about a broken ankle and she were t' virgin Mary, but she obviously knew summat of it for she said that cousins could marry as well as any… A think she's mad, me mother…"

"I think you do not always listen to your mother, my Love."

"Me not listen? 'Course A listen."

He was clearly offended by the notion, but then Cook brought in an apple crumble, his favourite pudding, so the moment quickly passed.

"A've made it a bit softer Sir, on account of thy teeth."

The captain was inordinately fond of Cook and thanked her kindly for her thoughtfulness.

****

As for the young lovers, they returned two weeks later, just in time for the sailing of the Fortitude, on her next whaling trip. By this time everyone had calmed down and they were welcomed by both families with the warmest of hugs and kisses. It turned out that when Hugo had carried Octavia home that day, by a quirk of fate, they were alone in the house save for the servants. Hugo had set her down upon a little sofa, Octavia kept her arms about his neck and kissed him with cousinly gratitude. Whereupon he had returned her kisses with manly passion, realised she was the love of his life and a plan to elope and marry was quickly hatched, both of them desirous to take their kisses and caresses to their natural fulfilment as soon as possible.

Octavia had crept out of the house with her bag, nearing midnight and they had hired a gig to take them on the first part of their journey, then it was several days on stagecoaches, staying in coaching inns as man and wife. Octavia had sensibly taken her Grandmother Franklin's wedding ring with her for this very purpose. When at last, they were actually married, then the tedious journey was undertaken in reverse to return home.

The happy couple had little time together before Hugo was off whaling, though as it happened it was to be his last trip to sea, for while he was away Octavia made herself very busy indeed. She rearranged the sleeping accommodation at the little house on Church Street, moving her mother-in-law upstairs to the first-floor front and her own marital bed up to the garret where Ged had once slept. Thus, vacating the front room downstairs, which in a matter of days became a shop, where bonnets were trimmed, as she claimed in the latest London styles. The business was started off with a large quantity of quality ribbons, lace and silk flowers which had once belonged to her wealthy Grandmother Franklin and had spent some years packed in a clothes press in her mother's Baxtergate attic. Steamed and pressed by the skilful Sarah and some of them dyed in new fashionable colours, they made a splendid opening display for her many curious customers.

By the time Hugo returned from whaling in early September, a prosperous milliner's business was firmly established, with new stock sent up from London almost every week. Sarah was still in charge of running the house and our mother-in-law, a kind of apprentice learning how to trim bonnets much more adeptly than one might at first imagine. Business was so good that Hugo started serving in the shop and never went back to sea. His easy charm and flattery ensured that none left the shop without a smile on her face and an expensive purchase in her hands.

One bright day in September, I visited with my dear little Gerald and sat with my mother-in-law. At once she put down the magenta silk which she was skilfully ruching and took him onto her lap, telling him he was the bonniest lad in all the world and marvelling that already he was walking.

"And what's tha think of me Idina, learning hat meking at my age?"

"I think it's good so long as it pleases you, of course."

"Aye, it does Hun, A love it. A nivver had chance ter do owt like this when A were a lass, but A wish that A had." I nodded, as she went on in her down to earth manner. "Gone through us all like a dose of the physick has yon Octavia, done us all good, she has. Bairns love 'er, she's a sister for our Sarah and she's give me summat ter look forward to ivvery day." She leaned forward and added confidentially. "And A think she'll keep our Hugo on a tight rein, as needs ter be done, afore he starts straying like his father afore him. Sniffing round ivvery skirt as passed him he did. But he were that good looking." She smiled to herself, "aye he were a bonny lad, were Jacob Curzon and no mestek."

I smiled too, thinking of Jacob now, a crippled old man with his devoted wife Lydia endlessly fussing over him.

But Octavia and Hugo were, in fact, a constant and loving couple, so much so that Octavia bore him eleven children over the coming years, never taking more than a couple of days off from her precious hat shop in order to fulfil her confinements. Though, as mother-in-law had sensibly advised, Octavia did always keep Hugo on a so called 'tight rein'.

And for ourselves, prosperity smiled very fondly upon us. My dear husband worked tirelessly on sailing, hunting, trading and investing. When we sat down together each quarter to reckon our books, I was always impressed at the very considerable way in which our finances grew and praised my dear husband for his ceaseless endeavours. But he would merely laugh and grasp my hand saying he could not earn a penny piece without me behind him to advise and support him. So, I think I can say we made something of an excellent team!

CHAPTER 23

Early on the morning of the elopement.
In which Annie is deceived.

I had hardly been gone more than ten minutes, leaving my Mr Thornton, Annie and Billy sitting around the kitchen table taking a cup of tea, chatting away, all as content as could be. But by the time I got back, our lives had turned quite upside down.

It happened that when I had got that days' shopping, I had forgotten to buy the sugar, I rarely failed to remember items we needed but it so happened I had met one of our tenants in the market square and I was so busy listening to her story of how her brother had come home from sea with the body of a baby mermaid, that my mind was quite elsewhere. I think I did not believe one word of it, but nevertheless she made such a fantastic tale of it, it quite slipped my mind to buy the last item on my list. So now I quickly ran across to the grocers' and bought two pounds of block sugar and hurried back home before the pot of tea grew cold.

What a sorry sight met my eyes, for poor Annie was weeping openly, a piece of paper clutched in her hand, Mr Thornton and Billy sitting on either side of her with arms about her shoulders.

"Eh whatever is amiss Annie love?" I asked, for it was rare to see her so.

She looked up at me, her dear face red and swollen with crying, but she could not speak so I looked to my husband.

"That young knave, has deceived her, deceived her good and proper," he said.

"What? Who, tha dunt mean our Hugo?"

For it was no secret that recently he had been taking his tea with us and afterwards been walking out with our Annie, indeed she had seemed much taken with him, though I had thought little of it with him having buried his wife very recently, and Annie being so young still.

"Aye, very same, that good for nothing, he's been leading her on, giving her reason ter hope wi' words of love and such."

"So, what has happened?" I asked innocently.

"The scoundrel's cheated her good and proper, run off with that hussy Octavia Curzon."

"What?" I was hardly able to believe my ears. Apart from anything else, though I loved Hugo with all my heart, him being my own flesh and blood, he was only a common sea man, and I would have thought Octavia Curzon would have been destined for something more of a monied young gentleman, though I will own they were always fond of each other as children.

"Aye, it's all in t' letter here, messenger lad's just brought it."

"What does it say?" I said weakly sitting down.

"A'll read it ter thee wife, though fancy words of it'll mek me want ter spit."

"Octavia must have written it last night afore she went…" Annie spoke through her tears.

My husband cleared his throat and held the letter at some distance, for he did not have his reading glasses to hand.

My Dearest Friend Annie,

Please forgive me, for I know truly how my words and actions will pain you.

I have never told you before, but since earliest childhood, I have loved my cousin Hugo and until now, I believed his love for me to be only that of a cousin. Today he has declared his feelings for me to be much more, to be those of a true and ardent lover. We plan to elope tonight and by the time you read this we will be on our way to marry in Scotland.

I know you had feelings for Hugo, and I hope our actions will not hurt you too much, though I fear they will. But I cannot turn my back upon my heart's true love.

If there is any hope for our friendship, which means a deal to me, please contact me upon our return.

Your loving and devoted friend,
Octavia Curzon

He almost did spit as he finished reading, screwed up the letter and threw it onto the hearth.

"Blatant hussy, false and not an ounce of feeling for any but herself."

He squeezed Annie to him and kissed the top of her head. I ached for I well remembered that awful pain of disappointed love in a young heart.

He went on, "A've no wish ter speak ill of t' lad when he's thy kin, but he's took advantage of our Annie, promising her all sorts and…and he's been pawing at her…"

"What's he done ter thee Lass?" Now my heart sank with dread.

"Kissed me Aunt Eliza," she said sniffling, "many times."

"And naught more than that Dear?"

She shook her head and I let out a sigh of relief. She stood up, walked around the table and I took her in my arms, glad enough to hide my own tears on her shoulder, for she was a good head taller than me now. For it struck me deep, that my poor Annie had had little happiness and so much loss in her life and that small scrap of joy that Hugo had casually offered and then snatched away, was so unfair. Annie with her simple, loving and trusting heart; Hugo handsome and charming, yet as shallow as his father, who had broken my own heart so long ago with his feckless philandering. As for Octavia, she had a dazzling prettiness and alluring manner that could have secured her any man she chose, not to mention her breeding and fine education to set her up on the right step of life. Yet she wanted the one man my poor Annie had fixed her heart upon.

Then our Billy spoke up, "tha'll meet another soon enough sister, maybes a better one, wait and see."

"Aye tha's reet enough lad, and one as deserves her too, eh Annie love?"

But this only brought on a fresh bout of weeping, "A don't want any but him, he said he loved me, how can he forget me so quick?"

She looked at me for an answer, but I fear I had none to that age-old question.

Whereupon my husband stood and reached for his coat, I looked at him questioningly and he said he was going to square up with those arrogant Curzons. I laid my hand upon his arm to pause him, for I knew him to be hot-headed in anger, but he shook my hand away.

"Tha knows Wife, when A've troubles in me mind A've ter square it up, we've all been slighted in this, not just our Annie. A'll look in every tavern in t' town till A find that Jacob Curzon and speak me mind, and if that lad Hugo weren't so far away, A'd show him just what A thought of him too."

I nodded knowing I had not the power to soothe his anger and he departed slamming the door behind him. But I well knew that whatever they thought privately of the matter, all those Curzon's would side together and there'd be little chance for my Mr Thornton to square up as he put it.

I think I hardly need add that Annie never spoke to Octavia again, even though Octavia always sent her flowers and a loving note on her birthday for years to come. As for Hugo, despite not being the most sensitive of souls, he only ever visited me when he knew me to be alone in the house. Try as we might, it took Mr Thornton and myself a good long time to lift Annie from her sadness; I've thought perhaps we never did, and she just learned to carry her pain quietly in her heart.

CHAPTER 24

1813.
In which a Christmas visit is made.

That same year, as it was nearing Christmas, Ged came in from visiting his brother and sister. Before he had taken off his coat, he put his arms around me.

"What's tha think ter this Darling, going away for the Christmas?"

"You mean this Christmas?" For it was only a couple of weeks away.

"Aye, A'm not sure about it meself, but A think it'd mean t' world ter our Hugo. He's wanting us ter go with him and his Octavia ter stop a few days wi' his other brother, Jack Curzon, him that's t' vicar."

"Oh," I felt unsure, for I'd been imagining us having a cosy time at Christmas with just the three of us, sitting around a good fire with some nice bits to eat and the last of our Sugar Spirit to drink, with perhaps sharing a meal at the little house on Church Street after the Christmas Service.

"A felt same meself but Hugo begged me ter ask thee, for he's wanting me ter meet his other brother and it seems the other sister might be there too, visiting…"

I did not want to be selfish if this meant much to Hugo. I also knew that they had a little boy at the vicarage, though I could not remember how old he was, and he might make a nice playmate for our young Gerald who was running about now. Then I remembered, Belle was Octavia's sister and of course they must surely want to see each other too.

So I said, "what do you think my Love?".

"A don't want ter go, but A'm thinking we should, it's just for three days, back home on t' Boxing Day."

"Of course, you are right my dearest Love, and it might be fun to meet new people and see a different place."

"Aye, but probably not, A've been all ovver t' world and there's nowhere A'd rather be than here…wi' me wife and bairn."

I smiled with happiness and started to write a list of things we would need to take.

The next day Lydia Curzon arrived in my parlour.

"My dear Idina, a little bird has told me you are to visit my dear Belle and Jack and my darling grandson… Of course. I should love to stay there for Christmas myself, but their house is far too cold for me, and dear Jacob has to be so careful of his bad leg now…"

"Is it very cold there?" I asked innocently.

"Lord yes, you'll need some warm clothes with you. Do you have some good furs to take?"

I nodded, for I had recently had some white fox furs made up into a hooded tippet and a fashionable large muff.

"Are you to travel on that dreadful stagecoach?"

"No, no, we are to go in a private hired coach, which Ged is booking as we speak, to take us first thing on Christmas Eve."

"Oh well that is something to be grateful for at least." She leaned forward and spoke confidentially,

"I feel disloyal saying this, for there are none dearer to me than Jack and Belle, but I have to warn you that their house is a touch cheerless, lacking the comforts that you and the dear Captain are so used to…" She lowered her voice, even though we were quite alone, "they have only the church stipend to rely on and it is a poor parish I fear." Here she shook her head somewhat sadly.

Laughing, I said, "Lydia remember that only last year, I sailed with my husband to the Greenland Fisheries, ice crystals froze on our faces daily and we had many days of eating bear meat and seal too towards the end of our voyage. So we are quite used to the cold and to a varied table too."

She nodded, but still looked doubtful.

However, I made a mental note to order a substantial hamper of festive delicacies to take with us for our hosts. I established that their little boy Jack was five years old and decided to buy him a large box of sweets, a whip and a top.

On asking my husband on the suitability of this gift he said, "aye grand, A'd 'ave loved owt like that as a lad."

He nodded with approval the day before our departure, when the large hamper arrived and helped himself to one of the oranges. Filled with brandy, wine, port, a full stilton cheese, ham, beef, cuts of veal and a selection of candied fruits, oranges and lemons, I hoped it would be a welcome addition to the Christmas fare. To this Cook added a pound cake, a fruit cake and a quantity of Whitby's own gingerbread wrapped in silvered paper.

The journey itself, though it required an early start, was really quite comfortable, the coach being well appointed with padded seats and heavy travel rugs.

There were shallow metal boxes filled with hot coals on the floor for us to rest our feet upon. Little Gerald was wakeful and fidgety, but Octavia and Hugo kept him diverted with a series of animal noises entertainingly acted out.

Octavia would say, "what does the piggy say Uncle Hugo?"

Hugo would reply with a snorting sound wiggling his nose and so on. Gerald was much delighted by all this, eventually joining in with the noises himself. Octavia then amused us with a hilarious story of when she and Hugo were still children and he had spent a full evening dressed as a ferocious polar bear to amuse his youngest sister.

Sadly, Ged was not well entertained on the journey, he sighed a great deal; bored he stared out of the window for most of the time and jigged his leg which he always did when he was agitated. And no one was more relieved than he when we finally arrived at the vicarage.

Of course, there was much hugging and kissing, while Ged and I stood back, waiting politely until we were introduced. But it gave me a chance to get a good look at our hosts without the rudeness of staring. I had always thought Octavia to be very pretty, with her sparkling dark eyes and profusion of curls, but her sister Belle was a true beauty, like a dark-haired Madonna with such a softness and quiet grace to her. The vicar himself had gentle grey eyes and apart from that, had a similar colouring to Hugo, with his hair perhaps a shade more reddish than his brother's. He shook our hands and welcomed us most warmly, but I could see Ged felt awkward, for I fear we rarely mixed socially with other couples. Our hired coachman unloaded the luggage plus the large hamper, which was accepted with thanks and some modest appreciation, though I could tell at a glance that neither the vicar nor his wife were given to exaggerated shows of emotion.

Their little boy Jack was quite a surprise to me, being so quiet and serious. Gerald stood too close to him and gazed up at him with the greatest interest, but I soon realised that they were not to be playmates, in fact I came to wonder during our stay, if young Jack ever played at all, for he seemed a bookish child and was already learning his Latin declensions.

A girl of about seventeen or so, showed us to our room, and a grim place it proved to be, overlooking the graveyard at the back of the house, the bare window had neither curtains nor shutters. Sparsely furnished, the room contained a bed, covered by a finely quilted coverlet in white, a chair, a wooden crate upturned and concealed with a cloth which served as a washstand and a row of iron clothes hooks on the wall.

Ged looked round the chilly room, "bet there's more bloody comfort in t' workhouse, eh?"

"Shh," I remonstrated, though there were none to overhear us.

We unpacked our clothes and washed our hands in the icy water poured from a rather pretty blue jug into an unmatching basin, dried them on a well-worn towel and descended to take our dinner.

I spent the rest of the afternoon in the kitchen, where at last there was some warmth from a good fire with its oven to one side. The task for Octavia and our hostess, was to bake one hundred mince pies to be handed out the following day after the Christmas Day church service, mainly to benefit the many poor parishioners.

I felt quite the ignoramus, for I rarely ventured into my own kitchen leaving such things entirely to our Cook. I had no notion of how pastry was made or how to prepare mincemeat, yet these two sisters did it with hardly a thought, they seemed to know exactly what to do without any discussion, measurements or a recipe. At last, Belle let her guard down a little as the two of them reminisced about their childhood and giggled over family escapades. They tried to include me in their conversation, with phrases like, 'listen to this one Idina' or 'you'll never guess what happened next Idina,' but essentially the stories belonged to them and their close sisterhood. I sat by the cosy fireside, listened and watched them fascinated, while my little Gerald played endlessly with a lump of dough and rubbed his hands in the flour that had spilt on the table, the afternoon being most pleasantly passed by us all. It culminated in some extra pies being set upon a plate and taken into the study where the men had spent the time drinking and chatting with young Jack carefully working at his copy book at the big desk there.

"Did tha mek these?" asked Ged in astonishment as I handed him a little pie, still warm, and I had to shake my head, feeling somewhat inadequate, even though he smiled at me and squeezed my hand reassuringly.

That evening after supper, the poor vicar had to turn out in the cold to sit with a dying parishioner, Belle sat beside the thin little fire with her knitting and there seemed to be little else to do save go to bed. I wished I had brought some needlework with me, but I had not for I had foolishly imagined our time would be taken up with Christmas festivities and games. So, we feigned fatigue after our journey and went up to our chilly bedroom. As for Octavia and Hugo, being still in the first days of connubial love, they looked like they welcomed an early bedtime, and we could hear their bed creaking rhythmically long into the night. Ged grinned and nudged me, for myself, I was far too cold to even think of such a thing.

Gerald was sleeping soundly, wrapped in my highland tartan shawl, Ged touched him and laughed, "hot as a bun, he is. Lucky for some, eh?"

"My love, I am thinking of wearing my fur tippet in bed, but I fear it getting crushed and spoilt?"

"Nay, tha cannot do that. A'll wrap thee in me greatcoat and tha'll soon be warm Darling."

Thus, ridiculous as it may seem, I slept in my shift and my husband's seaman's coat (designed to combat Arctic weather) under the pretty white quilt which was hardly thicker than the sheet itself. With my husband lying against my back, holding me tight in his strong arms, I have to say at long last, I was warm and slept like the proverbial log.

The following day, of course we all went to the church close by. The pathway was covered with a layer of ice and Octavia and I were slithering about, clutching on to our husbands who strode manfully in their strong sea boots. The Vicar was already at the front of the church with Belle and their little boy sitting nearby, but we all slipped quietly into a pew near the back. My husband and son hardly lasted ten minutes into the service with Ged fidgeting and Gerald trying to climb everywhere and then whinging when he was stopped, so with a quick nod to me, the two of them disappeared off outside. After that, I leant forward, tucked my hands well into my white fox muff and really enjoyed the rest of the service. Jack was a stirring preacher; his sermon spoke of Christ's coming to earth to give joy to transform our lives and how we must all open our hearts to let that joy enter into us. I was quite transfixed and hardly noticed the hour and a half passing. Though I did notice Hugo out of the corner of my eye, caressing Octavia's thigh in a very inappropriate manner as we listened. Afterwards I stood outside with Belle, holding one side of the flat basket full of hot mince pies. There were a few well dressed in the congregation, but most were poor, attired in greyish brownish clothes, their faces pale and wan beneath grubby bonnets and hats with linens that looked like they had never seen the wash tub. I could hardly tell one from another, though Belle seemed to know them all by name, but I found their hopelessness somewhat depressing, suddenly wishing myself home in Whitby. Of course, there were plenty of poor people there too, but somehow, they seemed on the whole noisy and cheerful, not desolate like these poor souls. A movement in the distance caught my eye, and I could see Ged in a far corner of the graveyard helping little Gerald balance on top of a tombstone. It made me smile inside my head to imagine what my father would have said if he had still been alive to see his grandson behaving in such a disrespectful way. In fact, I do not think he would have said anything, he would simply have exploded with the shock of it.

Together we all made our way back to the house, I found myself dreading the dull Christmas dinner to come, I only hoped my husband would remember to wait for the grace to be said before he started eating.

But how wrong was I, for Christmas dinner was not in the least dull, and in fact was one of the jolliest I had ever attended. As we approached the house, we saw a couple standing there with their horses and three young boys.

"Oh," cried Octavia, "it's Cousin Penelope and her Mr Harrison and…"

She could not finish her words for she was now kissing the lady visitor and her husband and all the boys. Hugo and Jack sprang into life, back slapping and hugging Mr Harrison and their sister, while the oldest lad took the horses behind the house where there was a sort of small farmyard, to bait and rest them.

"Now," said Penelope coming towards us and holding out her hands, "you must be Idina and Ged, our Hugo's new brother."

She was a small lively little person about my own age, with the most delightful dimples whenever she laughed, which was all the time, and I could see my husband liked her down to earth ways at once. She introduced her sons, who were strapping lads aged twelve, nine and seven.

Two tables were pushed together for our dinner and laden with food (most of it out of our hamper). There were only ten chairs, which meant Penelope's younger sons had to share a chair which they did agreeably enough, Gerald sat upon my lap and Belle reached out to take her son onto her knee, but young Jack shook his head and said he preferred to stand. However, this was not remarked upon as silence fell around the table, hands were clasped, and the vicar said a special Christmas grace.

"Heavenly Father, love brought Jesus Christ to earth on this day and love brings our family to this Christmas table. We thank you for this bounty before us and for the love that binds us together and may memories of today warm all our hearts for years to come."

Well, there could not have been more perfect words, I felt a lump in my throat as everyone said Amen and smiled at each other. And then of course our feast began; roasted beef, boiled ham, veal pies, mincemeat pies, dishes of potatoes, carrots and cabbage, three kinds of cheese, plum pudding, lemon cake, gingerbread iced in gold and a washbowl full of apples and oranges. The table was most enhanced by some fine linen, crystal glasses and a most elegant dinner service, almost out of place in that sombre vicarage. A great deal was drunk, and short work was made of the food, accompanied by chatter and laughter; the Harrison lads entertained us with juggling tricks using the oranges and I swear were quite as skilled as any circus performer I have ever seen. I was seated next to Penelope, and she plied me with many questions.

"Do tell Idina, how did tha meet thy husband?"

Before I could answer, my husband who had had quite a lot to drink, leaned across, "it were love at first sight, once A could get her ter look up from her book, eh Wife?" I smiled and nodded, and I think a flush crept up my cheeks at the memory of it. "A thought ter meself, A'll nivver get meself another lass as knows how ter sail a mizzen ship so A'd best snap her up quick."

"Is that true?" She turned to me in astonishment, "tha knows how to sail a big ship?"

"Well, yes I do just about, for I used to go to sea when I was a girl with my father for the whaling."

"Oh, my how very exciting, A've nivver heard of a woman doing such a thing, if A had, A'd have gone ter sea meself." She grasped my arm and spoke in a low voice into my ear. "Dunt mention owt about going ter sea ter my husband, for it's a sore point in our family."

"Really?"

"Oh aye, my eldest, Nathanial's a fancy ter go ter sea, but Harrisons have farmed on our land for two hundred year and his father just expected our Nat ter do t' same wi' owt question. But A keep telling him things is different nowadays and lads mek their own choices."

She looked at me for affirmation. Personally, I could not imagine anything more boring than a lifetime of tending muddy animals in muddy fields, but I did not say this.

"Tis a grand life going to sea Penelope, there is naught more exciting for a man than the sailing and the hunting, but it is a hard life and that must not be forgotten."

She nodded thoughtfully, and then she asked the question that I think she had most wanted to ask. "Tell me Captain, how came it that tha found our Hugo and knew him to be thy brother?"

"Well, A were serving as First Mate on t' Olivia Belle wi' thy cousin Robert, well A'd known him years, yet he'd nivver A'd cause ter mention he had a Cousin Hugo, though A'd probably A've thought nowt of it if he had. Any road, A were signing up crew for t' muster, when there were summat in his voice when he said his name as made me look up. Soon as A saw him A knew, A knew he were me lost brother, lost for twenty year... A could hardly write straight for t' shock of it."

"But our Hugo knew nowt of thee, did he?"

"Nay he did not, he thought A were a bloody madman for weeks, but he came round ter it in t' end and when we docked, he came home ter meet our sister and his natural mother too. Our mother were that shocked wi' seeing him again after so long, why she nivver spoke a word for two days after, though she's well made up for that since!"

"Now," I interrupted, "you have missed out the best bit of the story, my Love, through modesty I am thinking."

Here I explained how Hugo had slipped from the rigging and Ged had jumped into the treacherous cold sea to rescue him.

"Oh," said Penelope, her eyes wide with admiration, "he'd know tha were his brother then, risking thy own life ter save him."

"It were nowt," grinned Ged, "but A thought when A saw him fall, that A'd spent twenty year looking for him and A weren't going ter let him get away now and drown hisself."

Her face crumpled a little, "did tha look for him, did tha not know where he'd been taken?"

Ged shook his head, "Mother always said it best we dint know and none would tell us where he was, me sister wept for weeks ovver it, we searched all ovver Whitby for him and all that time he were only four mile away." He smiled ruefully, "but when yer youngsters nobody'll tell yer owt."

She reached out and touched Ged's arm sympathetically. "We loved Hugo from t' very first day; me and our Jack knew he were our brother even though no one would talk of it or tell us where he had come from. It were nivver spoke of at all, by any of our family."

"How did you know he was your brother if no one told you?" I asked with interest.

"A think just A kind of instinct, me and Jack used ter talk of it late at night when we was supposed ter be asleep and try ter work it out. Our Aunt Eliza's allus saying 'blood's thicker n' water,' and it's true."

"Aye," said Ged pensively topping up Penelope's wine glass, "tis a kind of instinct, that's exact how A knew him, an instinct as much as owt else."

"Thank you, Captain." She sipped her drink. "On her deathbed my mother asked that Hugo nivver be told, for she would not have believed that tha would ivver find him and she did not want him ter think she did not love him same as me and Jack, because she did love him so…everyone did."

The young maid, who looked rather tired now, was clearing away the empty plates and crumbs. Then the Harrisons jumped up; the older boys carried the two tables out into the hall and pushed the chairs against the walls, I was unsure of what was to happen until three violins and a drum appeared and Mr Harrison and his sons formed a little orchestra at the side of the room, (the youngest lad playing the drum). So, there was to be dancing, my heart lifted, for the last time I had danced was before my marriage.

"Eh we are grown too serious for Christmas wi' our talk," said Penelope, her dimples appearing again. "My resolution for this Christmas Day is ter get a smile for once on my brother Jack's face."

Then she looked across at her husband, sawing at his fiddle and he gave her the cheeriest of grins and winked at her.

With true good manners my husband asked our hostess to partner him but though she thanked him kindly, she declined and reached for her knitting again.

I was next to be asked, by the vicar himself, and I have to say he was a most accomplished dancer, perhaps wasted on the simple country dances that were chosen. Octavia with my husband, and Hugo with his sister Penelope, made up our set. Young Jack stood awkwardly to the side, his top and sweets lay untouched on the windowsill, though he had thanked us most courteously for the gift. Our dear little Gerald positioned himself very close to the musicians and stared hard at them until they made funny faces and stuck tongues out at him to make him laugh. The eldest boy broke off his playing for a moment to tweak Gerald's nose and then put his thumb between his fingers and showed it to him. Our little boy was astounded and broke into giggles, feeling on his face for his nose in case it had really disappeared; I think he had never seen this age-old game before.

We danced for more than an hour until everyone was out of breath and grinning with the delight of it. Penelope achieved her resolution and her brother Jack smiled broadly, enjoying the fun as much as anyone. Whilst the tables were brought back in and tea was being served, he regaled us with memories of the dancing master who had taught the older Curzon children to dance years ago and had caused much amusement due to his precious mannerisms.

Penelope pulled me to her and whispered, "he were a reet Molly Boy, A think he'd A've liked ter wear a ballgown hisself if he could."

Hugo did hilarious imitations of his false teeth which clicked every time the poor man spoke.

As we sat around and took a welcome cup of tea with buttered plum bread, I chatted with Penelope and her husband about their superb musical talents; it seemed the lads all loved music and getting them to practice was never any kind of a chore as it so often can be with lively children.

"Truth is they play a bit most nights unless they're ovver tired wit' farm work and that. And me husband's a rare singing voice." She smiled and looked down at her hands, "and that is how he wooed me Idina, he wrote a love song to me and sat at my Aunt Lydie's harpsicord and played it ter me singing t' words, all of thirteen Christmases ago."

"Why how very romantic, and did he win you at once with his love song?"

"Oh aye, A were won straight off, though A let him court me a couple of month just ter keep him guessing like." The dimples reappeared in her cheeks. "And tha sen Idina, did tha fall for t' good captain straight off, or did tha play coy wi' him?"

"Straight away I set my heart upon him, I had no time to flirt much for he was sailing away after I had known him only two weeks, but it was long enough, and I was always certain I loved him."

She squeezed my hand and went on, "my brother Jack always loved Belle, all his life, they were nivver apart as bairns. They used ter hide together in a dark cupboard in case anyone found out that they loved each other."

"Was it a forbidden love then?" I asked in surprise.

"Not as such, it was that Jack had years of study ahead of him, and more years as a curate before he could take a living, and I think my Aunt Lydie wanted her Belle married off at eighteen. But they were both true to one another always and waited faithful until they could marry." Here she sighed, and I was curious, for surely such a love is a reason for joy. "So sad it has turned as it has."

She looked at me and seeing my puzzled look, she whispered to me that Belle had rejected her little boy when he was born and had spent many months weeping and unable to care for him or even look at him. "A'll not speak out er turn, but A'll just say it's driven a rift between them that's hard ter heal. A'd say it's their duty afore God as keeps 'em together like, for A fear true love is quite lost between them now."

Now I was most surprised and indeed a little shocked, for I had never heard of such a thing as a mother not loving her own babe.

"Oh dear," I said, and somehow it seemed to explain the quiet studious little boy with his rather sad face, for surely every child needs a mother's love? No one had yearned for such more than me.

I glanced across the room and saw my husband looking most serious with arms folded, talking with the eldest boy Nat, who stood politely with his hands behind his back. Of course, there was no prize for guessing what they were talking about and soon enough they joined us, Ged pulling up a chair beside Mr Harrison.

"A'll come ter t' point straight off Sir, thy lad's telling me he's a fancy for sea life and A'd be willing ter tek him on, so long as he has thy approval."

Mr Harrison sighed and shook his head, "we're all farmers and we've been on t' same land for hundreds of year, fathers followed by sons. But our lad's allus had a fancy for t' sea, ivver since he could speak, dunt know where he gets it from." He shook his head again.

"Me mother's family were sea farers," interrupted Penelope, "though of course they had all passed afore our Nat were born."

Her husband went on, "but things is different nowadays, youngsters mek their own choices…what is it yer thinking Captain?"

"A were thinking, ter tek him on a trial for me next whaling trip, and if he shapes up, ter sign him up as apprentice for t' following season."

Nat's face lit up at these words, he did not speak but only watched his father's face intently.

This time Mr Harrison nodded thoughtfully as my husband continued, "A know tha'll be fretting for him Mrs Harrison but ease thy mind, for he'll sleep in me own cabin, there's a box bed in there what me wife slept in when she were a lass and went ter sea. And he shall tek his vittels at me own table, so there'll be no worries of him going short of good nourishment."

Here I laid my hand upon her wrist, "do be assured Penelope dear, he shall be properly fed, for the ship's cook, a Mr Briggs, keeps an excellent table."

"And if young Nat shows himself a hard worker, he can be my apprentice in good time, and if t' lad changes his mind at end of first voyage, then he's not committed hisself and there's no harm done."

"Please Father…"

His father somewhat reluctantly agreed to the proposal and Penelope clutched her son's hand excitedly.

"A'll write thee a list of what tha'll need Young Nat and tha'll report ter t' Fortitude, first week in March, we'll probably not sail till later, but tha'll need ter be aboard and at the ready just then." He shook the boy's hand vigorously, "good lad. And A'll tell thee tha'll soon mek friends, for there's nowt sailors like better than a bit of music on board so dunt forget that fiddle."

Now it was time to pack away the musical instruments, wrap up in scarves and heavy coats and after hugs, kisses and promises to write, the Harrison family mounted their horses and departed into a rather milder evening with an exceptionally clear sky. The Vicar stood holding his little son's hand, as he wished them all a safe journey.

I took Gerald in my arms to wave them off.

"Gerald like horse, nice horses."

"Yes Darling, perhaps you'll have your own horse when you're a big boy."

"Gerald big boy now," he said earnestly.

"But not big enough yet," I said firmly and kissed him.

As I turned to follow the others inside, I saw the Vicar slip his arm around Belle and as she laid her head upon his shoulder, they might have been any young couple in love. I had no desire to eavesdrop but could not help but hear him ask if she had enjoyed her Christmas day, she raised her head to look at him and nodded.

"Indeed, there has been much love and happiness in our house today," she said softly.

Together they looked up at the clear winter sky.

"Our house under the stars," he said.

"Our house under the stars," she replied, and they gently kissed one another.

And I knew for certain that whatever others may think, that Jack and Belle still loved one another deeply.

CHAPTER 25

Early 1814.
In which a wedding is planned.

On a crisp day in January, Ged Stone strode into Campion's Bank to make a deposit, there were smiles and 'good morning Captain Stone Sir' from all sides, for he was now one of the most prosperous ship owners in Whitby and thus a favourite customer in the bank. Though he looked dour and replied with nothing more than a grim nod, inside his head he was almost laughing, for he was remembering the day he had first opened his savings account, fourteen years before. He was twenty years old then and having been going to sea on the whalers and colliers for twelve years, he had managed to save the princely sum of three pounds (as well as supporting his mother and sister for most of that time), with which to open his account. The clerk had looked at him quite sneeringly, and repeated in an over-bearing voice, for all to hear, 'just the three pounds is it Sir?'. Nevertheless, Mrs Campion herself had stepped forward and taken his details for the docket. In her ladylike way she had said she welcomed his custom and had shaken his hand.

Now, his prosperity had given him all the respect and prestige he has always dreamt of. As he stood at the counter, he felt a nudge at his shoulder, and he turned round to see Robert Curzon behind him looking to be in a particularly good mood.

"Eh Robert, tha made me start then, thought tha were a thief ter tek me money…" he joked.

"Nay, as if. I've got a bit of news to tell and a favour to ask too."

"Give us a minute man and A'll be reet with thee."

Deposit made, the two of them crossed over to the 'Black Bull' and were at once served with ales, brandies and a bowl of water for the wolf dog, by a pretty young girl, who introduced herself as Molly, Mr Briggs' granddaughter.

Both men took a sup of ale and Robert said, "I'm to be married Ged and I'm hoping you'll stand as my best man."

"Course A will man, A'd no idea tha were courting though?"

Robert grinned rather sheepishly, "tis Louisa Coates, I met her last year, at several assemblies and dances and come New Year's Eve, she agreed to be mine and we've set a date for March."

Ged clapped him on the back in congratulations and they chatted on about it for quite some time after and how it fitted around another relationship that Robert had once had.

At dinner that same day, Idina was told the news of the forthcoming wedding, to be held a few weeks hence, in very grand style.

"How very exciting, I'm so happy for Robert."

"Aye well it's time he were wed, for he'll be thirty one this year. She's no Spring Chicken neither, Robert says she's twenty nine." Not noticing Idina's frown, he went on, "plain lass she is, all them Coates' girls look like horses ter me; good catch for him though, for she comes with ten thousand pounds and more than a few shipping shares. He's taken one of them grand new houses up bit' Beck, he'll be well set up, eh?"

On receiving no reply, he looked up from his plate and saw his wife staring at him; for some reason, she seemed to be on the edge of tears.

"What?"

"Is that why you married me?" Her voice was shaking now. "Because I came with a big ship and some money, you could put up with me being past thirty? That's what the solicitor said to me that first day you know, he said I was past the first flush of youth, and you were marrying me for my money…"

She got no further, for at this point Ged stood up, knocked his plate to the floor and shouted, "A'll not tek that wife, that tha should speak ter me so… when there's one or two things tha chooses ter forget ter mek thy little story fit…"

At this point Cook opened the door to bring in the pudding and quickly retreated, seeing it not to be a good moment, though of course she remained in the hallway to listen.

He stormed, "what's them things tha's forgetting, tell me that?" He saw tears ooze down her cheeks as she shook her head, but he could not stop himself now to comfort her, for he was far too angry. "Number one, when A asked thee ter tek me, tha dint have no bloody ship, tha dint have no money, tha told me that tha had nowt and couldn't change t' dressmaker because of it, remember?" He didn't pause for her to answer. He shouted, "A thought tha'd be coming ter live with me and me family, in t' house on Church Street, for a dint think thy father'd think too much of me as a son-in-law. All t' time A were at sea waiting ter wed thee A pictured thee there...in me own bed, us living off my money. A'd no notion it'd be other till A got back. A dint know thy father were ter die and A dint wish it so."

Idina put her head on her arm and wept into the tablecloth, knowing she had caused this row herself, for no good reason at all.

Her husband continued now with a hurt tone; his anger having subsided somewhat. He had not meant to shout at her, for he felt he had stooped to his own father's level. "And secondly, that first day when we walked out and A saw thee, why A could hardly speak fer thinking tha were t' most beautiful woman A'd ivver seen..."

"Not like a horse then?" she said through her tears.

"No, not like a bloody horse...A've A not shown me love for thee? For A've tried best ways A can."

Idina looked up at him, "always."

"A'll add another thing that tha also well knows, check our banking books and tha'll see A've nigh on doubled t' money what tha brought ter t' marriage with profits and that..."

She nodded, unable to speak.

"Well then, A want ter hear no more of it...ivver."

Cook, who greatly admired Captain Stone, was rather moved by his words of love and chose this moment to bring in the pudding. "Shall yer tek yer plum tarts now Captain and Mistress?"

"Aye, A thank thee kindly Cook."

Discreetly she picked the plate up from the floor (the spaniel having surreptitiously devoured the spilt food already), stacked it with the others and quickly withdrew, though she lurked for a few moments in the hall to see what was to happen next. Of course, she could not see the captain's face not looking up, yet reaching out his hand, which his wife took at once. Still not looking up, he drew her towards him, and she bent down to kiss him.

He held her head close and whispered, "a plum tart kiss is me favourite."

But Cook could hear nothing of this, only the sound of scraping of spoons on plates. However, she had hardly got down to the kitchen, when the parlour door opened, and she heard the two of them run upstairs and shut the bedroom door firmly behind them. So, Cook felt she could now take a quiet ten minutes in her chair as she smiled to herself, feeling all was mended and hoping the bairn would stay asleep a bit longer so that they could make-up properly.

****

The day of Robert's wedding was bleak and cold, on the edge of snow. It took place in the New Church, as it was always called, on Baxtergate, which was not so new now, being more than thirty years old. It was full to bursting, Robert was one of nine, most of whom were there, plus various cousins, all with spouses and their older children; at the back, a collection of devoted servants and sailors crammed together. The Coates were also a huge family, and soon the gallery was filling up as well.

Of course, Ged stood at the front with a calm and confident Robert.

Idina sat with Sarah and her mother-in-law, who as ever, had plenty to say for herself.

"Eh, it's that good of Robert ter have invited likes of me, ter sit with quality…"

"Hush Mother," whispered Sarah.

"Well, A'm just saying like, it's good of him. A've allus been fond of him, whenever he's been ter our house, he's allus had lovely manners, even when we lived in Nicholson's Yard, he were nivver condescending or owt wi' us."

"I should think not," said Idina firmly.

Sarah and old Sally both wore the most extravagant of bonnets, clearly Octavia had decked them out as advertisements for her hat shop. Octavia herself looked resplendent in royal blue velvet, she had somehow managed to dye her copious winter furs to tone, in a lighter shade of blue. She was very obviously pregnant now and in case anyone failed to notice this, her hand was always rested gracefully across her stomach.

Suddenly a hush rippled through the assemblage and Miss Coates was walked down the aisle. Idina chastised herself yet could not help but think of her husband's description, for indeed the bride had a long upper lip, a prominent nose and rather protruding teeth, though she looked pleased enough if not exactly radiant in a most expensive cream silk dress and smart matching wedding jacket with intricate frogging, piping and tassels too.

The service was overly long in the opinion of most and all were delighted to run over the road, dodging the first of the snowflakes, to the Assembly Rooms to embark upon the wedding breakfast, which was magnificent and also exotic, boasting a centrepiece of fresh pineapples, cut pomegranates and silver cherubs.

After the feast there was dancing, Idina managed to sit with Penelope and the friendship begun at Christmas, was enthusiastically renewed, but interrupted by the approach of a tall dark man, with twinkling eyes and an engaging crooked smile. He held out his hand to Idina, but she hesitated, not having the least idea who he was.

Penelope laughed, "why Idina Hun don't worry, this is me cousin, Ben Curzon, Robert's twin brother."

"I the elder by only ten minutes, yet it enabled me to inherit all the goodly farmlands and poor old brother Robert had to go to sea and sail the world to make his fortune," he joked. Then he lowered his voice and whispered to both ladies, "not to mention a propitious marriage to boost his funds a bit, eh?"

Idina shook his outstretched hand. "Pleased to meet you Mr Curzon."

"Nay, Mrs Stone, I do not come to shake hands, I come to ask if you would honour me with the next set? For though I am not the best dancer, I always try to make myself a most entertaining partner and sadly my good lady wife is not with me, so I must make my own amusement."

"Indeed, I should be most pleased to Mr Curzon." And the words were hardly out of her mouth than she was swept firmly onto the dancefloor. "Pray tell, is your wife unwell that she cannot be here?"

"No, she is well enough but expects her confinement any minute, so cannot travel away from home."

Idina nodded and asked politely if he hoped for a girl or boy.

"God forgive me, but I pray most earnestly for a son, for I have three daughters already; bless them but I am quite outnumbered at home."

True to his word, he did make a most amusing partner, they twisted and twirled their way through a couple of complex, yet fashionable dances, during which he regaled her with gossip and funny stories about his family. He pointed out Olivia, who he said was Robert's favourite sister along with her tremendously rich husband, then he told her that Belle was his favourite sister and what a rum do it was that things had turned out as they had. Idina nodded sympathetically when he said it broke his heart to see Belle so changed.

As the second dance was coming to its close, he joked, "now I have met your good husband, but who is that dainty lady with the pretty smile he is partnering now, quite the pocket Venus I'd say. She laughs so with him; surely she must be his mistress?"

"Most certainly not," Idina could not help but smile at his outrageous remark, "it is his sister Sarah."

"Then I must gain myself an introduction, do you think she would deign to partner me for the next Cotillion?"

"I am most sure she would be pleased to," for Sarah did not know many of the guests and Idina felt certain she would be glad of such a very entertaining partner.

And they had sat down again only just in time to be welcomed by the bridal couple who were doing a circuit of the hall in order to introduce Louisa to the numerous Curzons and likewise for Robert to meet her many relations. They were arm in arm and Idina thought they looked happy enough, though it was always difficult to tell with Robert, as he generally had a rather serious demeanour. He introduced his wife as Mrs Curzon, and she giggled saying she was not used to her new name yet.

Penelope complimented her on her cream silk outfit.

Idina wished them every happiness.

Octavia who had joined them, just smiled and nodded and smoothed her bump with her elegant, gloved hand.

Ben grasped the bride's hand and said she looked so lovely, that had he not already been spoken for, he would have married her himself. Whereupon they all laughed, and the bridal couple moved on.

Though they were barely out of earshot when Octavia whispered to Idina. "Idina dear, I have to say that I would never have chosen cream silk myself, had I such a pasty complexion as Louisa Coates. A pinkish colour or a soft lavender would have been a deal more flattering do you not think?"

Idina nudged her and had to smile, for sometimes there was something very middle-aged about the way Octavia spoke, even though she was not yet nineteen. She herself, having the most pretty 'English-Rose' colouring, especially enhanced by her delicate condition. The heat of the room had caused her to cast off her blue velvet and toning furs and now she sported a dress in peacock blue silk which could easily have been mistaken for the most expensive gown in the room, but in reality, was a dress her Grandmama Curzon had worn to a wedding many years before which Octavia had cleverly cut up and remodelled.

And indeed, Penelope remarked upon this, "did our Grandmama not wear a gown of this very shade when my father wed Aunt Lydie?"

"In truth this is the very gown itself. Of course, it was not large enough for me, so I cut up the matching turban and inserted strips down the side, added a bit of crimping to cover the mark where I let down the hem, altered the sleeves and the neckline and here you have it, as good as new. For 'tis my belief Grandmama only wore the dress the once."

"By tha's a clever one Cousin Octavia, what think thee, Idina?"

"I am endlessly impressed by our sister-in-law," laughed Idina squeezing her arm affectionately.

****

Later that same evening, Idina lay flat on her stomach on the bed, her husband trailed a quill feather slowly down her spine and she gave a little moan of delight. Both of them were naked, for the bedroom was warm with a fire lit and heavy curtains drawn against the falling snow.

Ged was deep in thought, "expect Robert'll be at his nuptial duties now…" He trailed the feather in circles.

"Mmm," said Idina, engulfed in pleasure herself. Then she murmured, "but will they not be his nuptial delights and not his nuptial duties?"

"Aye maybe, but…"

"But what?" Intrigued, she was up on one elbow now as the circling feather moved down to her buttocks.

"Well, it's dead secret is this, A wunt want Mrs Nosey Octavia or me big mouth brother ter know owt of it, for Robert's sake or for t' other party neither."

"Of course, my Love, whatever you tell shall remain between us only."

She turned to lie in his arms, for she felt an interesting story was about to unfold. He pulled up the white fur rug to cover them both and caressed her breasts idly as he spoke.

"A were going ter tell thee of it a bit ago Darling, but we got inter a row with each other and then there hasn't been time since." Indeed, the preceding weeks had been busy for both of them. "A came ter guess of it afore A knew facts of it; a few year back afore A knew thee, A used ter smoke a pipe now and again, any road, we'd docked 'Olivia Belle' and A'd come ashore when A remembered A'd left me pipe on t' deck, and as it were quite a good pipe A thought A'd best go back and fetch it like. So, A found it straight off, but A noticed a light on in t' captain's cabin, so A thought A'd say a 'goodnight' ter Robert thinking he'd be in there working on his charts and such. But as A got near A could hear a woman's laughter and A'll swear there were t' sound of a bairn, babbling as they do afore they can say proper words."

"So what did you do?" Idina was wide-eyed with curiosity now.

"Well Darling, A thought best leave it be. Robert were allus quiet about his private life and A knew he nivver went ter brothels or owt like that but A'd no clue as ter what he did for that side of things. So, nowt were said between us. But more recent, end of last year in fact, I were up in t' top of town, when A glanced down a dark little yard and A saw Robert's great dog lying there, gentle as anything with two bairns playing with it. Well, there's no mistaking that dog, A knew it were his and he wunt be far away. So next time A sees him, A asked him outright. He were quite open about it and said he should of mentioned it afore…"

"And what was the truth of it my Love?"

"Turns out he'd been keeping this lass as his mistress for years and none knew of it. He couldn't wed her for she's already married and husband's still living. This husband used ter beat her regular and badly, she had a little son she were afeared for and Robert found her weeping on t' quayside in Leith one day, when he were docked there, though she's not some low dockside lass at all, but she'd had ter run away from t' husband, with bairn under her arm, in nowt but t' clothes she stood up in. Robert can't stand owt brutal ter lasses, that A do know, so he just bundled her and her bairn in ter t' ship and brought them back here. Set 'em up in t' cottage and that would have been end of it, but ovver t' months he fell in love with her, and her with him. Afore he set ter marry Miss Coates, he made enquiries and found her husband were still living, shacked up bold as brass wi' another lass… Tha's not shocked about it Darling?"

"No, but…but amazed. Robert is so measured and calm, I can barely imagine him being so impetuous as to grab a complete stranger and take her on his ship."

"Aye, thought same meself, but sometimes yer just have ter act fast on yer instincts."

"Is this lady not hurt that he has married Miss Coates?"

"A dunt suppose she likes it, but she understands Robert's ter make his way in t' world, for he's no fancy inheritance ter come 'as he, not like his twin brother's had? And marrying well's a part of all that and Miss Coates has got herself a good 'un, for none'll treat her better than Robert will and there's none works harder than him ter build a good business."

"But a marriage without love?"

"Well, it wunt suit me," he said kissing her breast. "But she's got herself a good husband and he's got himself t' money ter push his business on. He'll be happy enough with all t' Coates family; they have these musical evenings, playing and singing and that, for Robert's a rare singing voice."

"Has he? I did not know that."

"Oh aye, he could sing in one of them operas on a stage and not be out of place."

"So, will he still see the mistress now he is married?"

"Aye he will, for he loves her true and…"

"And what?"

"Dunt be shocked Darling," for he saw the look on Idina's face, "dunt be shocked, this is real life, not a church sermon, she's had his bairn too, Robert's a little lass called Sylvie… He took me ter meet them all only two week since…"

Idina gasped, quite ignorant of much of life she had until now, thought all mistresses were trollopes or whores, not ladies who could be loved and esteemed.

"She's a sweet, kindly lass and yer've only ter look at them together ter see t' love between them. She's educated and such, had a big dowry too, but of course husband's kept all of that. Yer can't deny people love just because it's not respectable. It's a neat little home and bairns as good as gold. It'll allus be a haven for Robert when he visits, that A do know."

Idina thought about it, as far as secrets were concerned, she was as deep as an ocean and would never tell, yet it somehow gave her a little feeling of power to carry a secret that Lydia and Octavia would give their eye teeth to know of, not to mention the new Mrs Robert Curzon with her slightly equine features and her useful fortune. Falling asleep in her husband's arms she thought what an interesting day she had had and felt well-loved and cherished herself.

CHAPTER 26

The following November 1814.
In which young Gerald is bought a special toy
and the captain receives some surprising news.

Our little boy, Gerald Faichney Stone, had flatly refused to sleep in the beautiful cradle prepared for him. From the first, he roared his head off as soon as he was laid in it and continued so until he was lifted up again and would only consent to sleep if he was in the big bed with myself and his Papa. One day when our little one was about five months old; my husband had woken up with a baby foot actually in his mouth.

"Tis just a matter of teking a firm hand Darling."

"Yes, my Love," I had said, though I knew there to be a doubtful note in my voice.

Ged had lifted up our little son and gently laid him in the cradle, on the softest of pillows and tucked the warm blankets around him with such a tenderness. At once Gerald started a rising crescendo of bawling. 'Enough ter wake t' dead,' as Cook had once remarked.

Ged had sat on the bed beside me and taken me in his arms, he started to kiss me ardently, but had soon broken away, he had sighed, "by God he can go at it and no mistek."

"Yes, my Love I fear he can."

Ged had stood up and gone to the cradle. I knew that Ged had sailed a couple of slave ships in the past and his feelings had been little stirred by it, simply seeing it as business, he had many times comfortably ordered his own sailors to be flogged to within an inch of their lives as part of his on board discipline routine, yet now when he saw his little son, his heart had seemed to melt at once. He lifted him, put him on his shoulder and patted his back. Gerald clutched handfuls of his father's shirt tightly to avoid being put back in the cradle again, then he laid his weeping head upon his father's shoulder and fell fast asleep.

"Trouble is we dint plan this proper, yer can only fail if yer dunt plan proper…"

"Yes, my Love."

"A'll think on it, and mek a bit of a plan and we'll try again, eh?"

"Yes, my Love, that would be for the best."

Life was busy for us, my husband was away at sea for a good part of the time and no more thought had been given to young Gerald's sleeping arrangements, until he was just past two years old, though I had made up a bed for him in the dressing room adjoining our bedroom, just in case he ever changed his little mind.

Thus, my story begins on a chill day in early November, when my husband burst through the front door and said, "Darling, A've a bit of a plan come ter me."

"What my Love?"

But the Captain tapped the side of his nose and said, "wrap bairn up well, for tis freezing and we'll all be off out."

I was touched by his concern for his son's comfort, for in general he took little notice of the weather; I had seen him times many in Arctic climes in only his shirt sleeves and often heard tales of how when he had sailed in the tropics, he had been indifferent to the intense heat which floored most other men.

So, well fastened up in winter hats, warm jackets, knitted mufflers and gloves we set off. As soon as we were near the busy main road, little Gerald ran onto it, missing a horse and gig by inches, Ged only stopped him just in time. Even though he had been told off, a minute later he was running onto the road again. This time, his father caught him up and smacked him hard, at once his dear face crumpled to the edge of tears.

"Nah, our Gerald, tha's been a naughty lad and tha must tek thy punishment like a man."

My heart ached to see my son struck and told to behave like a man when he was but two years old. But in that moment, I had forgotten the great love between the pair of them, for next minute, Ged handed me his hat and lifted his son high up on his shoulders.

"A'll bet tha can see all t' world now, our Gerald, eh?"

"See all world," shouted Gerald in delight waving his arms about, his punishment quite forgotten.

And thus, we proceeded, me running after them to keep up with Ged's long strides, until we came to a new shop which I had not noticed before. Behind the small squares of glass was the most wonderful array of toys and dolls and all manner of things to amuse children. In front of the shop was a wooden stool for little ones to stand on, that they might look into the window. Gerald was set down upon it and as he leaned up, he gasped with wonder, because he had never seen such a sight before in his short life. The centrepiece of the display was a beautiful wooden horse, big enough for a small child to sit on, it was carved in a most lifelike way with real horsehair for its mane and tail and metal wheels attached to each of its hooves.

At once he cried out, "horse, horse, look Papa."

But Ged ignored him and said, "them coloured balls is nice, tha could have some fun with those eh Gerald?"

"Horse Papa."

"Look our Gerald, all them toy whips, if thar had one of them, tha could whip Papa when he's naughty."

Gerald was clearly amused by that idea, but he would not be deterred, and he grasped his father's cheek, turning it towards the centrepiece. At this I had to stifle a smile, so amusing was this little scene.

"Gerald like horse best."

"Oh aye," said Ged as if noticing it for the first time. "That'd be a grand present for some little boy, eh?

"Gerald want horse." As an afterthought he added, "please Papa."

"Ah no, tha couldn't have a horse like that, for where would it sleep? It couldn't sleep on its own, it'd be lonely without all its friends."

"Sleep with Gerald."

"Nay, there'd be no room, for in t' big bed there's Mama and Papa and Gerald." He counted out on his fingers to emphasize the point. "There wunt be room for a horse as well."

Gerald's lower lip quivered slightly in disappointment.

"Gerald and horse sleep in little bed," he tried hopefully.

"Ah, now there's an idea, so Gerald and t' horse would sleep in t' little bed in t' dressing room and Mama and Papa sleep in t' big bed, eh?"

Gerald nodded triumphantly.

"Well now there's an idea." Ged rubbed the side of his nose thoughtfully. "Shall we go in t' shop and ask how much it is?"

Already Gerald had climbed down from the stool and had run in the shop. With such confidence he asked to buy the horse.

"Indeed yes, young Sir."

And with great care, the shopkeeper lifted the horse out of the window and wrapped it up in large pieces of tissue paper.

"Fingers crossed Darling," said Ged squeezing my arm as we all left the shop.

And this time everything worked like a dream, for that night (and every other night after) Gerald was as good as his word and slept soundly in the dressing room bed clutching his horse rather awkwardly to his chest.

Ged and I lay in our bed.

"At last Darling we are alone in t' bed." He reached out to caress me.

"My Love, I have to tell you we are not actually alone, for I am pretty certain that we have another little one on the way."

I smiled at him, but he looked aghast and was up on one elbow, staring down at me.

"Bb but, t' doctor said that we should have no more bairns."

I thought to myself it was a bit late to be thinking of that now, for we must have lain together almost every night since his return in August.

"The doctor," I said scornfully, "that useless man, he did naught but tell me to push for three long days, a child could have managed the whole thing as well, you ask your sister. Besides, it is for God to decide how many children we have, not that useless Doctor Myers... Do you not want us to have more children my own Love?"

"Of course, A bloody do, A'd have twenty of our Gerald if A could, but it's not me as has 'em? A've ter stand by while tha's risking thy life, ripped apart wi' t' pain of it."

And I put my arms around him and comforted him with many kisses, touched by his concern and also, so very delighted that I was with child again. And I felt sure he would be pleased by it in time too.

CHAPTER 27

1815.
In which Ged has a welcome surprise
and Idina receives a welcome present.

Towards the end of March, Ged left home early, he had an appointment with the harbour master, then he took a breakfast in the Angel Inn with Robert Curzon who had been away for two months and had only docked the previous day. After this he called in on his mother who was struggling with a swollen window frame, to rectify this he called upon his ship's carpenter Davis, who was only too glad of a bit of extra work at this time of year as the sailing for Greenland had been delayed. Remembering that Sarah needed more pantry shelves he told him to carry out any work as required and to send him the bill.

"Davis, be sure tha speaks ter me sister on this, for tha'll get no sense outer me mother."

"Aye, Cap'n."

Ged then called in to see young Nathaniel Harrison who was lodging temporarily with the Briggs family. After a successful first trip the previous year, young Nat was finally to be signed up for his apprenticeship. The captain had 'taken' to the lad and always introduced him to others as his brother's nephew in order to emphasize a family connection. He had decided to continue to share his cabin and his table with him, for he had found Nathaniel had an unusual talent for map work and the neat plotting of charts, as well as being a conscientious worker in all of the more physical maritime tasks. After the signing and having taken a cup of tea with Mr and Mrs Briggs he went on to visit the Fortitude in its dry dock to check on some final repairs and lastly, he strode up to the ropery to order a quantity of cordage. Deep in thought he walked home and was amazed to find the parlour empty of his wife and the whole house unusually quiet. Cook appeared.

"Where's thy Mistress?"

"Upstairs Sir, she's got a bit of a surprise for thee."

Before he could ask what it was, Cook had turned on her heel and disappeared off down to the kitchen. So, he opened that day's post, wandered into the study, filed the letters carefully and made a note of his cordage order. Back in the hallway, he met Cook again.

"Not been upstairs yet, Sir?"

"On me way now Cook, on me way."

He went upstairs two at a time, suddenly anxious to see his wife, in the knowledge that her time might be near. Through the half open door, he heard her soft voice.

"Sit very still Gerald and hold her very carefully."

For a moment he could hardly comprehend what had happened. Before him stood his sister and sitting up in the bed was his wife, beside her sat his son and in his arms, held rather precariously, was a tiny baby.

"What, what, how did this happen?"

"Why, the usual way Brother," laughed Sarah.

"My Love, we have a daughter, and…"

But before she could finish her sentence, Gerald interrupted and shouted, "it is new baby sister Papa."

"So it is, by God."

He rushed to Idina's side and grasped her hand, "how was it Darling, did it pain thee much."

She shook her head, "not too much, and it only took a few hours, start to finish, no tearing like last time," she laughed ruefully.

For a moment Ged shuddered at the word 'tearing' and felt humbled by her bravery, as he looked at his little girl.

"Now Gerald let Papa hold the baby, it is his turn."

"No," said Gerald firmly and concisely.

They all laughed with the ease and carefree feeling that follows the fear and dread of a confinement. Gerald smiled cheerily at them, and Ged shrugged his shoulders in defeat.

"Brother, Doctor's been, though he only got here just in time, eh Idina?"

Idina nodded.

"He said that all were well, but he'll be calling in termorrow ter check up like. Poor man, he's a widower now and A think him not ovver it at all, for it were only six week since. He thinks t' bairn were born a bit early like." She leaned over to whisper to the baby, "but tha just wanted ter see us all, eh Darling."

"Oh aye." Ged was not really listening, he felt suddenly overwhelmed, he wanted to look at his daughter properly, he wanted to hold his wife close.

Seeing this at once, Sarah put her arm around Gerald and whispered to him about going downstairs to have some milk and cake. Gerald was a sturdy boy and always put his stomach first, he agreed at once, almost letting the baby roll out of his arms, but Sarah deftly caught her and passed her to Ged.

Filled with wonder at her tiny perfection, he rocked her gently in his arms. Privately in the preceding months, Ged had doubted he could ever love a second child as much as he loved little Gerald, he had taken no pleasure in the pregnancy, fearing for the life of his wife. But all that was forgotten now as he gazed at this tiny being; he saw his mother and sister's small, neat features in her little face and his own slightly unruly dark hair peeping from under her bonnet. For just as Gerald was a Faichney through and through, this little one was a Stone, and no mistake.

Idina asked, "might I choose her name?"

"Course, owt tha likes."

"My grandmother was called Sorcha, I named my doll after her when I was a little girl, and I always dreamed of having a real baby called Sorcha."

"Sorcha, eh? A've nivver heard it afore."

"It means brightness and I would like her to have a name that reflects her Scottish heritage."

"Aye, brightness, A like it, so Sorcha it is."

"After she drowned, I..."

"What thy grandmother drowned?" said Ged in astonishment.

"No, no..." Idina laughed at the confusion, "no, it was my doll that drowned, or rather fell in the sea. That first doll was called Sorcha Rose Peacock and one day when I was playing with her on the top deck, my father called to me to come down to the cabin at once. I don't know why I didn't grab her and run down, but instead I stuck her behind the windlass and thought she'd be safe. But there was a storm brewing and father would not let me go back to fetch her. It was one of those violent storms that come down so quick, and of course she must have been washed overboard."

"Did he get thee another doll then?"

"Dear me no, he thought my tears just girlish nonsense, and said I'd be better reading my bible than wasting time playing with dolls."

"Ahh," smiled Ged, always sympathetic to Idina's lonely childhood.

"But anyway, some of the sailor's heard of it and were so kind to me about it. And a few days later they brought me another doll, Mr Davis who was only a young man then, had carved it for me from a bit of wood and the others had sewed me little clothes for her out of scraps and Mr Briggs, who was also quite young then, had knitted little stockings and gloves for her."

Ged smiled, "and did tha call t' new doll Sorcha, as well?"

"Yes, I did, but just Sorcha, not Rose. For I had called the first doll after my grandmother and also after a little girl I admired very much. My father used to take me with him to visit a Captain Peacock and I was supposed to play with his daughter while they talked business. I thought Rose as beautiful as a princess, she had golden curls and big blue eyes and the most lovely silk dresses. She had a large doll's house, all full of fine furniture; of course, I longed to play with it, but she would only let me stand and watch. I should love a doll's house even now, you know. She used to say unkind things about me not having a mother as well…"

"A nasty little piece then? A'd have give her a bloody good slap for thee if A'd been there."

"Tis strange to think, my Love, about then, you must have been going to sea for the first time." She took his hand, thinking how hard his childhood must have been for him.

"So, what happened to 'er then?"

"Rose Peacock? Oh, she was made to marry a man much older than herself and died on the childbed, years ago."

Ged had to smile at her dismissive tone, which was quite without any pity.

"So, by the time I got my second doll, I realised that Rose Peacock was an unkind girl, so I just called that second doll Sorcha. I still have her in the drawer, though she was in no way fancy, I loved her, she had been made specially for me with such kindness from those sailors…"

Ged looked at the sleeping baby in his arms, he had been rocking her all this while, he looked at Idina and then at the cradle.

She nodded, "yes, try her in the cradle."

He laid her down and waited her till she was quite settled.

He rubbed his hands triumphantly, "see Darling, it's just a case of firm discipline wi' em. As Robert always says firm but fair."

"Yes, my Love," replied Idina, with her usual meekness.

"Well, that's his rule wi' t' sailors."

The twitch on Idina's lips made him laugh out loud at himself.

"I haven't thought about my doll for years, should you like to see her now?"

"Aye, A would."

Idina turned back the sheet and started to get out of bed. Ged pushed her back quite roughly.

"Tha's ter stay in bed for two weeks and rest up, even if A have ter tie thee down. Tell me where it is and A'll ger it."

"Second drawer down, right at the back, wrapped in a green handkerchief."

He found it at once and unwrapped it carefully while Idina sat patiently, as a person confined to bed for a fortnight.

He grinned at the wooden doll; it was so very much a doll made on a ship. She had been carved from a bit of mast wood, her hair painted on with black bitumen, the surprised expression on her face inked in, the hat and cape were stiff sail cloth, the other clothes were cut up handkerchiefs and the little socks must have been knitted on two of the pointed sail needles.

He waggled the doll and said in a high-pitched voice, "I am naughty Rose Peacock, and YOU can't play with my doll's house."

"She did sound just like that," laughed Idina.

"Nah then A'm going ter put her at end at cradle so our bairn can look at her when she wakes up."

Then he lay down beside Idina with his arms around her, at once she fell asleep, but he was thinking about various things and did not want to rest. It occurred to him that in all the time he had known and loved her, he had bought her hardly any gifts, (only that dog which he still hated, and which lay quietly at her feet now, partly concealed by the fur rug). He had not bought her any jewellery, for she had a large box of rings and necklaces that had belonged to her mother, and she never wore any of them, only wore her wedding ring and tiny gold ear studs which he often had to untangle from her long hair. As for clothes, fabric samples were regularly sent from Guisborough for her to choose from and then the finished dresses would be sent on a couple of weeks later.

Whenever he was asked which of the samples he preferred, he always said, "ger owt tha wants, in fact ger 'em all."

But these were not personal gifts that he had chosen to give to her. Ged was not one to dwell upon past faults and was soon hatching a plan to rectify things. He slithered out of her arms and when she stirred, he kissed her cheek, crept quietly downstairs and went out.

Upon his return he had a beautifully wrapped box tied with narrow blue satin ribbon; he met his son on the staircase, swinging rather dangerously off the outside of the bannisters.

"Our Gerald, this is a present for thy mama, shall tha give it to her, like a good lad."

"Is it for Gerald too?" he asked hopefully.

"Nah son, tis only for Mama, but A've got summat else for thee, if tha's a good lad and tek this nice for Mama."

At once, Gerald took the box to his mother, laid it beside her and allowed himself to be pulled up onto the bed as it was rather too high for him to climb on his own.

"Present for Mama."

"Why, what a lovely surprise, whatever can it be?" The box was the size of a shoe box, but Idina could not think that her husband would have bought her a pair of shoes. "Shall I open it now, Gerald dear?"

Gerald nodded vigorously as his mama pulled at the bow and took off the lid. At once she smiled with delight, that special delight that comes from a childhood dream being fulfilled. Nestled in soft paper was a set of doll's house furniture; chairs, tables, a little dresser and a four-poster bed. In a separate tiny box was a dinner service in pink and white china and two miniature brass candlesticks. She set them all out carefully on the upturned lid of the box.

"Oh Ged, it is a lovely gift and when we were just talking of such things…"

"Aye, well when tha said of that Rose's doll's house, A thought tha could have one now, better late than nivver, eh?" Idina nodded in delight. "If tha meks a bit of a drawing, then A'll get Davis ter mek it up, he's a good man, can mek owt, if instructions is clear. It'll have ter wait a few month though, for we need ter sail soon, now bairn's here safe. Then our little Sorcha can play wi' t' house when she's a bit older."

"Gerald want a doll's house 'swell."

"Nay, Gerald lad, such as that is fer lasses. A've summat else fer thee."

Ged felt in his pocket and produced a hard, shiny red ball. Gerald was more than thrilled with this, though it was hardly an ideal gift, because over the subsequent weeks it was responsible for the breakage of two windowpanes and a rather precious china figurine was smashed too.

Both his parents were quite tolerant of this, Idina said, "he's only little, he didn't mean to."

Ged said, rather more darkly, "troubles and hardships come soon enough in life, let t' lad enjoy himself while he can."

CHAPTER 28

1815.
Ged and Idina have a group portrait painted.

That year everywhere had a great feeling of euphoria and victory when at last England won its long war against France. The wondrous Duke had finally triumphed after more than twenty years of war, which was really all of their adult lives.

When Ged came back from the whaling later that same year, he clearly had a feeling of victory himself from this good news and also having completed the most successful voyage ever for the 'Fortitude', despite its late departure. He was buzzing with an idea he'd had.

"A've been thinking of this all t' time A've bin away, can't get it from me head."

"What my own Love?"

"Why, we should 'ave a picture painted of us, all of us like, in a row, A've seen them done…"

"A portrait?"

"Aye, that's it, a portrait."

"Oh, I think that would be so lovely, what a good idea, my Love."

Gratified, Ged went on, "A thought we'd have us in front o' t' parlour window and have Fortitude in t' background on t' sea."

Idina nodded enthusiastically, "we could have us side by side, with Sorcha on my lap, and Gerald to one side and our dog to the other…"

"And my horse, my horse in the picture Papa," interrupted Gerald.

Ged gave a defeated sigh, "aye lad, what picture'd be complete wi'out our Gerald's wooden horse… and that bloody dog."

Idina smiled her most loving smile and kissed her husband's hand.

The following week, Cook and Jane moved the big parlour table to one side and Idina sat on a chair beside the window with her baby sleeping on her lap, Ged stood behind her, to her right the spaniel sat briefly and to her left stood Gerald with his toy horse by his side. Facing them was the artist and his easel; there were to be four such sittings, plus two more without the family, in which the painter would block in the background and sketch in the Fortitude itself. The picture would then be finished off in the painter's own studio.

After only five minutes, Ged was shifting from one foot to the other and sneaking a look at his pocket watch, Gerald could not resist pushing his horse back and forth on its noisy little metal wheels.

"Might the young man stand still, if you please…"

"Gerald dear, please try to stop fidgeting and be still…" said his Mama without moving a muscle herself.

After which young Gerald confined himself to making donkey noises at the ceiling, though he did manage to stay fairly still.

"Sir, might I ask that you look a little to the left as you were before?"

Ged wrenched his head to the left and the painter stepped forward, taking Ged's chin in his hand to adjust its position. Ged twitched slightly, he wanted to knock the man to the floor for his impudence in touching him, but with some difficulty constrained himself and merely tightened his grip on his wife's shoulder.

Idina decided that if she counted backwards from six hundred that the sitting would be over by then, as indeed it was.

"I do thank you kindly Captain and Mrs Stone and young Master for your patience." The painter gave a slight nod and smiled, though in truth he felt a little challenged by achieving any kind of flattering likeness for such a ferocious looking man as the captain or for that very plain child who could hardly be right in the head making such strange noises without reproof. He felt however, that he could make a good likeness for Mrs Stone with her Rubenesque beauty.

After several weeks, the completed picture arrived, with instructions that it was not to be touched as the varnish was not yet quite dry. The good Captain and his wife were out at the time, so Cook supervised the clearing of the parlour mantlepiece and the painting was stood upon it, awaiting the patrons' return.

Cook clasped her hands and said, "eh it's beautiful, it's that like, it's as if they was all stood in t' room wi' us."

Gratified, the artist felt confident in leaving his bill and departing.

Upon their return, Idina stared sadly at the picture, "oh dear, I did not know I had grown so stout."

"Stout? Why there's hardly an ounce of flesh on thee."

Speaking more from devoted love than factual truth, Ged discreetly caressed her left buttock.

Then he inspected the painting himself, "by God, our Gerald's no beauty, but he's nivver that ugly, eh? And our Sorcha, she's laid like a bloody corpse, she allus has her little hands up ter her mouth when she's sleeping, dunt she?"

Idina smiled and nodded.

Ged went on, "look at me face, A look as if A'm ter tek strap to yer all. A nivver look angry like that…do A?"

"No, my Love, never."

"A'll say one thing though, he's caught a good likeness for our Gerald's horse."

At this they both laughed out loud, kissed each other and turned to sit to the tea-table, though Idina had firmly resolved not to have any of the cake. However, when she saw that there was her favourite lemon cake fresh baked, she decided she would wait until tomorrow to cut back on such things.

The painting rested on the mantle for several months, no arrangements were ever made to hang it on the wall. Ged paid the artists bill with good grace, though he privately referred to him as a 'bloody joker'.

Towards the end of the year, Mr Davis called round to gain instruction as to what required for the making of Mrs Stone's dolls' house.

"Morning Davis, A've ter be off ter see ter t' caulking so A'll leave thee in t' capable hands of me wife and she'll explain what's wanted exact."

"Aye, Cap'n. Mrs Stone?"

"Thank you for calling so promptly Mr Davis."

Mr Davis nodded, and Captain Stone kissed his wife and left.

"I was hoping it would fit into this alcove Mr Davis, about twelve inches from the floor, then six rooms with a staircase and hallway up the middle. Could you make a little turned balustrade and newel post, and little doors going off the hallways?"

"A can mek owt tha likes Mrs Stone." He made a note of this with a stub of pencil.

"So, for the front, it needs to have two large opening doors with windows set in and a front door...and a fancy porch," she added remembering Rose Peacock's dolls' house. With a certain lack of imagination, Idina was ordering an identical one to the one she recollected from all those years ago.

"Reet Mrs Stone, A'll measure up and mek a bit of a sketch for thee ter check afore A leave."

He sighed, though glad of the work, he had never heard of such a nonsense as making a fine house for playthings to sit in, when most people he knew had only two or three rooms for themselves and numerous children to live in. However, he also knew that it was said that the Stones had so much money now, they hardly knew what to spend it on.

"Please do be seated Mr Davis and make yourself comfortable while you work." She indicated a chair set at the parlour table and without asking she poured a good measure of rum into a glass for him.

"A thank thee kindly, Mrs Stone."

Then a silence ensued while he drew an extremely detailed and competent plan of the proposed house. This silence enabled Idina to initiate a subject which had intrigued her for some time.

"Mr Davis, my husband tells me you lived for a while in Greenland ...with the native people."

"Aye A did, A were nigh on two year afore A could get a passage home."

"It must have been a most interesting time for you Mr Davis, I think?"

He glanced at her, perhaps wondering what she had heard and said, "Aye."

Sensing she had been too intrusive, she said, "how very useful it must be for all that sail with you that you have learned the native language."

"Aye, A dare say."

His drawing completed, he pushed it forward for her perusal.

"Oh Mr Davis, that is exactly as I pictured it, how splendid."

Gratified he stood up and folded the paper carefully.

"Mr Davis, before you go, I must show you something from many years ago, that you may not even remember…"

She reached into the toy chest and took out her Sorcha doll.

Davis had to grin as he turned the doll in his hands, "A do remember it well Mrs Stone, bye A were a young man then, hardly out of me apprenticeship. A can remember it as if it were yesterday. Briggs made most at' clothes, course he were only young then too, a couple of years older an me; and James, t' sail maker made little hat and that. Hope A don't speak outer turn, but in them days tha reminded me so much of one of me little sisters at home playing wit' dolls and that."

Idina smiled, "as you see, I have treasured her all these years and now my own daughter plays with her, and shares the same name, Sorcha."

He nodded thoughtfully, promised to come back the following week to fit the doll's house and departed.

Later on, at dinner, she told of the morning's activity and her conversation with Mr Davis.

"I was most interested in his time spent with the natives, but he would not speak of it…"

"A'm not bloody surprised," laughed her husband. "He'd be wondering what tha'd heard. His wife thinks he spent two years shivering and suffering on a wrecked ship, if she knew he'd been having a high old time wit' lasses, living with 'em and fathering a bairn, why A think she'd kill him. She's built like a brick wall is Mrs Davis, there's not many as would want ter cross her."

"Oh dear, I did not think, I was just so fascinated. Yet it must have been terrible for him wondering if he would ever see his home again."

"Maybes not as bad as what tha thinks, A've heard he lived in one of those little huts made of ice bricks with two young lasses and both of 'em were his wives like…"

Now Idina was rather shocked never having imagined such a way of living, but it certainly gave her something to think about and she resolved to ask Sarah to point out the formidable Mrs Davis, as Sarah seemed to know most people who lived on the East side of the river.

CHAPTER 29

1816.
In which a great deal happens.

Both of them ignored the family portrait until the following year when the captain bought an expensive and complex clock in a mahogany case, which showed the movements of the moon and stars, as well as the time itself. He and Idina were both fascinated by this, explaining it as best they could to little Gerald. Immediately, upon its arrival, the painting was put on its side in a corner of the room and the new clock took pride of place upon the mantle shelf.

Ged said, "nah, dunt that look grand now."

Idina said, "oh what an interesting piece, I like that much better than the painting."

Gerald said, "I like the big clock, tick tocking." He waved his hands in imitation of the pendulum.

Sorcha was too young to say many words but made appreciative noises and reached out her little hands, when her father held her up to see it.

Cook said, "eh that beautiful picture just stuck in t' corner."

Jane did not consider it her place to speak out, but privately sighed at the thought of yet more dusting.

When the Captain had returned from that year's whaling, all attentions were spent on two very exciting matters. First, was the conversion of the old Captain's bedroom into an upstairs drawing room, where guests could be elegantly and fashionably entertained and Idina could gain a little peace and quiet from Gerald and Sorcha, both of whom were exceptionally boisterous children. Ged was never bothered by these high spirits, being a man of boundless energy himself, he thought of his children as great good fun. He often played vigorous games with them and occasionally, when pressed, sat them upon his knee and told them a story. Insisting he only knew the one story; he always told the tale of the house falling down on Henrietta Street.

It started with, "me and Aunty Sarah were nobbut bairns..." which was a concept neither child could possibly imagine. When their Papa came to the bit about the cliff falling down, Gerald would bang on the table to make thunderous noises and Ged would say, "Aye that were about t' sound of it, Son."

Then came Sorcha's favourite part, when the neighbours ran naked from their houses. Here she would giggle and squeal with laughter, covering her eyes and saying, "no clothes on, Dada."

Both of them loved the story's finale, when Papa ate a delicious, sweet orange and then thought he'd try a lemon and made the most monstrous of faces to indicate it's sourness. This involved both children shouting, "make the lemon face again, again Papa pleeease."

The second matter to occupy everyone's attention, occurred that very same week. A most unexpected visitor arrived, it was Dr Myers himself. Idina was in the hallway with the children, about to take them upstairs for their afternoon nap when Jane answered the door and announced the doctor. Idina could not imagine whatever had caused his visit, thinking perhaps they had forgotten to pay his bill, for he had recently attended little Sorcha and Gerald for a particularly nasty bout of measles.

"Good to see you Mrs Stone, keeping well I hope?"

"Yes, I thank you Dr Myers and yourself?"

"Never better Mrs Stone, never better." Indeed, the doctor did seem to be in fine spirits. He went on, "and pleased to see your little ones looking a deal brighter. I wonder if I might have a quiet word with your good husband?"

"Of course, please make yourself comfortable in the parlour while I fetch him."

Thus, the doctor settled himself and Idina fetched her husband from his study.

"What?" he said silently.

But Idina had to shrug her shoulders and shake her head. Then she ushered her children upstairs to rest, Sorcha had been tying a baby's bonnet onto the reluctant dog and Gerald was picking away assiduously at some crumbling paintwork on the hall walls.

Every day after dinner, Idina lay on her bed with the two of them until they fell asleep. Every day she would read a story and without fail, Gerald always chose "The Amusing Tale of Dame Trot and her Cat." Sorcha clearly found this boring and was asleep by page two; Gerald on the other hand, loved the story start to finish and if his mama ever paused, he would shout, "what happens next Mama, what happens next?"

Then, when the book was closed, he put his hands behind his head and fell asleep at once, 'just like a true sailor,' his father always said.

Idina was quite tired herself this day, and lay there with eyes closed, thinking of this and that, with the fox fur rug and Bella the dog covering her feet. She was quite content, yet only a month since, she had been most fearful for her children. Both covered in red blotches with raging fevers; Gerald had slept soundly for most of the illness giving his body chance to heal itself, but little Sorcha had lain in her father's arms wakeful and burning with fever, her eyes with a horrible, glazed brightness, two scarlet spots upon her cheeks and every inch of her covered in an angry rash. Always a dainty child, her arms and legs looked like sticks as she lay there listless and staring in the gloomy room carefully darkened to protect their young eyes.

She would gaze up at him, touch her throat and say, "sore Dada, sore."

And how it had broken his heart that he could do nothing for her, save dip his finger in the milk and brandy mixture and moisten her mouth when she could not swallow, for he could not bear to let her be bled or purged as Dr Myers wished. Here Idina was in agreement with her husband, thinking her too weak to stand such intervention. Both of them had feared for the life of this frail little girl for several days and nothing could equal the joy they felt when she finally sat up, put her hands on Ged's face and said, "love Dada."

At once he had jerked out of his doze, felt her forehead and realising the fever had broken turned his head to wipe away tears of relief.

Idina was just thinking of this very moment when he put his head round the bedroom door, she smiled at him but could not sit up as she had a sleeping child on each of her arms.

He crept towards the foot of the bed, sat down carefully and spoke in a low voice. The dog shuffled discreetly to one side.

"Well, Darling, seems we're ter have a doctor in t' family."

"How? Whatever do you mean?"

"Yon Dr Myers has come after our Sarah. He came ter ask my permission first off, like a true gentleman and him being widowed for a decent time now."

Idina was quite astonished, having had no notion of such a thing. "Have they been courting? And us knowing naught of it?"

This seemed unlikely as Idina and Sarah were quite close, and even if Sarah had had a secret lover, Mother-in-law would have got wind of it and would have had a few bawdy remarks to make about it.

"Nay, not at all, he's off round there now ter ask her."

"Do you think she'll accept him?"

"Oh aye, she'll have ter if she wants a husband like, for there's no others queuing at t' door is there?"

"No," said Idina thoughtfully.

"Turns out, he came ter admire her during thy first labour and says he came ter love her during thy second time."

"How very strange…" Idina could not imagine anything less conducive to romance than a confinement.

Then Ged forgot about whispering. "Touch and go whether he'll ivver get ter her."

"How do you mean?"

"Well think on it," he laughed. "Poor man, he'll get ter t' house, and he's ter get past our Hugo and Mrs Nosey Octavia in t' hat shop, then past all of them children, Tommy and Sukey and little Hugo and that new bairn that's allus screaming its head off int' cradle. Then there'll be that dog running about and barking away, then me mother and it's anyone's guess what she'll come out with. All that afore poor man even gets ter me sister."

Idina had to smile, because of course it was a true picture of any visit to that busy household.

But it seemed that the good Doctor mastered all obstacles, declared his love, proposed and was accepted. It turned out, Sarah had secretly harboured feelings for Dr Myers for some time. A wedding was planned for early in the New Year, whereupon all stops had to be pulled out for the proposed redecoration of the house, for Miss Stone was to be married from her brother's abode and the wedding breakfast was to be held there afterwards.

As well as the creation of an upstairs parlour, it was decided to distemper the hall and stairway and also the grim dining room in readiness for the aforementioned wedding breakfast.

Lydia Curzon was brought in to advise upon the colour schemes.

"I'm hopeless at that sort of thing, Lydia," confessed Idina.

"Fear not, my dear Idina, upstairs is an ideal room with its delightful sea view, and I guarantee we can make it the most beautiful and stylish drawing room in Whitby. As to the hallway and dining room, well it is an easy matter to make them fresh and bright with lighter colours."

Whereupon she showed a book of paint shades to Ged, but he quickly turned away with a dismissive wave of his arm.

"A don't know owt about colours, ger owt tha wants, but dunt stint, there's nowt too good nor too costly for my Idina."

With that he grabbed his hat and disappeared out of the front door. In fact, he spent most of the next three weeks away from home, in his new harbourside office which he shared with Robert Curzon, they both having formed a business partnership together. The office seeming greatly preferable to the upheaval and paint smells at home, and also the mess of the lime plaster, for it turned out that the hallway needed replastering before its colour wash, as for some reason the lower part of the wall was crumbling away.

"The dear Captain," sighed Lydia, "what a perfect generous husband he is."

Idina smiled happily, though she was fairly baffled by the paint colours herself. But here Lydia was on 'home ground' and confidently chose shell pink to brighten the dark wood of the dining room, silver grey for the hallway and cerulean and sea green distempers for the new drawing room panelling, the floorboards washed in a pale tint, were mostly covered by a large, expensive silk rug in shades of aquamarine. The new drawing room furniture was mainly white, picked out in silver which Lydia insisted was more fashionable than gold. And lastly, when the decorating was finished, carpet laid and furniture installed in the new room, a most beautiful china teaset in a Grecian pattern was unpacked, to be serviced by a silver tea kettle and a Chinese lacquer tea caddy.

Idina was thrilled by the whole ensemble.

"What think you, my Love?"

Ged grunted and said it did not look comfortable to him and he preferred the old parlour downstairs, but on seeing the disappointment in Idina's eyes he quickly corrected himself and said, "but A've nivver in me life seen owt so beautiful, tis a deal finer than any drawing room A've ever been in. Robert and that Louisa have nowt like this in that big house of theirs. Tha's made a grand job of it Darling."

As for the family portrait, it still remained on its side in the downstairs parlour.

A few weeks later Octavia came to take tea in the newly decorated room; she brought with her, her stepchildren Tommy and Sukey, her firstborn son Hugo who was now two years old and her new baby Benjamin. Apart from the new baby, the other children decided on a lively game of pirates while their Mamas took tea upstairs and discussed the forthcoming wedding. It was a loud and vigorous game which involved much shouting and hurtling about, with the spaniel running round in circles and barking. Toy swords and pistols were employed by the boys and the little girls as well. Sorcha was experimenting with shouting, her father often shouted and her brother did so all the time and Sorcha found she liked shouting too, even though she been repeatedly told that it was unladylike to make loud noises.

Ged arrived home halfway through the game and young Gerald ran at him with a wooden sword, his father fought back valiantly, throwing him up in the air quite roughly but then allowed himself to be 'killed'. At this point Idina came downstairs to find her husband lying on the hall floor with his eyes closed and Cook standing there weeping.

"I have killed Papa," yelled Gerald triumphantly.

"Goodness me," said Idina mildly, stepping over her husband. She almost tripped in doing so, because despite being 'dead', he shot his hand up her skirt to caress her leg as she stepped over him.

"Whatever is it Cook, what has happened?" Idina put a kindly arm about her shoulders.

"It's all them bairns, Mistress. A cannot cope wi' em, A've done me best but there's another windowpane broke, and Master Gerald's put his foot through that beautiful picture of yer all." Here Cook broke into open sobs, "A cannot cope no more."

The captain leapt to his feet in one swift motion, "Na then our Gerald, tha's upset Cook, say tha's sorry like a good lad."

Gerald hugged Cook's legs tightly, "very, very sorry Cook, don't cry…"

"Eh Master Gerald, A'm just a silly old woman," she said, wiping her eyes on the corner of her apron and ruffling his little ginger curls with her other hand. "A just cannot cope wi' it all no more."

"Cope," roared Ged, "it's us as can't cope wi' out thee Cook, if tha gets upset and gets tha self laid up."

"Absolutely Cook," said Idina, "now why don't you go down to the kitchen and make yourself a good pot of tea and put your feet up and take a rest. Jane can bring the bread and cakes up for the children, and you can gather yourself, for Mrs Curzon and I can easily serve the children's teas ourselves."

Octavia herself appeared at the top of the stairs, her new baby flopped on her shoulder, "now what is going on, what is all this noise, Tommy and Sukey?"

The two children quaked, for though Octavia was an efficient and much-loved stepmother, she rarely hesitated in handing out a sharp slap when required.

"I think the little ones are ready for their teas," said Idina calmly, guiding them all to sit at the parlour table.

Cook dried her eyes, went down to the kitchen and put a decent measure of brandy into her cup of tea.

Jane staggered up with a heavy tray of bread, butter, cakes and milk. At once the captain stepped to the table and made a surprisingly good job of buttering bread and cutting it into small pieces, as the children all climbed onto their chairs and held out hungry little hands.

"Am A cutting it right Sister Curzon?" he asked.

"Indeed you are, 'tis done exactly right dear Brother Stone," she replied, "why indeed it is so well done, I fear you may have missed your calling in life."

"By tha's an acid tongue…" he grinned.

"Well, I should say, it takes one to know one, Brother Stone," she twinkled.

And by now, Ged was as fond of Octavia as any brother-in-law could be, although they always addressed each other in a most formal way.

When all were settled, he strode across the room and held up the family portrait. There was now a large tear in the canvas at the top. He laughed out loud, "aye, looks more interesting wi' a hole in it."

"We never really liked the picture much," said Idina confidentially to Octavia. "I look so stout in it, and Ged looks so angry and…" here she lowered her voice, "and poor dear Gerald is made to look so plain…"

"And our Sorcha looks bloody dead," laughed the captain, "but toy horse is a good likeness."

CHAPTER 30

Not long ago.
Rob and Penny go to the Saleroom.

Slowly they walked up the steep hill and turned onto Silver Street.

He nudged her hard, "child free, we can run wild now, can't we?"

"Mmm," she smiled up at him, "no stopping us now."

Rob took her hand and squeezed it.

They intended to make the most of the few precious hours while Penny's mum looked after the two babies. And the thing they both loved to do best was to go to the local auction room and buy something old and interesting.

He looked at his watch, "we've a good half hour to view before it starts."

They walked up the steep ramp, past the abundant fig tree brushing against them and into the large room crammed with the lots of the day. Furniture was set around the edge, long tables stood at the far end, laden with china and glass wares, metalware to the left, objects d'art to the right and a multitude of pictures hanging behind. A motley collection of chairs and sofas were set out in rows in the middle of the room for the bidders and onlookers to sit on.

"Ooh, there's loads of stuff," gasped Penny in delight.

Rob nodded, pulling her towards an old pine dresser, "some age there, I'd say."

The wood, delicately inlaid with simple bands of ebony, had been lovingly polished over the centuries.

"Just what we need, it's got loads of storage at the bottom and we could get just about all our nice china on those shelves. What d'you think, three hundred?"

"Maybe a bit more," said Rob who was given to extravagance at auction sales.

"Three fifty then?" Penny took out her notebook and carefully wrote, 'Lot 214 dresser £350.'

They listed a large mahogany chest of drawers, which Penny privately doubted would fit up the narrow staircase of their cottage, but Rob, with his usual optimism, thought it could be hauled up the outside and fitted through the bedroom window.

Penny fell in love with a beautiful set of glasses engraved with grapes and vine leaves, for wine, water and sherry. She wrote down, 'Lot 19 glasses £60.'

"Darling, do we really need eighteen glasses?"

"Yes," she replied firmly, "we do."

"Write these down," he indicated a pair of old prints of Captain Cook's ships. "I know they'll be a lot, but I LOVE them,"

"How much? What's our limit?"

He grinned, "one hundred? No one hundred and twenty."

"Oh Rob, they're only small prints."

"But there'll be collectors wanting them."

She dutifully wrote it down in her little book, as well as two bedroom chairs and a stone garden trough.

"Don't forget the boxes."

Rob squatted down to look at the miscellaneous low value goods randomly grouped together in boxes under the long tables. It was here that everyone hoped to find a bargain, something of real value that the auctioneer had somehow missed. Penny bent down and fingered some enamel kitchen cannisters which still had bits of old sugar and tea inside them.

"Yuk," she said wiping her hands on her jeans, "they're all sticky."

"What about this Darling?"

Rob was on all fours and dragged a large box towards him, of mainly broken picture frames. He pulled out an old canvas with a large rip in it and rising to his feet held it at arm's length.

"My this looks ancient." He flattened the tear and stared at the painting of a couple with their children and dog, behind them a ship on a gloomy sea.

"They look very serious and dour," smiled Penny. "D'you think they ever had any fun?"

Rob turned the picture over and Penny read the label on the back.

"Captain G. Stone and family. Whitby 1815."

"That's a good name for them, 'Stone'. They look like stones the lot of them," he laughed. "Wish they were some of our ancestors, then I'd buy it even though it's such an unattractive picture."

With that he shoved it back in the box and the Auctioneer mounted the rostrum and banged down his gavel. Quickly, Rob and Penny squeezed into the last two seats, a saggy old sofa.

"I'll not be buying this," whispered Rob, shifting uncomfortably over an escaped spring.

Now the porter was holding up the first item for sale and the auctioneer began his patter.

"You're attention please ladies and gentlemen. Lot number one, a particularly fine figurine. What am I bid?

Thirty pounds, twenty-five surely, well twenty to get started, thank you Sir, fifteen pounds bid, do I see seventeen…"

Slowly the bidding for that first lot limped up to a final thirty pounds, the gavel thundered down, and the sale was now in full swing.

"Let's get on now ladies and gentlemen."

The auctioneer then sped through the next three hundred lots.

"Oh no," whispered Penny, as the engraved glasses went for ninety pounds.

They were disappointed on the dresser which was knocked down for only one bid after theirs, as were the chairs and the chest of drawers. They never even got in on the bidding for the garden trough, as it quickly shot up to a staggering four hundred pounds.

"Never mind," murmured Rob, "leaves a bit more for the Captain Cook prints.

But Penny had to hold Rob's hand down as he bid way over his limit for these, and then in the end, they went to an Australian on the internet. He was cross and Penny saw a sullen frown on his face as he folded his arms. Many of the bidders started to leave as the last lots came up, the miscellaneous junk boxes on the floor.

"Now to our final lot of the day, number three hundred and forty."

The auctioneer peered at the box that the porter was pointing to.

"Ah, selection of picture frames and an unusual painting, perhaps seen better days…What am I bid?"

He looked round at his diminished audience.

"I'm not going home empty-handed," whispered Rob raising his hand, fingers splayed to indicate five pounds.

The gavel banged down for the last time.

"Maiden bid, five pounds to the gentleman at the back…Ah to Mr Curzon," he added recognizing Rob as a regular. "And that concludes our sale for today, ladies and gentlemen, I thank you."

"What have you bought that for," laughed Penny, as they stood up and joined the queue to pay.

"No idea," grinned Rob.

Outside, the broken frames were stuffed into a rubbish bin and Rob put the painting under his arm as they walked on for a late pub lunch.

"I think I could put a patch across the back, and then touch up the front with some oil paints," said Penny when they looked at the picture again later. "I wonder who they all were." She examined it more closely, licked her finger and rubbed it across the ship. "Look Rob, I can see the letters Fort…something. It must have been called the 'Fortune', d'you think? I bet we could look that up in the library and find out more about it."

He nodded thoughtfully, "it's growing on me this painting you know, I think I quite like it, though it's not very well painted. She's a stout old bird and no mistake and he looks like he's about to take his belt to them all."

"The child is very plain."

"That baby looks like it's dead, the dog's alright though, is that another dog next to the kid?"

"No," smiled Penny, "it's a horse, a toy horse, look it's got little wheels on its feet. That's the artist's signature in the bottom corner isn't it."

"Well he was a bloody joker and no mistake," he laughed, "I hope he didn't charge them much for it."

List of characters

Lydia Curzon (nee Franklin) married Benjamin Curzon 1781
                      Married his cousin Jacob Curzon 1799

Children of Lydia and Benjamin:

Belle born 1782 married her cousin Jack Curzon (a kindly vicar) 1806-one son Jack born 1808.

Benjamin born 1783 (a successful farmer, heir to the Curzon Estate) married Phoebe 1804- 3 daughters.

Robert twin brother of Benjamin (a sea captain) married Louisa Coates 1816.

Olivia born 1785 married wealthy Hartley Fairfax 1802- 2 daughters.

George born 1787- (a brave soldier).

Frederick born 1789- (a brave soldier).

Francis born 1791- (a curate).

Octavia born 1795 (a beautiful, clever and determined daughter).

Child of Lydia and Jacob Curzon (both in their second marriage). Martha Jane born 1800.

Children of Jacob Curzon and his first wife Susannah:

Jack born 1780 (see above)

Penelope born 1782 married Mr Harrison 1800- 3 sons.

Child of Jacob Curzon and Sally Stone: Hugo Curzon (a sailor) born 1789 married Margaret Ann 1809- One child Susannah (Sukey). Married Octavia Curzon 1813- 11 children in this his second marriage.

Children of Sally Stone:

Gerald (Ged) Stone born 1780 (a sea captain) married Idina Faichney 1811- Gerald born 1812, Sorcha born 1815.

Sarah Stone born 1778.

Hugo Curzon born 1789 (see above).

Other characters:

Eliza Lawson born 1747 (devoted servant to three generations of the Curzon family). Cousin to Jacob Curzon on his mother's side and so related to Jack, Penelope, Hugo, Baby Jack and Martha Jane Curzon.

Thomas Thornton born 1750 (coachman and owner of Thornton's Yard). Married Eliza 1809.

Louis Franklin born 1765 (brave Captain, fighting in the French wars). Lydia's younger brother married to Lydia's Cousin Chloe.

Tommy born 1808 Margaret Ann's son from her first marriage and so Hugo's stepson.

Annie and Billy, the adopted children of Eliza and Thomas Thornton.

Mary and Lizzie devoted former servants to the Franklins who now run a sweet shop on Sandgate in their retirement.

Janet, Betty and James devoted servants at Moorhome Farm.

Elizabeth Jane born 1795 (devoted servant at the Vicarage) and sister of Margaret Ann.

Captain Faichney born 1730 (owner of the Fortitude) and father to Idina.

Cook born 1750 (devoted servant to the Faichneys).

Jane born 1796 (servant to the Faichneys).

Mr Briggs born 1765 (cook and surgeon with many years of service on the Fortitude).

Mr Davis born 1767 (ship's carpenter with many years of service on the Fortitude).

Doctor Myers born 1768 (doctor to the Curzon, Faichney and the Stone families).

Sylvie born 1809, illegitimate daughter of Robert Curzon and his long-term mistress.

Rob and Penny and babies Jake and Suzie, 21st century descendants of Lydia and Benjamin Curzon.

Lightning Source UK Ltd.
Milton Keynes UK
UKHW010752180822
407492UK00002B/327